Cast of Characters

Miss Rebecca Hampton was nearly 80 and the mistress of Hampton Court. A fierce Protestant, she had her will altered to forbid her heir to marry a Catholic.

Captain William Hampton, her cousin and closest relative, was to inherit Hampton Court upon Miss Hampton's death. An ardent Irish nationalist who did not suffer fools gladly, he not only changed his first name to the Gaelic **Lia** ~~~~~~~~~~~~~~~~~~~~~~~~ a Catholic girl.

Meriel Booley Brown ~~~~~~~~~~~~~~~~~~~~~~~~~ affections, was so lovely that the rector ~~~~~~~~~~~~~~~~~~~~~~~ it "providence had not seen fit to besto ~~~~~~~~~~~~~~~~~~~~~~

Priscilla Hoyle, a Dubliner, couldn't bear to stay at home with her know-it-all mother after she was deceived by a lover, and answered an ad in the *Irish Times* to become Miss Hampton's secretary-companion.

Tim Linacre, a Trinity College student home on vacation, dabbled in many things, from snail cultivation to science, and was a distant relative of Miss Hampton's. Second in line to inherit the estate, 20-year-old Tim enthusiastically turned detective after the old lady is poisoned.

Lizzie Shegog was the town witch, kept an errant goat, and was a self-proclaimed expert on herbs, including poisonous ones. She put a curse on her archenemy Miss Hampton shortly before the old woman died.

Dr. Claffey, Bainsborough's only doctor, was the first to cry "murder." He was stoutish, youngish, unceremonious, and "inclined to be prejudiced against rich old ladies."

McGuirk was Miss Hampton's gardener and usually won the hardy cut flower division at the local fair.

Cuddy, the Booley Brownes' gardener, usually took the honors in vegetables, although this year there was some question about his onions.

Plus assorted other villagers and policemen.

Books by Sheila Pim

Crime Fiction

Common or Garden Crime (1945)
Creeping Venom (1946)
A Brush with Death (1950)
A Hive of Suspects (1952)

Novels of Irish life

The Flowering Shamrock (1949)
Other People's Business (1957)
The Sheltered Garden (1965)

Non-Fiction

Getting Better (1943)
Bringing the Garden Indoors (1949)
The Wood and the Trees (1966, 1984)

Creeping Venom

An Irish gardening mystery by
Sheila Pim

The Rue Morgue Press
Boulder, Colorado

TO MY FATHER
For whose sake I took to crime

Creeping Venom
Copyright © 1946
Copyright © 2001
ISBN: 0-915230-42-9

FIRST AMERICAN EDITION

The Rue Morgue Press
P. O. Box 4119
Boulder, Colorado 80306

Printed by Johnson Printing
Boulder, Colorado

PRINTED IN THE UNITED STATES OF AMERICA

MYS
PIM

About Sheila Pim

SHEILA PIM took to crime, as she put it in the dedication to her second mystery, *Creeping Venom*, for her father's sake. Frank Pim loved his thrillers but was unable to get as many as he would like in neutral Ireland during World War II. Her first effort, *Common or Garden Crime*, was set in 1943 and published in 1945, followed a year later by *Creeping Venom*. *A Brush with Death* appeared in 1950 and *A Hive of Suspects* was released in England in 1952 and the following year in the United States, the only book of hers to appear in the U.S. in her lifetime. Two other books, *Other People's Business* (1957) and *The Sheltered Garden* (1964) had some mystery elements but were primarily novels of Irish life, prompting some reviewers to describe her as the Irish Angela Thirkell. Gardening was a key element in all of her books.

She was born in Dublin on September 21, 1909, of a Quaker father and an English mother. Her twin brother Andrew survived only two weeks. She had a second brother, Tom, two years her senior, who was born developmentally disabled and would need constant supervision for most of his life. Sheila bore the brunt of this care, as well as the maintenance of her father's home, after her mother died in 1940. Prior to this, she was educated at the French School in Bray, County Wicklow, and "finished" at La Casita in Lausanne, Switzerland, where she perfected her French. In 1928, she went to Girton College, Cambridge, where she took a Tripos in French and Italian and passed some of the happiest days of her life. Shortly before finals, her mother took ill and Sheila returned to Ireland to look after her and to provide some diversion for brother Tom.

Although she was forced to abandon any thought of formal training in botany, she became an enthusiastic amateur and contributed many essays to the Irish magazine, *My Garden*. Several of these were collected and published in 1949 in a slender volume entitled *Bringing the Garden Indoors* (a selection from which can be found on page opposite the opening chapter). Her major work in this field, however, was the biography of another gifted horticultural amateur, Augustine Henry, an Irish doctor who was one of the foremost plant collectors of his age. *The Wood and the Trees* was published in 1966 and revised and reissued in 1988.

After her father's death in 1958 and Tom's in 1964, Sheila threw herself into her activities at the Historical Society of the Religious Order of Friends, researching and conserving archival embroideries and portraits. At about this same time, she began an involvement with the Irish Travellers which she would continue for the rest of her life. Ostracized by much of Irish society, the Travellers are a nomadic people native to Ireland who follow a gypsy-like life and speak their own language, Shelta, which is closer to English than to Irish. Travellers are sometimes known as Tinkers—now considered a derogatory term—partly because many of them worked as tinsmiths, as well as itinerant farm laborers and door-to-door salesmen. Pim took many Traveller children into her home and eventually adopted an entire family which had been abandoned to the care of their travelling grandfather.

In Sheila Pim's last years, her growing deafness forced her to move into a sheltered housing complex where she still managed to grow a few herbs by her door. She fell ill and died on December 16, 1995, at the age of 86. For more information on Pim and her books see Tom and Enid Schantz' lengthy introduction to *Common or Garden Crime* (Rue Morgue Press, 2001).

Contents

Garden tips from Sheila Pim's
Bringing the Garden Indoors

<u>June</u>

For Weddings:

In Japanese flower arrangement a combination of roses with a branch of old pine symbolizes eternal youth and is considered appropriate for festive occasions, especially weddings.

For wedding guests who must throw things, provide bowls of rose petals, or peony petals, anything rather than confetti. It is kinder to the happy couple and to the charwoman who sweeps up.

Miniature Roses:

Under this heading I count every kind of rose with a small flower, whether it grows on a full-sized bush, like the "Threepenny-bit" rose, or properly belongs, like *Rouletti* or *Peon*, to the dolls' house garden.

The "Threepenny-bit" rose is the briar type, single, white, with pink-tipped petals, and not much larger than a coin. It is delightfully free flowering, but hardly one to cut. More suitable for miniature vases is a kind of small rose the same shape as modern hybrid teas. I can give only one name, "Bouton d' or.' They are worth enquiring for from specialist nurserymen.

At a show recently I saw an exquisite small rose labeled "Maltese Rose." Now, if this was the true Maltese Rose, it is not supposed to be taken out of Malta, and must have been smuggled away. Having seen it, I can understand the temptation and will not strike a moral attitude. Is it fair to forbid the spread of varieties if they can be propagated from slips without injury to the parent bush?

CHAPTER ONE
It Starts at the Flower Show

OLD Miss Hampton was wonderful. In other words she was over eighty and did not die, although she had been expected to at any time during the last five years. When she did die it took everybody by surprise. They all said how wonderful she had been on the day of the flower show.

This was the flower show held in Brainborough in June, 1945; not allowed to be called the Victory Flower Show because of Irish neutrality, but indicating all the same that Brainborough knew the war was over. Brainborough is a small place, sequestered, calm, not like anywhere you read about in the newspapers, and not less satisfied with itself on that account. But Brainborough people do take an interest in the outside world. The war in Europe was over. There had not been a local flower show since it began. Everybody felt it would be nice to hold one, and that it would fill a certain need of something to talk about.

As things turned out, the flower show was hardly used up as a topic before it was eclipsed by the mystery of Miss Hampton's death. Not long after that was cleared up came the first news of the atomic bomb. Luckily these events were evenly spaced out, as Brainborough does not like too many things happening at once.

The town of Brainborough (which visitors sometimes mistake for a village) is situated within the Pale. It may once have had another name in Irish, but to the English settlers it was Brian Boru's town, and after English had been spoken there for some centuries it was Brainboroughston, as it cumbrously appears on eighteenth century maps. Then somebody who thought they knew decided that "borough" and "town" in one name were redundant, so the end of the word was cut off, and the modern form, like many things that are slightly incorrect, turned out more convenient.

The two chief houses in the neighborhood nowadays are Hampton Court and Spangle Hill. The Hamptons arrived at the end of the seventeenth century, acquired land at the expense of some imprudent supporters of James II, and built their fine stone mansion in the best period of the eighteenth century. Sturdy Whigs, they put their own name on it, feeling they had as much right to a house called Hampton Court as the British royal family. Since then there had been ramifications of Hamptons throughout the county. Brainborough had had a Hampton hockey team and a Hampton harriers. But the family was dying out, and now the only people of the name left were old Miss Hampton at the Court and Liam Hampton of Hampton Lodge, who was her cousin and generally looked on as her heir. Some other cousins were called Linacre, and lived at Glenwood.

Spangle Hill was another eighteenth century house once owned by Hamptons, into which a cheerful family called Booley Browne had recently poured themselves, like new wine into an old bottle. Miss Hampton did not take much interest in the Booley Brownes because they were Roman Catholics. But there was rivalry between the gardens, for when it came to classes like "Hardy Cut Flowers, 12 vases; 12 distinct varieties," or "Vegetables, Collection of. To be shown on a space not exceeding 12 ft. by 4 ft.", McGuirk of Hampton Court and Cuddy of Spangle Hill were the only two gardeners with enough material to make an entry.

By happy chance, or possibly tactful judging had something to do with it, the two chief awards at the June flower show went one to each garden: McGuirk beat Cuddy in the Hardy Cut Flowers, but Cuddy beat McGuirk in the Assorted Vegetables.

One novelty was the class for Medicinal Herbs ("Class for Noxious Weeds, I call it," said old Miss Hampton). Since the war, Mrs. Linacre of Glenwood had been taking an interest in vegetable drugs. She talked gravely about the shortage of imports, and reproached her neighbors with letting the very stuff of healing go to waste in the fields and hedgerows. She had been corresponding with the Department of Agriculture, and was planning a herb-gathering picnic to make money for the Work Depot. Being on the flower show committee, she had insisted on herbs being introduced into the schedule, and the class attracted quite a number of entries, as all you had to do was to dig up some mulleins or foxgloves or deadly nightshade, all of which grew wild in the district. Most people were vague about the properties of these plants. Mrs. Linacre's own exhibit, in which each plant was labeled with full particulars, easily took first prize.

Vegetables, bottled fruit and honey were important features of the show, for they were what would bring in the money at the auction afterwards. Anything that was left over after paying expenses was to go to the Work Depot, a sewing party that met at Hampton Court. Several firsts in the smaller Vegetable Classes had been carried off by Mrs. De Vigne, who was a tenant of Miss Hampton's in a small house called Prospect View.

"My grandfather called it that," Miss Hampton explained to her secretary-companion, Priscilla Hoyle. "He had his own peculiar sense of humor. The house overlooks a graveyard. I think that's why her vegetables do so well. It's good Protestant soil."

Priscilla Hoyle laughed. She was not very experienced in the duties of a companion, but she knew one laughed at one's employer's jokes.

Priscilla had only recently been engaged by Miss Hampton, and this was the first time she had met so many Brainborough people all together. She was having an anxious afternoon, trying to sort out the people she was supposed to know from those to whom she had not yet been introduced, and trying to sense her employer's attitude to all of them. In general it seemed to be an attitude of contempt. Contempt was mitigated by family solidarity in the case of a cousin like Mrs. Linacre, but Mrs. De Vigne, her tenant, bored Miss Hampton very much by always having some question of repairs she wanted attended to, and Priscilla had instructions to head off this subject whenever it approached.

Miss Hampton was going round the show in great detail, leaning heavily on her stick and on Priscilla's arm. On her other arm Priscilla carried Miss Hampton's mackintosh and furs. It was a very hot day for having anything on your arm at all, even an old lady who could hardly weigh more than seven stone, but such are the duties of a companion. Priscilla glanced anxiously at Miss Hampton from time to time, wondering how she could bear the heat and the exertion, but she knew that nothing annoyed her employer more than being advised to rest.

While Miss Hampton was peering suspiciously at an exhibit of Old Roses, Priscilla had a chance to look round. There did not seem to be many young, or even youngish, people present. She wondered if Captain Hampton of Hampton Lodge came to flower shows. She could see Mrs. Linacre's boy, Tim, home from Trinity, sitting on a table in a corner with a very pretty girl. The girl was hatless and stockingless, and Priscilla envied her; companions have to wear their stockings.

"How nice to see you here, dear Cousin Rebecca!" said Mrs. Linacre, coming up to them. "Don't let her tire herself," she whispered to Priscilla,

who did not see how she could help it. "I see you are looking at Miss
Tench's Old Roses," said Mrs. Linacre to Miss Hampton. "Such darlings,
aren't they? Is that the real old York and Lancaster?"

"No. *Rosa mundi*. And stolen property too," snapped Miss Hampton.
"It's a cutting off mine. Three years ago she got into my garden and broke
off half the bush. I didn't notice at the time, unfortunately, but when I
found it rooted with her, I knew what to think."

"Really? How annoying!" said Mrs. Linacre. "Of course, people have
no consciences about cuttings."

"Nobody has a conscience nowadays," said Miss Hampton. "Not even
the Protestants. So I took my own measures. I presented her with a root of
Tussilago farfara variegata and advised her to give it a good position on
the rockery. I don't suppose she'll ever quite get it out again."

She reminded Priscilla of a bad fairy, laying up trouble for somebody
who had not invited her to a christening. Mrs. Linacre changed the subject, but not too tactfully, by admiring some fine lilies from Spangle Hill.
Miss Hampton regarded them with pinched nostrils.

"Very fine blooms," she conceded, "if you care for Madonna lilies.
Do you know, my dear, I always think they're very R.C. flowers."

II

"Have you seen my exhibit?" Tim Linacre demanded of Meriel Booley
Browne.

"I'm afraid I haven't, Tim. Did it get a prize?"

"Not for competition," said Tim. "It's educational." He took her
arm and led her to a table a little apart from the other exhibits. On the
table was a wooden box with a glass over it. A card lying on the glass
read:

HELIX POMATIA (edible snails)
Not found in Ireland
Lent by T. Linacre, Esq.

Tim took off the glass to give Meriel a better view. The snails were
enormous, nearly as large as hens' eggs. Some were striped in brown,
some a pale tawny shade all over. They were lying in a heap at the bottom
of the box, and one or two perked up vague inquiring horns, or squeezed
out their fat shapes and went crawling slowly over the others' shells and
up the sides of the box, leaving behind them trails of slime.

"Ugh!" Meriel went all feminine. "Fancy bringing those to a flower show!"

"Why not? They're garden produce. Lots of people eat them nowadays."

"I'd like to see you eat one. Where did you get them?"

"Chap I know called Marshall, who's at school near Cheltenham. There are Roman remains there, and these little pets are probably descended from snails that were imported by the Romans. It's int'resting, you know." Tim was a person of many interests. "In France they have regular snail farms where they raise them for market. It's called *Héliciculture*."

"And is that what you're thinking of going in for?"

"Might do worse. I don't see why there shouldn't be money in it. All you R.C.s could eat them on fast days when you can't get fish. One would have to create a demand by advertising to begin with. I should need some capital. . . ."

Tim Linacre was on the lookout for a suitable opening in life. So far, in his third year at Trinity, he had not found anything that appealed both to him and to his mother (his father had died some years before). Mrs. Linacre thought perhaps research, or an estate agency, something to keep him near her in Ireland. Tim thought perhaps diplomacy or journalism, or crime investigation. But nothing was yet decided; Tim had another year to go before taking his degree, and Mrs. Linacre cultivated family ties with Miss Hampton while waiting for something to turn up.

Meriel Booley Browne, the girl whom Priscilla Hoyle had thought pretty from a distance, was a little older than Tim and the acknowledged beauty of Brainborough. She was a perfect Irish type, with dark hair and gray eyes and the lovely complexion that seems to be one compensation for a rainy climate. She was bad at games, but rode well and danced beautifully, and she was very sweet-natured and her parents had money. Tim could hardly expect to monopolize her, even in that limited society. As he proceeded to outline his latest financial project, he noticed that her attention had wandered, and from something concentrated in her expression, he guessed, without looking up, that his cousin Liam had entered the tent.

Liam Hampton was, like Meriel Booley Browne, a person who would be noticed anywhere. With him it was something more than good looks; he walked as if he was somebody, and he had a head like a poet's, if you like poets. In Brainborough he attracted rather particular interest because of his future prospects and past career.

Hampton Court and Hampton Lodge had once been all one property.

Then two brothers had divided it, the elder taking the big house and
the gardens and the younger the small house and the farm. Miss Hampton was free to leave Hampton Court as she liked, but it seemed logical for her to leave it to Liam and reunite the two halves of the estate.
She would also have to leave him the money for its upkeep, or it
would be a white elephant, and a white elephant with a hearty appe-
tite. Rising taxation and two generations' death duties had diminished
the resources of Liam's branch of the family, but fortunes made by
deceased uncles and brothers had increased Miss Hampton's. The old
lady kept up no style and was growing miserly in her old age, but
people imagined her fortune all the larger the less evidence there
was of it.

Liam himself, scion of an old Ascendancy dynasty, had displayed an
indifference to the ideals and tradition of his ancestors that was almost
overdone. Christened after William of Orange, he had changed his name
to the Irish version, and, at a time when all his kinsfolk and connections
were rallying to the British forces, Liam Hampton enlisted in the army of
his native land. This had caused a quarrel between him and Miss Hampton, for the old lady, if she had been the British, would not have hesitated
to invade Ireland and seize the Treaty ports, and Liam would have had to
do his best to prevent her.

But no invasion came, either of British or of Germans, and in due
course Liam was exempted from further service. A few months ago he
had come back home to resume farming. It seemed as if he was now old
enough to stop being quixotic about his future. When he generously let
McGuirk get the better of him in an argument over a boundary fence,
Miss Hampton commented that he was counting on both sides soon being
his own.

On the other hand, as Mrs. Linacre pointed out to her cousin Rebecca,
Liam was also of an age to marry and settle down. That was where Meriel
Booley Browne came into the picture.

IV

Other people besides Tim were aware of Liam's arrival. From either
side of a bank of flowering shrubs, which hid each pair from the other,
Miss Hampton and Priscilla Hoyle, and Miss Tench and Mrs. De Vigne,
watched him walk straight over to join Meriel. There was nothing in the
encounter that a film producer would have thought worth shooting; nevertheless, Miss Tench remarked to Mrs. De Vigne:

"That looks to me like a 'case'."

Mrs. De Vigne made gentle twitters of distress. "Oh dear, I hope not," she said.

"It would be a slap in the face for Miss Hampton, wouldn't it?" said Miss Tench, in a tone of some satisfaction. "I wonder if he means to turn. I met him twice last week coming from Father Lawrence's."

"He's been helping on this Muintir na Tire movement," said Mrs. De Vigne, being fair.

"Huh," said Miss Tench. "That might be the thin end of the wedge."

On the other side of the flowering shrubs, Priscilla tried to edge Miss Hampton away. But the old lady's fingers closed on her companion's arm like a kestrel's claw, and she held her to the spot while she listened shamelessly. Priscilla was not allowed to move until Miss Hampton had heard enough, and then they bore down direct on the group by Tim Linacre's snail box.

Priscilla was rather in the dark about the circumstances, but anyone could sense a family crisis. She prepared to make herself invisible, for companions ought to be like furniture during a crisis. To her relief it all passed off quietly, at any rate on the surface.

"Ah, Miss Booley Browne," said Miss Hampton, rather as one identifies an aphis. "We have not seen you at the Work Depot lately. Well, William, you seem to have time to spare."

"An odd day away does no harm," said Liam easily.

"Then perhaps you will come and see me one afternoon. I should like to have a little talk."

"Would tomorrow suit you, Cousin Rebecca?"

"I prefer not to discuss business on Sunday."

"I'm going up to town on Monday."

"Indeed. Then we must defer the matter till your return. In any case, Monday is our Work Depot day. Shall we see you, Miss Booley Browne?"

"I'm afraid not next Monday, Miss Hampton," said Meriel, blushing unnecessarily. "I—er—I shan't be here that day either, I'm afraid. I know Mammy means to go, though."

"Then I shall look forward to seeing your mother. I think she is trying to attract your attention at the moment."

Mrs. Booley Browne, a capacious, comfortable matron, was certainly looking in their direction, and Meriel, feeling several years too young for her age, obeyed an impulse to take shelter under the maternal wing.

"Shall we say Tuesday morning, William?" said Miss Hampton, turning again to her cousin. Liam jumped and looked vague for a moment, then said, not too gladly, "Very well, Cousin Rebecca, I daresay I can make it."

"Eleven," said Miss Hampton. "I do not come down to breakfast nowadays, but I shall be ready by that hour."

"I'll hardly be back by eleven," said Liam. "Wait though, you mean eleven, old time?"

"Eleven, God's time," said Miss Hampton, who had never approved of the government tampering with the clock.

"Twelve, in fact," said Liam, and made a note of it. Then he chose to consider himself dismissed and sauntered off.

V

Meanwhile Miss Tench and Mrs. De Vigne pursued their artless way round the tent.

In spite of all her own first prizes, Mrs. De Vigne sighed with envy over Cuddy's Assorted Vegetables; his emerald green peas, his iridescent onions, smooth new potatoes, firm round lettuces, all fittingly mounted on black velvet and bordered round with parsley.

"My onions got the mildew," remarked Miss Tench, "and McGuirk told me so did all his at the Court. I don't know what this man does to them. Do you think would it be holy water?"

"McGuirk beat him in the Hardy Cut Flowers," said Mrs. De Vigne. "Did you notice that fine dark red *Verbascum*?"

"I did. I wonder now, whereabouts McGuirk had that growing. I don't remember seeing it before."

"I do, but not at the Court. Paddy Shankey has it in his little back garden. Perhaps McGuirk gave him a root."

"I'm sure Miss Hampton didn't, anyway," said Miss Tench. Miss Hampton had the reputation of not being generous with "bits."

Suddenly Mrs. De Vigne caught Miss Tench's arm with an exclamation. "Eily, look there! Do, you see it, or am I imagining things?"

She pointed to McGuirk's rival exhibit of vegetables. It was disfigured by a trail of slime right across a row of new potatoes, and, following the trail to its end, their eyes fastened on an enormous snail.

Other visitors to the show were suffering similar shocks. A girl going round with her "fella" saw another snail crawling up a lupin, and gave an affected scream. A child's voice shrieked: "Mammy! Would ya look-a-the-snayul! Janey! The size of him!" Snails two inches high are startling things to be faced with if you are not prepared for them.

Tim Linacre said afterwards that there could not have been more fuss made over Hitler's secret weapon.

Tim had taken the glass off the box to show Meriel the snails, and had forgotten about it for a few minutes while they were all talking to Miss Hampton. It could not have been more than about ten minutes that he left the box uncovered, but snails can, apparently, show more speed than they are given credit for. Some of them turned up yards away. A hunt for them spread to the remotest corners of the tent, and while Tim tried several times over to count the ones left in the box, people kept bringing snails back to him, with much giggling and remarks that he did not think funny. Then while he was still all hot and bothered, McGuirk pitched into him because a snail had eaten one of his lettuces, and he seemed to blame Tim for sabotaging his exhibit, whereas anyone could see he had had no chance against those onions of Cuddy's. But McGuirk was working off his resentment at Miss Hampton's commenting on those same onions and saying it was a pity they could not have them at the Court, and she would buy up Cuddy's at the auction at the end of the show. It was a good thing the show was nearly over. It seemed to have been going on and on and on, and the stuffiness in the tent was telling on people's tempers and their intelligences.

Tim gave up the idea of *Héliciculture* and let the snails go in the auction too. But although Shankey, the auctioneer, wrung all the humor he could out of them, they did not seem likely to be much in demand. To everybody's surprise, old Miss Hampton bid a shilling for the lot.

"Properly cooked, they are delicious," she informed Priscilla, in her high, authoritative voice, to which bystanders listened with awe. "Yes, indeed, I have eaten them many times at Prunier's. *Escargots à la poulette* or *à la Bourguignonne*. I should like to taste them again, it would bring back the old days."

Nobody else wanted to revive Continental memories, so the snails were knocked down to Miss Hampton, and she told Tim to put them in her pony trap. The last office he could do for them was to fill the box with greenstuff off his mother's herb exhibit to give them provender for their final journey.

CHAPTER TWO
Hampton Court

WHEN Priscilla Hoyle decided that she could not live with her mother any longer, she answered the first advertisement in that day's *Irish Times*, and that was how she came to be at Hampton Court.

Priscilla was a Dubliner. She knew the Wicklow hills at Easter, the West in August, and Rathgar all the year round. She knew what Hampton Court would be like as well as a New Yorker knows what to expect in the South: aristocratic owners, amusingly faithful servants, relics of grandeur, bygone elegance, antiques, horses and all the props. It would be "the big house," as seen from trains and buses at a distance in a demesne, and closer on the stage. It turned out to be just like that only different.

You came to Hampton Court through large iron gates, inside which stood a house you might take for a little church before you knew it was a lodge. This was the appropriate home of the McGuirks, who, as befitted retainers of Miss Hampton's, were strong Protestants. McGuirk himself was a dour and stiff-necked man, especially so on Sundays when he wore a high white collar for best. Mrs. McGuirk was a subdued woman. She came up to the house each day to do the cooking, and it was evidence of Miss Hampton's strong attachment to her faith that she would rather have Mrs. McGuirk's food than more digestible results produced by a Roman Catholic. The rest of the staff at the house was one house parlormaid called Mary, who was very young and unimportant and did most of the work. McGuirk's son Billy, aged ten, did Miss Hampton's boots and brought in turf for the fires. Outside the house there was McVittie, in charge of the pony; a man like a gnarled old thorn tree if a thorn tree could spit. There were also two or three men under McGuirk in the garden and grounds.

From the lodge you approached the house by a narrow pass between high walls of laurel, laurustinus, holly, ilex, arbutus,, and rhododendrons all grown together in a continuous mass of evergreen. So deep and dark was the drive that it might have been a corridor in a labyrinth. Priscilla always had a feeling that on plunging into the drive she left the surface of the modern world.

The rhododendrons in the drive were clipped back, but around the house they were free to flower and, in June, were a mass of pinkish mauve. They straggled round the lawn and up to the wall of the flower garden. In their midst was a rubbish dump, past which a branch of the drive cut off to the yard. Most of the lawn was occupied by three or four Wellingtonias, which had grown much taller than anyone expected a century ago when they were planted. Their spreading arms, dark green to the fingertips, cut off light from the house.

The house was a fine old house. It had a pillared portico and flight of stone steps, and the eighteenth century rightness in its proportions. But more than half the windows faced you with blank shutters. As for the interior, none of it matched. There were eighteenth century busts and Victorian beaded woolwork; Adams bookcases filled with Edwardian novelettes; African weapons and Italian peasant pottery; expensive knickknacks given by the Hamptons to each other as Christmas presents, and cheap modern plates and utensils that Miss Hampton had picked up as bargains. Priscilla's strongest first impressions were of dirt. The McGuirks and Mary were an adequate staff to look after the day-to-day needs of one old lady, but not enough to dust the high gilt picture frames, wash the turf smoke off the marble mantelpieces, take down and shake the hangings, or sort the heaps of rags and papers that lay about in corners like drifts of fallen leaves. Miss Hampton did seem aware that the house had been somewhat neglected, for she told Priscilla she had not thought it worthwhile to have any spring cleaning done during the war. "What was the use, when at any moment one might have to fly?" She was obsessed by the fear of an invasion, and used to make lists of things she would take with her if she had to be evacuated.

Except for a drawing room that had been cleared of furniture and fitted up to accommodate the Work Depot, the only rooms in use were bedrooms and a small back parlor off the hall. Miss Hampton had her writing bureau in the parlor, and there was a small table with folding leaves that opened out for meals. If company came it was not often let in any further than the hall, which was a large room full of objects like stuffed fish, spare parts of foxes (the Hampton Harriers owed its name to alliteration, as it had really been a fox hunt), relics of all England's wars from Napoleon to 1914, and a great many plants in pots. Among these were to be found chairs and tables, two oak chests, and an old-fashioned circular sofa of the kind on which you have to sit back to back. Some of the things out of the hall had overflowed into the kitchen; and here the general background of history, botany, zoology, and cooking utensils of unfathomable uses, was like a stage setting for "The Sorcerer's Apprentice." And the day after the flower show, Priscilla went into the kitchen and found the maids entertaining a real witch.

Old Mrs. Shegog had glided inconspicuously in across the yard, and the dogs, which usually made a great fuss about visitors, never gave one bark at her. Priscilla knew she was a witch because she had been pointed

out as one by Miss Hampton herself. She lived alone with her goat in
a cabin at the demesne back gate, like the poor man in the hymn,
whom the rich man in his castle would probably have evicted if he
could. Miss Hampton said she was an obnoxious old humbug and her
goat was a public nuisance, but that she knew more about herbs than
Mrs. Linacre.

Mrs. Shegog was the beggar of all past ages, whatever may be to
come. The type is out of place in a modern community, but in old-fashioned countries it is still cherished as a kind of object lesson to the mate-
rialist. Beggars both demonstrate the superfluousness of worldly possessions and offer you an opportunity of discarding some of your own surplus. This point of view would not have appealed to Miss Hampton, however, smacking too much of Catholicism.

"Many's the time I ate a dish of snails myself," Mrs. Shegog was
informing the kitchen audience. Mrs. McGuirk was beating a cake mixture; Mary was polishing silver.

Mrs. McGuirk stopped beating: "Is that so? Well, now, and how do
you cook them?" This was a problem she supposed she would soon have
to tackle, and she was glad of expert advice.

"I boils them," said Mrs. Shegog. "Put a drop of milk on to boil, and
when it's mad boiling drop them in. Then if you drink the milk after it'd
cure a consumption. If you had T.B. as they say now."

"Is that so?" said Mrs. McGuirk again. She was not really much of a
believer in Mrs. Shegog, but the snails did seem to be more in the old
woman's line than her own. Any cook not nailed to her post by marriage
would have given notice on the head of them.

"I never seen any the size of them," said Mrs. Shegog, poking
about among the leaves in Tim Linacre's box. "Wherever did they
come from at all?"

"From England, I'm told," said Mrs. McGuirk.

"Ah, the poor creatures!" Mrs. Shegog meant the English, not the
snails. "I suppose they'd eat anything there, as things are at present." All
three women wagged their heads compassionately.

It was some time since Mrs. Shegog had been up to the house, as she
was aware of Miss Hampton's prejudice against her. What brought her
now was partly interest in the snails, for she was genuinely a bit of a
naturalist, and partly her other great interest, gossip, for the gossip of
Brainborough was running just then on the Hampton family.

At this point, however, Priscilla came forward.

"Good evening, Mrs. Shegog," she said, and firmly replaced the lid on the snail box. "You know, I don't think Miss Hampton likes you coming into the kitchen."

"Good evening, Miss." The old woman made Priscilla a little bob that might have been meant for a curtsey. "Miss Hoyle, isn't it? Sure the people is all talking of the lovely young lady from Dublin. God bless you, Miss, and may you never want in your old age. I only came to see if Mrs. McGuirk could spare a heel of an old loaf. Sure it's not for myself, it's for my poor old goat."

"The mistress says I'm to give nothing without I'd ask her," said Mrs. McGuirk.

"Miss Hampton was complaining about your goat," said Priscilla. "She says if she finds it tethered on the back drive again, she'll hand it over to the Guards."

"Ah, she's a hard woman, God help her!" said Mrs. Shegog, grieved to think that anybody could harbor such ill intentions. "My poor old goat's giving nothing this long time, on account of the poor grass it gets. You couldn't spare me a little cup of milk? Sure I wouldn't ask you for tea, in these times."

One of the things that distressed Priscilla in the domestic economy of the Court was the waste of milk. A gallon can was sent over every morning from Liam Hampton's farm, and sometimes half of it was thrown away. Against her better judgment, she took the battered tin can Mrs. Shegog held out to her. In the time her back was turned, two carrots and half a dozen potatoes rolled out of the vegetable rack into the large pocket of Mrs. Shegog's skirt. She had often mentioned to Mrs. McGuirk that to carry a potato in one's pocket was a preventative of rheumatism.

Priscilla returned with the milk, and Mrs. Shegog immediately began calling down blessings which she seemed to expect in a shower from the ceiling. Priscilla's hope that, having got something out of her, the old woman would go, was doomed to disappointment. Mrs. Shegog took the greatest interest in the new young lady from Dublin. She peered closely into her face, and discovered there an opening for her professional services.

"That's a bad old spot ye have there, Miss," she said sympathetically. "I'll tell ye what to do for that now. Take your starving spittle, an' put it on a board, an' make the sign of the Cross on it, an' rub it well in, an' say, 'In the name of the Father and of the Son and of the Holy Ghost, Amen.' That'll take all the bad out of it and it'll be gone by morning."

She nodded reassuringly at Priscilla, who was too horrified to reply. "They do be troublesome in the spring," said the old woman, "and the girls all wanting to look their best. Ye'll be giving the ball a kick yourself, Miss, one of these days. And is it true now, what I hear of the captain? Is he courting at last?"

The question, the real object of Mrs. Shegog's visit, went unanswered. Somehow, in the interest of the conversation, or because the old witch held them spellbound, no one had noticed Miss Hampton's step in the passage. Now they all jumped as the old lady rapped angrily with her stick on the threshold. Mary raised the silver tea tray she was polishing as if it was a shield. Only Mrs. Shegog kept her composure and curtseyed. There was no knowing how long Miss Hampton had been there. She surveyed them with beady eyes and addressed Priscilla.

"Miss Hoyle, I told you I don't allow begging at the back door. What is this creature doing here? I saw her goat in my fields this minute from my bedroom window, and she may take it out of there before I set the dogs on it." This was an empty threat, for the Hampton Court dogs, a fat old springer and an Irish terrier, never took violent exercise. However, it conveyed Miss Hampton's attitude on the goat question.

"Ah, you're very bad, Miss Hampton," said Mrs. Shegog. "I'll say a prayer for you, Miss Hoyle. You've a hard mistress, God help you!"

The two old woman stood measuring each other, and it struck Priscilla that there was quite a resemblance between them: they were both so old and crabbed and wrinkled, and dressed in much the same kind of shapeless old black clothes.

Mrs. Shegog had had two husbands and ten children, who had all died or gone away. All her life she had worked and foraged and scrounged and never had quite enough to eat. She had learned to suspect most people's charity of having strings to it, and to see through people and get things out of them. Miss Hampton had been the richest woman in the district for eighty years, and had grown richer and richer through losing one kinsman after another. She had always had enough to eat, but had completely missed sex life, had found that most people sooner or later asked her for subscriptions, had learned to see through people and order them about. So they had come by different routes to the same level of lonely old age. Miss Hampton had blood pressure and refused to diet; Mrs. Shegog could not keep off the drink. But they both meant to hang on to life as long as possible, though they knew most of the worst of it between them.

In spite of their long cherished animosity, they had a kind of contemporary respect for each other, and an understanding from which Priscilla and Mary and middle-aged Mrs. McGuirk were shut out.

Priscilla almost thought Miss Hampton had met her match, but it was not likely she would be outfaced on her home ground.

Mrs. Shegog dropped another curtsey and retreated.

"I'll be going now," she remarked, reserving to herself the right to leave at her own pleasure. "Ill luck does be on them that turns the poor and needy from their door. Many a one that's rich and easy now will be twisting and turning in torment till the end of time."

She tossed back this parting shaft from halfway across the yard. Miss Hampton sniffed, and ordered Mary to open all the windows and air the room after her.

CHAPTER THREE
Work Depot

THE Work Depot made Priscilla laugh. She could not imagine how it came to be established in a house like Hampton Court. The fact was it was there because of Mrs. Linacre's insistence that in good works the "big house" ought to give a lead. Otherwise, she warned Miss Hampton, things would get into the wrong hands, by which she meant Mrs. Booley Browne's instead of her own. Mrs. Linacre originally had her eye on a room upstairs, known as the music room, and empty except for a grand piano, which would do for cutting out on. But the floor was found to be unsafe (much of the old mansion was in bad repair), so they had cleared the drawing room below of countless small chairs, tables, cabinets, whatnots, footstools, palms and pot plants which now cluttered up other corners. Eighteenth century spaciousness returned for a moment when there was nothing left in the room but the two mantelpieces of inlaid marble and the shimmering cut-glass chandelier. Then Mrs. Linacre brought in a sewing machine, a plain deal cupboard, some kitchen chairs, and a long table covered in American cloth.

The idea was to make clothes and hospital dressings for various charities. On the two Work Depot days Priscilla had come in for so far, nothing very much had been done. Priscilla liked to get things done, and it occurred to her that it might help if she did the cutting out beforehand, so as to have everything ready for the helpers to sew when they arrived. But she could not find the cutting-out scissors, and had to ask Miss Hampton about them.

Miss Hampton was sitting at her desk in the back parlor, making a list of things she would lay in if ever there was another war. Around her lay scattered newspaper cuttings, and a genealogical table she had drawn up on a sheet of cartridge paper. She was a very littery old lady.

"Scissors?" she said. "Oh yes, I have them. I was just cutting out this obituary notice of old Sir Howard Gower. Five years younger than me," she added with satisfaction. "You may take the paper now, I've done with it."

"You oughtn't to use cutting-out scissors on newspaper," said Priscilla. "It takes the edge off them." She said "You oughtn't" to Miss Hampton for practice, because lately she had been afraid she was getting too servile.

"I don't care if it does," said Miss Hampton. "I wish you would put some flowers in the hall before people come. Rhododendrons. In that big brass jug. I will attend to the cutting out, but first I must put away my papers. One never knows who will turn up on these occasions, and it does not do to leave things lying about."

It was one of the old lady's ways to think of something different for you to do as soon as you suggested anything yourself. Priscilla could not feel that the hall needed flowers on top of everything that was there already. She knew Miss Hampton would cut the Work Depot materials to waste, and draw down on them the reproaches of the Dublin Center that had supplied them. But companions are not paid to argue, so she went off to the shrubbery.

As she came back across the drive with her arms full, Miss Hampton put her head out of her bedroom window and announced: "Here's that De Vigne woman. I don't know why she comes so early. Hold the fort, Miss Hoyle. I shan't come down till some more arrive."

Mrs. De Vigne was at that moment tattling out on to the gravel, and Priscilla, seeing that the visitor had been well within earshot, tried to be extra civil in her reception. She explained that Miss Hampton was "changing." Whether this referred to her clothes, her mind, or the inevitable change that goes with decay in the hymn, it was unnecessary to say.

The visitor seemed in rather a fuss. Priscilla thought it was probably her nature. Mrs. De Vigne was nothing like so old as Miss Hampton, but had become venerable rather early through having masses of lovely snow-white hair. She was old-fashioned too; she wore a hat with a veil, and gloves, and bracelets over her gloves, and various ornaments that were obviously heirlooms. She had been a widow so long that she was more like an old maid.

She put up her veil to look at Priscilla, and took off one glove in order to shake hands. She apologized for being so early, and apologized for being hot—it was a beautiful day—and begged Priscilla not to disturb

Miss Hampton. Might she just have a look round the garden? It was a long time since she had seen it, and it must be looking lovely. Had not McGuirk carried all before him at the show? "That lovely red *Verbascum,*" said Mrs. De Vigne. "I should like to see that again. I think flowers are exquisite, don't you, Miss Hoyle? I mean, one gets such pleasure from them, at least I do."

Priscilla had not got any particular pleasure from the rhododendrons; they were all the dreary magenta ones, and she had had to push through the shrubbery to get at them, and twigs had yanked off her hair net and pulled out strands of the neat roll she wore all round her head. She excused herself in order to arrange the flowers and tidy up. Mrs. De Vigne knew her way to the garden and padded off there. Miss Hampton afterwards spoke severely to Priscilla for taking her eyes off her; as she was certainly after "bits". But she was mistaken; this time Mrs. De Vigne was after something else.

In due course the rest of the work party assembled: Mrs. Linacre; Miss Tench; Mrs. Booley Browne; Mrs. Gahan, the bank manager's wife; with one of her daughters; Ursula Owler, the rector's daughter; and Miss Counsel, whose father was Miss Hampton's solicitor.

There was a great taking off of hats and putting on of white overalls and caps, standing on tiptoe to look in the mirrors over the drawing-room mantelpieces. Then a procession to wash hands with carbolic soap in a basin in a little cubbyhole by the garden door. Then Mrs. De Vigne discovered that she had forgotten her glasses, and Priscilla invented a job for her that did not require them. She also found thimbles for two other ladies who had not brought their own. At last they all settled down, sitting round the long table, which Priscilla had punctiliously wiped down with disinfectant, and stitching away at dressings of gauze and cotton wool. A little later, Miss Hampton made a royal entrance, greeted the ladies ceremoniously one by one, and made them all sit down in different places.

Mrs. Booley Browne made her daughter's excuses. Mrs. Booley Browne was a round, jolly woman, looking in her white overall like a pleasant grocer's wife. She had been a lovely girl and felt that all allowances ought to be made for the young. She said: "Meriel's gone up to town for the night, to my sister, but her aunt won't see much of her, she's off to this big dance. I said to her, 'My dear child, gather ye rosebuds while ye may.' "

Most of the older ladies smiled sentimental smiles at the picture of Meriel gathering her rosebuds, and looking, no doubt, like a rosebud about due to be gathered herself.

Priscilla thought the Gahan girl and Ursula Owler looked a bit wistful, as if they did not get enough rosebuds, but she may have been mistaken, as Ursula was a very serious girl, and Biddy Gahan was engaged to a young Gaelic leaguer who did not approve of "foreign" dances.

But some people's rosebuds can be other people's thorns, as it appeared when Miss Tench casually remarked, "Mr., or should I say, Captain, Hampton has gone on that train too. I met them going to the station together."

"Oh yes," said Mrs. Booley Browne. "He's taking Meriel to the dance." In the pause that followed most people could not help glancing at Miss Hampton.

"I am surprised that Meriel did not choose a younger partner," said Miss Hampton.

"Well, I suppose it was the other way round," replied Mrs. Booley Browne, laughing. "It's usually the gentleman does the asking. But of course Meriel was delighted to go."

"Naturally," said Miss Hampton. "In your place, I should be inclined to discourage such outings in the case of a friendship that is unlikely to lead to anything."

Mrs. Booley Browne turned red. She was not a touchy woman, and would ordinarily have taken Miss Hampton's attitude as a joke, but she was just awakening to the fact that her pretty daughter was a responsibility, and it made her nervous. She was not going to have it said that Meriel was flirting with Liam Hampton, but neither was Miss Hampton to say she shouldn't if she liked.

The other ladies thought that, if the friendship was not likely to lead to anything, Miss Hampton would not be showing such anxiety to discourage it. Mrs. Linacre thought Liam was foolish to prejudice his prospects. Mrs. De Vigne feared he was being got hold of. Miss Tench thought it would be good for Miss Hampton not to get her own way. Biddy Gahan and Ursula Owler thought it was romantic. Miss Counsel thought Meriel was a minx. Mrs. Gahan, the bank manager's wife, thought of something her husband had let drop once about the old lady's financial position, something she still remembered because he had told her to forget it.

Just when the little scene was developing into something for the whole town to talk about there came a lucky diversion. "A goat!" exclaimed Mrs. Linacre, who was nearest the window. "Cousin Rebecca, there's a goat in the garden!"

The drawing-room windows looked out on the precious walled enclosure of the flower garden proper. The ladies, all keen gardeners, dropped their sewing and crowded to look. Miss Hampton rapped with her stick on the glass. Mrs. Linacre detached Mrs. De Vigne from the window catch with which she was struggling, flung up the sash and shouted "McGuirk! McGuirk!" But all the gardeners, like all gardeners when you want them, were out of sight.

"They're all out cutting the long grass in the park," said Priscilla. "I'll send Mary." She slipped away to the kitchen, and then out into the garden by the side door. The other ladies, still in their white overalls, climbed actively over the low windowsill and launched a mass attack against the intruder. Priscilla thought it would be a good idea to turn it into a pincers movement, so she made a detour round an area of rockery. She forgot that goats climb rocks. This one jumped from rock to rock like a chamois, then bounded gladly into a clump of lupines.

"Grab hold of the rope!" called Mrs. Linacre, for the goat had a broken tether rope hanging from its neck, and this offered the best chance of controlling it. Priscilla reached out, but the goat moved briskly on from the lupines and blitzed its way into a hedge of old roses. Beyond, there grew Miss Hampton's greatest treasures, irises grown from crosses she had made herself, which were now about to open their buds in flowers never yet seen by collector or commercial grower. Miss Hampton visited them first thing every morning to try and detect the first signs of color.

The ladies advanced, and tactical theories mingled with adverse comments on the smell of goat. "Don't try to catch it," advised Mrs. Linacre. "Let us drive it out of the gate." By means of tactful bustling they headed the goat away from the irises and on to a path that led to the open side gate where it had got in. Unfortunately, just as the goat was trotting quietly off to the outside world, McVittie, the pony driver, fetched by Mary, appeared in the gateway. The goat reversed, glared at the work party with slit yellow eyes, and suddenly came at Priscilla, who found herself sitting among the old roses, reflecting, in a dazed way, that that was how it felt to be butted. The old varieties of roses grow much more dense and prickly than the modern ones. While Priscilla extricated herself the chase went on; Mary screamed, McVittie shouted, and the white-clad ladies fluttered in all directions. At last McVittie got hold of the rope and things quieted down. The work party clustered together; and the animal was led up to judgment.

"It's Mrs. Shegog's goat," said McVittie, and spat.

"You wicked creature!" said Miss Hampton to the goat, prodding it with her stick. "You ought to be ashamed of yourself. McVittie! This mustn't happen again."

"No, ma'am."

"I won't have it happen again," said Miss Hampton. "Take the animal and tie it up. Shut it up in one of the stables. I shall write to Sergeant Carty about it."

"Very well, ma'am;" said McVittie.

The goat was led away in disgrace, both it and McVittie looking extremely disgruntled. McVittie did not want the trouble of tying it up and looking after it, and a trail of spit along his route to the yard testified to his disgust at goats and employers and the world in general.

"Why, it's four o'clock !" said Mrs. Booley Browne breaking in on a solemn hush. Everybody followed her line of thought. Priscilla sent Mary ahead to the house to hurry on tea.

II

The heavy silver tea tray, with soda bread and seed cake, was set out on one of the old chests in the hall. Priscilla poured out and Mary carried round milk and sugar, while the guests found places for their cups among the bric-a-brac and plants. Miss Hampton made no attempt to play hostess, but deliberately dodged Mrs. De Vigne, who was trying to have a word with her, and beckoned Mrs. Linacre out to the stone portico.

Over tea various people made a point of being nice to Priscilla. Brainborough people were inclined to be shy with strangers, but they had seen her now at two or three Work Depots and the flower show, not looking in any way dangerous, and they were inclined to be sorry for anyone who had to live with Miss Hampton. They soon found that she knew nothing about gardening, so they asked if she played tennis or was fond of reading. Mrs. De Vigne, who did not feel safe with anybody till she knew just who they were, recalled meeting a Mr. Hoyle once at Parknasilla, who might be a relation, but Priscilla was not able to tell much about her family, and it did not seem as if the Hoyles had been anywhere around at the time when the De Vignes came over with the Huguenots.

Out on the portico, in a dazzle of pillar shadows and afternoon sun shafts, Miss Hampton was indulging in her favorite hobby of raising Mrs. Linacre's hopes.

The Linacres were connected with the Hamptons through descendants of a younger sister of the two brothers who had divided the property. Mrs. Linacre had traced the relationship, though it was all through a female line, to show that her Tim was Miss Hampton's third cousin once removed, and only a degree more distant than Liam.

Miss Hampton knew quite well that Mrs. Linacre cherished beneficiary hopes of her. Having always had people after her for money she took that for granted. Beyond that, she had never found anything particular to dislike in this cousin; she was a charming woman by Brainborough standards, that is, she dressed nicely and was in no way odd. She had soft gray hair and a soft voice and a sweet, sad face, and although she was always getting up something or other, she went about it tactfully. Miss Hampton almost respected Mrs. Linacre for the way she had wished the Work Depot on to her. At the moment she was chatting away about her new idea of herb gathering, but Miss Hampton had not listened and made no bones about interrupting.

"Your boy's growing up," she observed. "I suppose you've made plans for him."

Mrs. Linacre's fine eyes lost their animation and looked for a moment rather vague. Always full of detailed work for some good cause or other, she had not lately had much time to give to the problem of her son's future, apart from her settled policy of cultivating Cousin Rebecca.

"I want Tim to feel free to choose for himself," she replied slowly. "So far we haven't talked much about it. One should be careful, don't you think, not to force their inclinations?"

"Nonsense!" said Miss Hampton. "Young people never know what they want. People say 'Youth must be served,' I say, 'Youth must be spanked.' Would you say country life suits him?"

"Oh yes, he loves it. Tim is a very simple soul, really." Tim's mother placed no importance on his boyish craze for tough literature and crime detection.

Miss Hampton drank her tea and called her fat old springer up for a bit of seed cake. She seemed to have lost interest. Her next remark was, "Isn't this a good year for the flowering shrubs? Have you noticed the rhododendrons? *Ponticum is* out of fashion now, I believe, the craze is all for new colors. I often wonder what will happen to the garden here when I am gone. Will they plant it all with double cherries and polyantha roses, like that vulgar display at Spangle Hill?"

Mrs. Linacre was too discreet to say anything. She knew her expression was sympathetic.

"Yes. Well," said Miss Hampton, "it's no use trying to talk to you now, with that De Vigne woman hovering." (Mrs. De Vigne, who had ventured to the doorway, hastily backed indoors again.) "Will you and Tim come to—let me see—to lunch on Wednesday?"

"Thank you, Cousin Rebecca," said Mrs. Linacre. She had never before been invited for anything more than tea.

"You are my nearest relations next to William," remarked Miss Hampton. "You ought to be here oftener. Now I am tired. I'm going round by the yard to dodge all these gobbling turkey hens. You can tell them I am lying down, and perhaps they will go. I am quite exhausted by that affair with the goat."

Mrs. Linacre did not immediately take the hint, but remained by herself, leaning gracefully against a stone pillar, gazing out to where the green of a small hill shouldered up beyond the shrubbery. She nibbled on a seed out of the seed cake. They were caraways which she grew herself and presented to Cousin Rebecca in a little silk bag every Christmas. It began to look as if they had been a good investment.

CHAPTER FOUR
Melodrama

THE next morning, a little after eleven, Liam Hampton strolled into the hall to keep the appointment Miss Hampton had given him at the flower show. Priscilla was there on her knees, stitching on a button that had come off the upholstery of the circular sofa. She had sized up the situation as regarded Liam by now, and could not help being interested because he was so handsome. He was like Rochester, or Mr. Darcy. She could not resist mentally fitting him out with the appropriate whiskers.

Their conversation was not prolonged.

"I think my cousin's expecting me," said Liam.

"Yes, she is," said Priscilla, and showed him into the back parlor.

In other places than Brainborough, young men may take girls to dances without meaning anything in particular. In Brainborough it always arouses comment, and in any case, Miss Hampton did not think her relation was a person to perform unmeaning actions out of sheer sociability. At this season of the year a farmer ought not to be wasting his time. There was the haymaking, and the silage, and the thinning of the root crops. Was it possible that William could take Miss Booley Browne more seriously than sugar beet, and hay, and silage?

In spite of disagreements, Miss Hampton had always regarded William Hampton as the proper person to live at Hampton Court after her death. Whatever she might or might not do for Tim Linacre, William was the representative of the family and bore the family name. But she was not going to have a Roman Catholic installed as mistress in the home of her ancestors.

The trouble was that William might not care about inhabiting the home of his ancestors. There were young men like that nowadays, Bolshies, no family pride. But unless he was fundamentally unsound (which she sometimes suspected) he must want to come into the land and reunite the place and the farm in one sizeable estate. She was not offering him "the differ of the price of a heifer to choose 'twixt the purty and the plain." If he had to give up one pretty girl, God knows, there are always plenty left. Thinking it over, Miss Hampton felt she had all the winning cards, and as she loved that, she was looking forward to her interview.

The two Hamptons looked each other in the eye with identical expressions. Liam's chin was firm and obstinate, but, what displeased Miss Hampton more, this morning it was blue. Liam was a man who needed to shave twice a day. He had shaved the previous night, before the dance, and not since, because his hotel had failed to call him and he had only just caught his train. To go home and achieve a proper pinkness would have made him late for his appointment, so he was hoping his toilet would pass. The effect was to harden Miss Hampton's heart against him. Shaving was to her a hallmark of caste, and a man who could break this taboo must indeed be unworthy of his origins. It was disrespectful to her and a sign of moral decadence. She would not have dreamed of mentioning such a matter to Liam, so he never knew she had noticed, but whereas she had intended to quarrel with him and forgive him, she now gave him up for lost.

"Well, William," she said. "A nice fool you're making of yourself."

"It's kind of you to say so," said Liam. "In any particular way?"

"You know what I'm talking about. I suppose there are no nice Protestant girls in Brainborough."

"Aren't there?" said Liam.

"Well, you don't seem able to find one to take to dances."

Liam did not reply. He turned to look out of the window, in an effort to keep his temper. His profile looked bored, which infuriated Miss Hampton.

"Tell me this," she cried, rapping her stick on the fireplace to recall his attention. "Is it behind the altar you mean to marry her, or are you going to turn and shame your Church?"

"What the hell business—" Liam began, and stopped himself. "What has that got to do with you?"

"It's my business what happens to this place when I'm gone," retorted Miss Hampton, playing her ace of trumps without delay. "It should be yours, and it will be yours if you make a proper marriage. But if not, I tell you I'll leave the Court and the land away from the Hamptons. I'll have no Rome rule here."

"You can leave it to the Holy Rollers for all I care," said Liam, and walked out of the house.

Mary the housemaid, whom Priscilla had chivvied into the hall to iron some candle grease off the carpet, reported to Mrs. McGuirk: "The captain come out with a face like murder."

II

By the time Mary nerved herself to ask the mistress if she might lay for lunch, Miss Hampton was in a black calm. It made everyone more nervous than if she had been her normal cantankerous self. Disregarding her afternoon rest, she ordered the trap round to drive her into Brainborough. Priscilla had to go too, as whenever the trap went in there were errands to be done. It was a grim drive. News of the family crisis had percolated to McVittie. They jogged along for an hour in such a silence that it was a wonder the dog roses did not wither in the hedge. Miss Hampton went straight to her solicitor.

Priscilla's chief errand was to Shankey's garage, where Miss Hampton told her they would do a black market deal in paraffin. With her mind full of this delicate negotiation, she did not pay much attention to a farm tractor drawing up outside the garage, until Liam Hampton climbed down from it.

Priscilla's idea was that companions passed their employers' offending relations with cool nods. But Liam stopped her.

"How are you?" he asked. "That's to say, how's my cousin?"

"Quite well, thank you," said Priscilla, and nearly added: "No thanks to you."

"I'm afraid she overexcited herself this morning, and it's not too good for her."

"She's been very cross ever since."

"She has, has she?"

"She's here now," said Priscilla. "I mean she came in with me and she's gone to see Mr. Counsel."

"Has she, by God? To cut me out of her will, I suppose."

"I shouldn't wonder," said Priscilla coolly. "Do you have to upset her like that? Couldn't you apologize? After all, she's very old."

"Old?" said Liam. "She ought to be dead."

Shankey came out and he and Liam became occupied with the tractor. Priscilla made a long detour and did all the other shopping before coming back about the paraffin. By then Liam had gone.

One other untoward incident marked that Tuesday. It was a day of melodrama.

Priscilla and McVittie sat for some time in the trap in front of Mr. Counsel's Georgian house, till at last the door opened and Miss Hampton came out. The solicitor came with her, hopping like a bird, chirruping about the weather, proffering a handshake which the old lady ignored, and looking hot and bothered.

"James Counsel's more of an old maid than his own daughter," Miss Hampton remarked audibly. "I don't know why the man can't do what I say without arguing with me. As if I didn't know my own mind. I've lived long enough."

Priscilla helped her into the trap and she settled herself laboriously, instructing them to rearrange most of the parcels. While this was going on, Mrs. Shegog came out of the door of Devine's, the principal Brainborough pub, a few doors down the street.

The old woman was a long way from home. In spite of her age she walked the five miles to Brainborough every week to collect her rations. But her more important business this time was to complain to the Civic Guards about the loss of her goat. Before she accomplished it melancholy had driven her to Devine's, where she had found sympathizers to treat her to the handiest remedy. In Devine's she heard that Miss Hampton was in town.

"There's that old wretch, Lizzie Shegog," said Miss Hampton. "I never wrote to the police about that wretched animal. I'll do it when we get back and Billy McGuirk can take it. We could go round by the barracks now, but it would take time and I'm tired. I don't see why the old woman should put us to the inconvenience."

Priscilla ventured to suggest that they might now give the goat back to its owner. "She's such a poor old soul," said she.

"Old age is no excuse," said Miss Hampton, apparently sharing Liam's views about that. "Why, the old faggot's raging drunk! Go away, Mrs. Shegog, I'm not going to listen to you!"

But Mrs. Shegog planted herself right in front of the trap and started talking, not in any strain of apology or conciliation. She was hurling time-honored abuse at the oppressor. Miss Hampton met it with a cold stare.

Getting no reaction, Mrs. Shegog worked herself into a fury. Suddenly she went down on her knees, railing, and raising both hands to heaven. She cursed Miss Hampton's seed, breed and generation. She called down every possible misfortune on her. She prayed that the evil Miss Hampton did to the poor would turn in on her and fester, and bad weather be over her fields and her crops rot, and her body rot on her bones, and the devil fly away with her, and have his way with her, and set her up with Hitler on the hob of hell. As a witch, Mrs. Shegog had special gifts for cursing. The people of Brainborough came to their shop doors to hear it professionally done. Some laughed, others crossed themselves and called their children in out of range of the evil eye.

It made an extraordinary picture, the one old woman shrieking in the dust, her gray hair streaming back from her upturned face, and her shawl slipping off her upraised arms; the other old woman sitting up straight in her pony trap, as unmoved as her father was when a Land Leaguer's bullet took his hat off. The Hamptons had always believed in their rights, the Shegogs as firmly believed in their wrongs. Priscilla, child of the twentieth century, shuddered at this old antagonism and even felt a superstitious tremor lest such an outpouring of hatred should indeed produce some occult effect.

Miss Hampton did not speak till Mrs. Shegog ran out of breath and lowered her gaze far enough to catch her enemy's eye. Then: "You are drunk," said Miss Hampton. "Out of the way, please. Go on, McVittie!" The pony woke up and trotted straight at the old woman, so that she had to leap aside. Naturally Mrs. Shegog redoubled her curses, running and shouting after the trap the whole length of the street.

Brainborough could talk of nothing else that evening, and recalled many a story in evidence of the powers of crazy old women, and the way that curses come home.

CHAPTER FIVE
Hospitality

WEDNESDAY, when the Linacres were invited to lunch, was another lovely day. Priscilla was condemned to spend the morning cooking. When she went into the kitchen, after taking the day's orders from Miss Hampton, she found Mrs. McGuirk bent double on a chair, groaning. The pain had come at her like a knife, and she bending down to rake out the ashes. It was her lumbago; last time she had it for a week.

Priscilla called McGuirk, and between them they got her back to the lodge where Priscilla left the husband to put his wife to bed. She had no confidence in McGuirk as a nurse; it seemed very callous to leave the groaning patient to his grudging ministrations. But you could not be in two places at once, and when anyone on the domestic staff drops out, companions do their work. She told McGuirk to give his wife a really *hot* hot jar and promised to look in again later on.

Then she hurried back to press on with preparations for guests. Nobody had been to lunch at Hampton Court since Priscilla was there. Nobody ever did come, except, occasionally, the Bishop. But Miss Hampton believed in keeping up a formal standard of entertainment. Lunch would be in the big dining room, with all that that implied in the way of a damask tablecloth, table napkins for all, and the best glass and silver. Luckily Mary knew where things were kept.

The lunch menu was drawn up by Miss Hampton, and Priscilla did not think the Linacres would half like it. Worse again, Miss Hampton intended to descend on the kitchen and supervise the *pièce de résistance* herself.

Priscilla was just getting together the ingredients for the *pièce de résistance* when she heard the dogs barking in the yard, and looked up to find Mrs. De Vigne on the doorstep.

Mrs. De Vigne was veiled, gloved, very neat and slightly fussed as usual. She apologized for coming in the back way, and for coming at an inconvenient time, but she could not find anybody at the front, and she thought perhaps this was a time of day when she might have a word with Miss Hampton alone.

Mrs. De Vigne's habit of apologizing was catching. Priscilla, in her turn, made excuses for Mary not being there to let anyone in (not that she ever was), and explained how the cook was laid up and guests expected for lunch. The cook's lumbago momentarily diverted Mrs. De Vigne's mind from her own business. She knew so well what her late husband had suffered. Had Miss Hoyle never tried ABC Liniment? Priscilla had not. It was wonderful for lumbago, and obtainable at any chemist's. Mrs. De Vigne could not have said more for ABC Liniment if she had been selling it on commission, which was unthinkable in a lady of her extreme refinement. In the end she talked Priscilla into sending Mary off on her bicycle to buy some. There was just time for her to ride to Brainborough and back before lunch.

Afterwards Priscilla wondered what on earth induced her to give in to such an idea on such a busy morning. The truth was that besides having

Mrs. McGuirk's groans still ringing in her ears, she was too hot to argue. Also it was like her to feel that she would get on better if she had the kitchen to herself.

Whatever Mrs. De Vigne's business was with Miss Hampton, she was in a flutter over it. She would not stay sitting in the hall with the newspaper that Priscilla offered her, but came trotting back to the kitchen to explain that she need not keep Miss Hampton long, but that she really must see her, and it was a delicate matter, and she wished she could ask Miss Hoyle what she thought, but she had better not say anything in case Miss Hampton preferred it to remain confidential. Priscilla would have been greatly intrigued if she had had time to think about it, but she was wishing to goodness the woman would go, and let her get on. She had just found a large pin sticking into an onion; one of the onions they had bought at the flower show. She was used to the idea that anything might turn up in Mrs. McGuirk's kitchen, but it unsettled her, and she picked over everything carefully twice for fear of other superfluous objects.

Miss Hampton came downstairs later than usual, owing to the complications of putting on her best dress. So far, she was blissfully ignorant of the dislocation of the household routine. When she heard about it, what annoyed her most was Priscilla's sending Mary off to Brainborough. Miss Hampton felt that a cook who chose to have lumbago at such an inconvenient moment, might very well go on suffering for an extra hour or so till somebody was at leisure to attend to her.

The old lady made short work of Mrs. De Vigne. Ten minutes after they had gone into the back parlor together, Priscilla heard the visitor being ushered out again. She heard Miss Hampton say: "I don't know what you expect me to do about it now." Mrs. De Vigne twittered some reply which was drowned by the dogs barking and Miss Hampton ordering them down till the visitor was off the premises.

Then Miss Hampton and Priscilla gave their full minds to the lunch, and achieved the culinary masterpiece which Priscilla regarded with misgiving. The table was laid, the napkins folded into cocked hats, the resident bluebottle driven out of the dining room. Finally, Miss Hampton went to a locked cupboard and brought out a bottle of port, which had been recommended to her by Devine as the same kind Mr. Owler bought for the Communion Service. It was three and six a bottle before the war. She did not uncork it, as it was possible Mrs. Linacre would not drink wine at lunch, and Tim was too young.

Mary came riding back two hundred yards ahead of the Linacres, bringing with her a little bottle of liniment sealed up in white paper, which she deposited on one of the oak chests. Priscilla showed it to Mrs. Lina-cre, while they were waiting for the house parlormaid to reappear in her black frock and announce lunch. It was reassuring to find that Mrs. Lina-cre also knew of ABC Liniment and could recommend it, and this some-what restored Priscilla to Miss Hampton's good books.

II

The table looked imposing; it was large enough for twenty. The four places were laid at one end, and the rest of it stretched away into the distance between a row of high narrow windows on one wall and a row of stiff dark portraits on the other. The walls, the heavy plush curtains, and the Turkey carpet were all different shades of red. It was a room that ought to have reeked of cigar smoke and good living, but didn't.

Mrs. Linacre, sitting on her hostess's right, suitably dressed as ever and enjoying her own social manner, looked politely expectant at the sight of the dish Miss Hampton uncovered before her. Something in mushroom sauce, a kind of fricassee. What could be more delicious?

Miss Hampton said graciously: "I ordered these out of compliment to Tim. The recipe was given me many years ago by the chef at Prunier's. May I offer you some *Escargots à la poulette?*"

"There are scrambled eggs as well," murmured Priscilla, lifting the lid of another casserole. Miss Hampton raised her eyebrows. She had not ordered scrambled eggs. It was Priscilla who had smuggled them on to the table at the last minute.

Mrs. Linacre was no cosmopolitan. She did not at first grasp what she was being offered. She saw that one was not meant to take scrambled eggs, so she accepted a generous helping from Hampton's dish. Only then did it dawn on her that *Escargots à la poulette* was snails.

She stared at her plate, covered with a grayish brown mess with lumps in it. Mushroom sauce was a thing she was rather fond of, but how to tell which of the lumps were mushroom and which were snail? In cooking they must have got intimately blended. Mrs. Linacre glanced wildly round and caught Miss Hampton's eye on her. Fearing that her son's whole future might be at stake, she speared a morsel on her fork, shut her eyes and swallowed quickly. But the idea was too much for her. Mushroom or snail, the lump stuck in her throat, she got it down, and kept it down, only by a determined effort. Swallow another she could not. Some things are too much even for mother love.

"I hope you are not eating those just to please me," said Miss Hampton.

"It is a pity to take them if you do not care for them. Some people find them a treat. I will gladly finish that plateful if you do not want it. Miss Hoyle, give Mrs. Linacre some scrambled eggs."

Mrs. Linacre felt disgraced, and dreaded lest she had prejudiced her cause. But Tim was redeeming the honor of the Linacres. He had taken snails and appeared to be enjoying them; at any rate he had nearly emptied his plate. His mother's eye dwelt on him fondly. Really he was behaving very nicely, and how nice he looked, she thought, when for once he was clean and tidy and had on a collar and tie. Tim was not exactly handsome, his mother acknowledged, studying his cheerful, childish face, under its crest of dun-colored hair. Not exactly handsome, but prepossessing, and she would not for worlds have had him turn out the film star type like Liam. Tim caught her eye and winked at her, and then she saw that the wretched boy was slipping spoonfuls of snails into his pocket handkerchief, intending no doubt to take them away in the pocket of his best trousers.

Priscilla Hoyle had been let off with scrambled eggs. Companions do not have to be gourmets. As for Miss Hampton, she consumed Mrs. Linacre's helping and her own with no deception and evident appreciation. It seemed to have made her thirsty, for she drank two or three glasses of water afterwards.

The last course, strawberries and cream, was acceptable to everybody. Mrs. Linacre made no objection to having a second helping, and began to feel better. A crisis had been weathered. They had coffee at the lunch table. Then Priscilla excused herself in order to go down to the lodge and rub Mrs. McGuirk with liniment. Miss Hampton brought the Linacres out into the garden.

III

It seemed that Tim was not to share in the conversation between his cousin and his mother. Miss Hampton suggested that he would like to look over his great-uncle's stamp collection. Tim expressed enthusiasm, and settled down with five large albums in the back parlor, but shortly afterwards he might have been found in the kitchen, where he ate up a tin of sardines provided by Mary to avert the consequences of lunchtime malnutrition.

Having got Mrs. Linacre out in the garden, Miss Hampton proceeded from force of habit to take her round it, showing her the old roses, the buds on the hybrid irises, the place where *Veronica hulkiana* perished in the frost, the *Tricuspidaria* which survived it, the lupines suffering from drought, the way McGuirk would fill the greenhouses with Arum lilies, till her guest began to think she was never coming to the point. Miss Hampton was quite capable of doing it on purpose. At, last she began to talk mournfully about what would happen to the garden when she was gone, and Mrs. Linacre's spirits rose again.

"Doesn't Li—William take an interest?" she inquired ingenuously.

"I am disappointed in William," said Miss Hampton. "He has come under unfortunate influences. I expect you know what I mean."

Mrs. Linacre could not pretend she didn't.

"That is why I have sent for you," Miss Hampton went on. "I am afraid I cannot bring myself to look on William as a true Hampton. There have always been Hamptons at Hampton Court, but if the continuity and the traditions are preserved, perhaps it makes no great odds for the property to pass to a female line. One should not make a fetish of these matters. And then again, a change of name might be arranged."

Mrs. Linacre began to feel excited and nervous of saying either too much or too little. She agreed that changing one's name on coming into property was often done.

"I took it for granted that there could be no serious objection," said Miss Hampton, "in talking the matter over with James Counsel yesterday. I had not really intended to discuss it with him before seeing you, but circumstances arose—dear me, I am very thirsty this afternoon. It must be from so much talking."

Mrs. Linacre was thinking that better is a dinner of snails where love is than omelet, or even roast chicken, and hatred therewith. It sounded as if everything was settled as satisfactorily as could be already, and there was nothing left for her to say. She murmured attentively, "Don't tire yourself with talking, Cousin Rebecca. Let me get you a glass of water."

But Miss Hampton preferred to get it herself and set off independently across the lawn. Halfway across she wavered and seemed as if she was going to walk right into one of the Wellingtonias, Mrs. Linacre's anxiety was aroused. She hurried up to her and took her arm.

"Are you all right, Cousin Rebecca?"

"Of course I'm all right," snapped Miss Hampton, "I felt a little giddy for a moment, as anyone might in this heat. It seems to have affected my eyes, I can't see quite distinctly. Now don't fuss me. All I want is a drink of water. This heat is quite phenon . . . phenom . . . phenollimal." The word bothered her.

Tim and Mary stared at them as they entered the kitchen. Miss Hampton drank three tumblers of cold water, though Mrs. Linacre begged her to stop. She spilt some of the last tumbler, and clutched at the edge of the sink as if she was afraid of falling. Mrs. Linacre caught her arm to support her, and called to Tim: "Oh, do go and get Miss Hoyle!"

Tim met Priscilla on the drive, coming back from the South Lodge with the liniment bottle in her hand. She and Mrs. Linacre between them got the old lady up to her room. She drank more water, said her throat was parched and she felt sick and could not see clearly. Mrs. Linacre suggested taking her temperature, but there was no thermometer in the house, and this seemed to amuse the patient. She was inclined to chatter about the heat and about the garden, and tried to tell them something very amusing about Mrs. De Vigne and McGuirk and the flower show, but it was all so rambling and incoherent that they could not follow the sense, or even make out the words. At first Priscilla and Mrs. Linacre tried to respond to this seeming gaiety, but it was a thin pretense, for they were growing frightened.

Mrs. Linacre said she would send Tim for the doctor. Priscilla put Miss Hampton to bed, in her huge old Gothic bed of carved oak with a feather mattress and brocade hangings. She kept on asking for water. Priscilla fetched a carafe and left it beside her, then withdrew to hold an anxious consultation with Mrs. Linacre.

"What can it be?" said Priscilla. "Sunstroke?"

Mrs. Linacre had no idea. "Whatever it is, it might be serious at her age."

A crash brought them back to the bedroom, where they found that the patient had knocked over the water. She was tossing restlessly on the bed, muttering to herself.

"How queer her eyes look!" whispered Priscilla. They did. The pupils were large and black, and though she stared at Priscilla it was evident that she could not see her properly. She was flushed too, her skin reddened with a rash like that of scarlatina.

"I don't like to leave her," Priscilla whispered, mopping up the water which had been emptied over the floor. Mrs. Linacre nodded and whispered back that she would stay till the doctor came. It seemed to her that the situation was critical and a relative ought to be at hand.

She drew the window curtains, changing the afternoon glare to a red-tinged gloom. It did not quiet the patient. Her restlessness was increasing, and in the next hour their anxiety mounted as they struggled with her, rescuing the coverings that she tossed aside in her delirium and trying in vain to make out the babble of half-formed words.

CHAPTER SIX
Untimely Death

ABOUT half-past four a bicycle wheel scrunched on the gravel and Tim's cheerful voice broke in on their vigil. Mrs. Linacre went down to him. The doctor was coming, but he had been out at a farm where a man had had his leg taken off by a hay cutter that same afternoon. He had to arrange for the man to be taken to the county hospital, then he would come straight back to Hampton Court, Tim had got directions at the doctor's house, found the farm, found the doctor, and then found a clever shortcut back. He was telling his mother all his cleverness when he suddenly noticed her expression.

"I say," he exclaimed, "is Cousin Rebecca really bad?"

His mother nodded.

Not knowing what to say, Tim was silent for an unusually long time. His mother moved back into the shadowy part of the hall, found a low chair and sat down and closed her eyes. There was no sound from upstairs; for the moment the patient was quiet. Presently Tim asked if they had had tea yet. As he spoke they heard the doctor's car.

Dr. Claffey was stoutish, youngish, unceremonious. He was inclined to be prejudiced against rich old ladies, and his mind was still full of his other case. But when he saw the patient he said they were quite right to send for him at once. He stayed just ten minutes, then dashed off in his car to fetch things. He was back sooner than he had said he would be, and then began an endless time of struggle and suspense. The struggle was all upstairs. There were rapid comings and goings, boards creaking, water running, doors shutting, whispers, instructions, occasionally groans. The rest of the house sank into an awed silence. The kettle Mary had boiled for tea was requisitioned for the sick room. She and Tim hung about .the kitchen feeling superfluous. Mrs. Linacre had gone up with the doctor. Presently she came down looking agitated. She sank on to a chair and asked Mary to heat her a cup of milk. Then she beckoned to Tim.

"Tim," she said, "I've been talking to the doctor. He thinks Cousin Rebecca may not get better. Now, I want you to ride straight over to Brainborough and fetch Mr. Counsel. The doctor agrees with me that, if she is conscious again, she ought to see her solicitor. There's a lot of property involved, you know. It would be awkward if her affairs were left unsettled."

Tim was off like a shot, delighted to have something to do. His mother followed him down the steps.

"Tell Mr. Counsel to take Shankey's taxi. Tell him it's life or death!"
But she knew very well it was the second alternative.

Tim wasted no time. It was not easy to hustle Counsel, who was nearly
as old as Cousin Rebecca, but Tim got hold of the taxi for him and tied his
own bicycle on to the back of it while the solicitor was assembling his
papers. Shankey, who was a terrifying driver, rushed them through the
lanes, and they were back at the Court by half-past six.

Mrs. Linacre was on the steps looking out for them. She took Mr.
Counsel's hand and whispered

"How good of you to come at once. She's conscious, and the doctor
thinks she could see you now. He won't let you stay long."

She took him straight upstairs and returned alone. She was looking
more cheerful, and Tim asked if she did not think Cousin Rebecca might
recover after all. His mother replied, "One must never give up hope. But
if the worst comes to the worst, at least we can feel we have left nothing
undone."

Mr. Counsel came down in less than ten minutes, looking very grieved.
As a client, Miss Hampton had been a nuisance to him for years, but he
was used to her, and he valued her as one of the few remaining links with
the good old days before the two world wars. He shook his silver head
sadly at Mrs. Linacre and murmured, "This is very sudden. A great shock
for you all. The doctor does not hold out much hope."

"She's over eighty, you know," said Mrs. Linacre.

"Seventy-nine," said Mr. Counsel, who was seventy-five himself, and
felt that a year or two made a difference even at their age.

"Well, well," he said. "However. At the moment there is a slight im-
provement. The doctor thinks all may be well at least for some hours. You
would not wish me to stay?"

"No, no," said Mrs. Linacre. "We'll let you know at once if anything
happens."

Mr. Counsel said, "Quite right, quite right," and, thankful not to have
to delay his own dinner hour, he got back into the taxi and drove away.

The dust of the taxi had hardly settled on the drive when a strange cry
rang out in the hushed quiet of the big house. The dogs set up a howl. Tim
and his mother exchanged startled glances. There was a bustle upstairs.
Mrs. Linacre ran halfway up, then stopped, listening with a strained expression. Silence prevailed again. In a minute or two the door of the sick
room opened and the doctor and Priscilla came out together.

It seemed as if the last effort demanded of Miss Hampton had, after
all, been too much. Or else, having settled her earthly business, she had

ceased to struggle. On that last cry her spirit had departed.

The doctor briefly told them the news and then went into the kitchen, where they heard him talking in a low voice to Mary. Priscilla Hoyle sat on the circular sofa looking worn out. Mrs. Linacre began to cry quietly. Tim was horribly afraid he might start crying too because the whole atmosphere was so depressing, though he was really only sorry he could not feel sorrier about his cousin, who was, after all, eighty. He managed to control himself, and said to his mother in a responsible tone. "We had better go home. Poor Cousin Rebecca, there's nothing we can do for her now."

"There's still plenty to be done," said the doctor, coming back. "This girl," he indicated Mary, "will help. Have you anyone else at hand? Mrs. McGuirk's laid up, is she? Wait now, isn't there old Lizzie Shegog?"

Priscilla looked up to protest, but he did not listen to her. "You've done enough," he told her. "You get something to eat and get to bed early. Take an aspirin." He put his hand on her shoulder and smiled down at her. "Ever think of taking up nursing?" he asked her. "You know, you're the type for it." That was Dr. Claffey's idea of handing her a bouquet. Priscilla only shook her head wearily. The doctor turned back to Mary and sent her off to fetch Mrs. Shegog, for the "wise woman" of Brainborough was experienced in laying out the dead. The doctor had not heard about the cursing episode, or perhaps he would not have thought fit to put the old woman whom Miss Hampton had spurned from her carriage wheels in such a position of ultimate superiority.

Tim asked Mary afterwards how Mrs. Shegog took the news, and he could not gather that she showed either remorse or surprise. Whether or not she felt that her cursing had anything to do with the catastrophe, she came along and did her work and got paid for it.

When Mary had gone the doctor had something more to say. He looked as if it was something disagreeable, and it was. He jerked out abruptly: "I'm afraid I can't give a certificate."

Tim did not grasp the point at first, but his mother gave startled gasp.

"Oh, Doctor! You don't mean there'll have to be an inquest?"

"I'm afraid so."

"But it's—it's indecent. I mean, the publicity."

"It's just a legal formality," said the doctor, but Mrs. Linacre was not reassured.

"Is it necessary?" she demanded. "Don't you know what she died of? You said heart failure."

There was a pause in which you could not hear the least sound of movement inside the house. There was not even a clock ticking. Outside, woodpigeons were calling, and the evening breeze had started the trees rustling. Tim waited eagerly for what the doctor would say next. He did not share his mother's objection to an inquest; he thought it might be interesting. That was an old one about heart failure. Heart failure is what people always die of. The question is, what makes your heart fail?

"She died," said the doctor, "of heart failure brought on by poisoning. The poison was atropine. Belladonna. I'm afraid the police will have to investigate how she came to take it. Now, I know you all had lunch together, but I think it's as well for the remains of that last meal to be analyzed. We'll just lock them up until the police can take charge of them. According to Miss Hoyle, there's no such thing as belladonna in the house."

"I said I didn't know of any," said Priscilla. Nobody could say what there might not be in a house so swamped with flotsam and jetsam.

A ray of evening sun, slanting through the pillars of the portico and one of the narrow windows at the side of the hall door, illuminated some dusty books, a pen tray, letters, bits of string, a cartridge case, a broken seccateurs, an egg and a mousetrap, all lying on the hall table. Finally, it dramatically spotlighted a medicine bottle. The doctor stared.

"ABC Liniment," he said. "Don't you know what that is? Aconite, belladonna, chloroform. One drachm of this stuff is a fatal dose. There's enough gone out of this bottle to poison the lot of you."

He put out his hand to grasp it, then stopped himself and took it up cautiously, with a finger on top of the cork, and a thumb on the bottom of the bottle. Tim Linacre knew that he was thinking of fingerprints.

"The police'll have to look into this too," said, the doctor.

"Beg pardon, sir." It was Mary, the housemaid, not gone yet. She had looked in with her coat on to mention a detail she had forgotten.

"Please sir," she said, nervously approaching the doctor. "Please sir, there's a Guard in the kitchen. He's been waiting this long time."

CHAPTER SEVEN
Enter First Policeman

HE was a very young, handsome, bashful Civic Guard, whose boots creaked. He stepped out of the kitchen and filled the whole of the back passage. He looked earnestly round the company, not sure who was the correct person to address, decided on the doctor, and mentioned diffidently that it was a matter of a goat.

"I feel bad about intruding on you," he added nicely. "I hear I've come in a time of sorrow."

"Goat? What goat?" snapped Dr. Claffey.

"Oh dear," said Priscilla Hoyle, "he means that goat of Mrs. Shegog's."

"Ah, never mind that now," said the doctor, who was anxious to get away. "Look, you can take charge here. There are some things to be locked up till your Super asks for them. I'll attend to that now and leave you the key. I'll stop in at the barracks on my way back and have a word with Sergeant Carty."

The Guard looked bewildered.

"It's a case of an inquest," the doctor explained with some impatience. "Very painful for the relatives. I daresay the sergeant will want to take statements. I'll send in my report to him in the morning."

The young policeman looked very much at sea, but he meekly accepted the doctor's arrangements and accompanied him and Mary into the kitchen to see to the business of putting aside everything that was left over from lunch. Tim disregarded his mother's signals that she was ready to go, and followed after them. For it had dawned on Tim, and he felt a fearful joy in the prospect, that there was going to be a police enquiry, and he, Tim, was on the inside.

Straight away he was able to be helpful.

"I've been thinking it over," he said to Dr. Claffey confidentially, "and I think whatever it was at lunch must have been in the *Escargots à la poulette.*"

Dr. Claffey had been told about the lunch menu already, and he had been at the flower show.

"My God, yes," he said. "Those snails were yours, weren't they? Well, you said they were edible."

"Of course they are. There's nothing wrong with snails. Lots of people eat them in France and England. What I mean is, anything else there was at lunch we all had, but when it came to the snail dish, Cousin Rebecca was the only one to tackle it."

"There's nothing left, only the shells," said Mary, "and I threw those out."

"That's where you're wrong," Tim told her, and turned out the repulsive contents of his trousers' pocket. Mary giggled in the house of mourning, and guiltily clapped her hand over her mouth. The doctor looked at Tim's handkerchief with distaste and asked, "Is that how you T.C.D. boys generally behave when you're out? Putting the food in your pockets?"

"Isn't it well I did?" said Tim. "I don't mind you keeping the handkerchief, I've another at home."

Mary found a drawer with a lock to it. They tipped out its very miscellaneous contents and put away the snails, also the cruet, bread, sugar, samples of the stock the soup was made of and that was the foundation of the mushroom sauce, the peels and stalks of the mushrooms and the coffee grounds, which last they had to scrape up out of the pig pail. The scrambled eggs and strawberries had all been eaten, and Mary had kindly given the rest of the cream to the yard cats. She was fond of the cats.

"Are the cats all right?" Tim inquired. Mary said you couldn't kill the like of them ones. Hampton Court, like most country houses, reversed the city custom with domestic animals: the dogs had the run of the house, while the cats led untamed lives in the yard. It would have been difficult to check up on them.

Tim was recalled to the hall by his mother, who wanted to get home. A thought struck him.

"Somebody ought to tell Liam."

Mrs. Linacre had thought of it herself, and had been occupied in writing a note in which she broke the news gently, and referred in the most tactful terms to her own action in sending for Mr. Counsel, which Liam was bound to hear about before long. There was a certain delicacy in this part of the subject, and the letter was one of her epistolary masterpieces. She had intended to give it to Mary to deliver, but Dr. Claffey volunteered. He would be passing Hampton Lodge on his way home.

"I've borne worse news in my time," he remarked. "Good thing you got everything legal fixed up. Nuisance, when people die intestate. Hampton ought to be obliged to you." Mrs. Linacre said nothing. After all, she did not know for certain how much Liam's prospects had been affected by her interposition. It was a pity Mr. Counsel had not stayed a bit, longer. However, she would get in touch with him early in the morning.

When they had all gone, and Mary and Mrs. Shegog were going about their business upstairs, Priscilla summoned up energy to make herself a cup of cocoa in the kitchen. She had had nothing since lunch time and it was nearly eight o'clock. She was sipping her drink thankfully when she was startled by a heavy tread across the flags. It was the young Civic Guard again, entering from the yard.

"If you'll pardon me for disturbing you, Miss—" he said.

"I thought you'd gone," sighed Priscilla.

"I just stepped down for a word with the man at the lodge. I—er—told him the sad news."

"Oh, thank you for doing that. I suppose I really ought to go down there."

"No need at all, Miss. They'll understand. Sure you're tired out. Time enough in the morning." The young Guard was sorry for Priscilla. She looked to him a nice girl. It was a shame to bother her, but he had his duty. "About that goat, Miss—"

"Oh yes. About the goat. I suppose Mrs. Shegog wants it back?"

"She does that. It's a kind of a pet like. And the animal has no right to be here at all. I was sent here to take it away out of this. You see, Miss, Miss Hampton, God rest her, was an old lady and she didn't know the law, but the way of it is, by shutting up a goat belonging to another person she made herself liable for damages."

Priscilla had an opportunity to marvel at the workings of Providence, far it seemed to her likely that if Miss Hampton had lived to be served with a summons on such a count she would have had a stroke anyway. She said, "Do you mean to say Mrs. Shegog was going to sue her? Then what happens now?"

The Guard reassured her. He was evidently a diplomatist. He had had a word with Mrs. Shegog himself, and the old witch was ready to let bygones be bygones. Then he had gone round to get the key of the stable from McGuirk. It only needed some responsible person such as Miss Hoyle to give the O.K. and he would let the goat out of its prison and restore it to its owner.

"Oh yes, do," said Priscilla, thankful to be rid of the matter. Then something occurred to her for the first time. "Goodness, I do hope it's all right. I don't think we ever arranged for anybody to milk it."

"Ah sure," said the Guard, "it wouldn't require it."

"Wouldn't it? Dear me, I hope it didn't. I think Mrs. Shegog did say it hadn't been giving milk for a long time."

"It was the truth she told you," said the Guard solemnly. "She only keeps it as a pet, like. Ye see, it's a billy-goat."

II

After that, Priscilla felt that, early as it was, she might as well go to bed, for things were getting beyond her. She suddenly felt completely exhausted.

It was not easy to sleep. After all the commotion of the afternoon, the old house had sunk back into uncanny quiet. Mary and Mrs. Shegog had finished; Priscilla heard them come out of the room, which was next to her own, and go down the passage talking in low voices. The kindly Guard had left. The stout front door was locked and bolted, and the shutters were up in all the widows, but though a house is built to stand a siege, night with all its terrors can get in. Priscilla had never in all her life felt so lonely and unprotected. A self-reliant young woman was discovering her limitations.

Suddenly she was startled broad awake by noisy barking from the dogs, which she had forgotten to shut up for the night. She jumped up and looked out of her window. There stood Liam Hampton on the gravel, looking up at the shuttered facade, while the old springer and Irish terrier wheezed and growled round his feet. Priscilla had been thinking about Liam Hampton. She supposed he was her new employer. She wondered if he would remember what he had said about Miss Hampton at their last meeting. He ought, by rights, to be overcome with self-reproach, but somehow she doubted if he ever suffered much from that.

She slipped on her thin dressing gown and went down. It was still daylight outside, but the house was strange and shadowy, and she quaked as she passed the door of the room where the body lay. She knocked painfully against the corners of furniture in the hall. At last she got .the door open to admit the new master of Hampton Court.

Liam looked at her in a preoccupied way and said, "The dogs ought to have been shut up."

"I forgot," said Priscilla. Then, as if his implied reproach, coming at the end of the ghastliest experience she had ever had, was one thing too much to bear, she quite unexpectedly dissolved in tears.

Liam Hampton was the last man on earth Priscilla would have wanted to weep over, but she did not seem able to stop. Once having let go, she luxuriated in it. It seemed to do her good.

Liam caught her by the shoulders. "Why, how cold you are!" he exclaimed, and picked up a rug and put it round her. It was a rug sacred to the dogs, that was always spread over their particular armchair. It had certain disadvantages which did not strike Priscilla till afterwards.

Liam kept his arm round her and let her cry, and though horrified at her own behavior, she did find it comfortable. At last the flood abated and she disentangled herself.

"I'm awfully sorry," she said. "I don't know what's the matter with me."

"That's easy," said Liam in a matter-of-fact way. "It's shock, you know. Might happen to anyone. After all, you're very young to have had to cope with all this."

"I'm twenty-five," said Priscilla.

"Are you really? Well, that's young. I'm thirty."

She thought for a moment he was laughing at her. It annoyed her. She said, "I've never seen anybody die before."

"Haven't you?" He spoke absently. He moved away from her out of the dark hall on to the portico, and began to pace up and down it. Presently he said, "There seems to be some kind of mystery about my cousin's death. I suppose you haven't any idea how she came to take this poison?"

Priscilla shook her head.

"I can't understand it. It isn't as if she was the kind of person who takes things. Pills or tonics, I mean. And we didn't find anything in her room. And really I don't see how anything could have got into the lunch. As for the bottle of liniment, she never touched it. Don't you think the doctor might be mistaken?"

Liam said it had been known to happen.

"The curse of it is," he said, "apparently we've got to have this police inquiry. I don't know exactly how much the law requires us to put up with. If I were you I shouldn't stand any nonsense. If you find them worrying you, let me know and I'll talk to them."

Priscilla could not picture herself appealing to Liam Hampton for support against bullying officialdom. She thought he was just the person to put the law's back up. She said the only Guard they'd had so far seemed a nice young man, and she didn't expect they'd be much trouble.

"Hope you're right," said Liam. "Anyhow, I'm afraid you'll have to stay on here till the authorities are satisfied. Look, have you got a mother or something?"

Priscilla admitted to having a mother.

"Get her to come down. Can she, do you think? You ought to have somebody with you. I should send her a wire first thing tomorrow."

Priscilla looked grateful but dubious.

"What's the matter with that?" Liam asked.

"Well——" Priscilla found explaining difficult, "you see, Mother and I don't always get on. We have rows sometimes. Quite often. Last time we didn't speak to each other for three days, and then I came down here."

"And what was it all about?"

"Oh, nothing much."

There was no point in telling Liam about Hugo Everard. He was only a young man who had broken Priscilla's heart. Her mother had been in a position to say "I told you so" about Hugo, and had said it too often.

"All families have rows," said Liam. "I sometimes lose my temper too. Your mother's probably forgotten all about it by this time, and I think you ought to have her here to be company for you. Well now, it's too late to settle anything more tonight. Mr. Counsel will be here again tomorrow and we can go into details then. You get back to bed. I'll shut the dogs up on my way out."

It was pitch dark on the stairs by now. Liam lit one of the candles that always stood on the hall mantelpiece and the shadows leapt back into their corners.

"I'll light you up," he said, and walked beside her up the staircase, along the passage and past Miss Hampton's door to her own room.

Priscilla crept straight into bed, and by this time her nerves were steadier. She lay and listened for Liam's retreating footsteps. They went a short way down the passage and then she heard a door opened and shut, the door of Miss Hampton's room.

She pictured what he would find there and shuddered, and shrank down closer into the protection of blankets and pillows. She fell asleep without having heard him go, and never knew how long he stood there, looking down by candlelight on the small withered thing that was all that was left of human in the enormous ancient bed.

CHAPTER EIGHT
The Inquiry Opens

BY the middle of next morning there was hardly anybody left in Brainborough who did not know that Miss Hampton of Hampton Court had died suddenly of poison, with a bottle of it open on the hall table. The women thought first of what they would wear to the funeral, and whether there would be a Sale. But already that evening some of the men talking it over in Devine's had the idea that Brainborough was at last the scene of a murder.

"Look at all the money there," they said.

The police never said anything of the kind, but embarked on the investigation in the most open-minded spirit. Tim Linacre found them very decent sort of chaps.

Tim had a feeling as if Providence might have arranged the whole thing for his benefit. Detection came high up on his list of possible careers, and it seemed as if this might be the very opening he was waiting for.

The heat wave continued; the early mornings were glorious, and Tim was out next day when the country was still fresh with dew. He passed farmhands going to work, cows being driven out from the milking sheds, a horse drawing a hay rake. But at Hampton Court it was like a Sunday. At first he thought there was nobody about, then he found all the men in the yard with McGuirk telling them the news.

McGuirk was in his element, wearing his good suit and his high starched white collar, with a black tie and a crepe band round his arm. He loved moralizing and appeared to be improving the occasion with a sermon. The men stood round looking solemn and shocked. McVittie growled to himself and spat in a corner.

In the kitchen Priscilla Hoyle was having her breakfast along with Mary. Priscilla was wearing a gray coat and skirt. Tim began to think he ought to have put on a black tie himself. However, he was not going all the way back for it, especially as a car came up the drive almost on his heels, and two policemen got out.

An inquiry into a case of poisoning in a well-known county family was too big an affair for the local barracks to handle. Brainborough was, in police jargon, only a one and three village; that is, one sergeant and three Guards were the barracks staff. Carty, the sergeant, had phoned through to the superintendent of the county town for directions how to proceed, and the superintendent had come himself, picking up the sergeant on his way. If it looked to the superintendent like a complicated business, he would send for a member of the detective branch from Dublin. They had already got in touch with the state pathologist, who was coming down to do the post mortem. For this the body would be removed to the county hospital.

The superintendent was lean and gray-haired, with a badly scarred face which made his appearance intimidating, but a pleasant, quiet manner. He spoke kindly to Priscilla Hoyle, who was looking scared at the idea of the post mortem. He explained that an ambulance was arranged for, and everything would be taken off her hands. The sergeant from Brainborough, whom Tim knew well by sight, was big, beefy, self-important and hot. It was hard on a man of his build to wear a uniform in this weather. The superintendent wore it too, but he was the kind of man who never seemed warm. The sergeant frequently mopped his forehead and looked as if he had all the cares of the world on his shoulders, but could take it so long as everybody knew what he had to put up with.

The two policemen first took a look round the garden and ground-floor of the house to get their bearings, and then asked Priscilla Hoyle, Mary and Tim himself to come into the kitchen. Tim had expected that they would be interviewed one by one and made to sign statements, but the superintendent explained that, though he would have to take a statement from each of them later, at present he was only concerned with getting a general picture of what had happened.

Priscilla Hoyle told about the morning, from Mrs. McGuirk's collapse to the time when Mary brought back the ABC Liniment. Tim told about lunch, and what he knew from his mother about the way Cousin Rebecca was taken ill. The superintendent took them over the story in detail, and asked about Mrs. De Vigne's visit, and made a note to interview her. Priscilla could not tell him what that visit had been about. He was naturally interested in the ABC Liniment, but the more they talked it over, the less it looked as if that could have had anything to do with the tragedy. The bottle had not arrived in the house till lunch time; Tim distinctly remembered that when Priscilla first showed it to them it had the wrapper on, and Priscilla herself said she had only unwrapped it after lunch, down at the lodge. Later on in the morning the sergeant verified this by finding the actual wrapper crushed up in a ball in Mrs. McGuirk's bedroom grate.

Mary was asked if she knew of any other bottles of poison anywhere about the house, and she swore she didn't, but Tim distinctly remembered a huge empty Lysol bottle in the bathroom, so that showed how much the housemaid's evidence was worth. He supposed the police would have to make a thorough search, and, glancing round the big untidy kitchen, he did not envy them the job.

Then they got on to the question of what the deceased had for lunch, and Tim braced himself for the inevitable funny remarks about eating snails. But the police are beyond being surprised at anything, and they appeared to take snail eating quite for granted. On the grounds that Tim had already indicated to the doctor, they were inclined to regard the snails as more likely than any other dish at lunch to have been the vehicle for the poison.

Priscilla had to explain very carefully how the dish was cooked. Tim wrote down the recipe on the back of an envelope.

Escargots à la poulette

Drop the snails into boiling water, stir in a handful of wood ashes, and boil for fifteen to twenty minutes. Then remove shells, and boil snails ten minutes longer in salt and water. Drain and wipe clean. Pour round the snails white wine and stock, chopped mushrooms and parsley. Let them bake gently for about half an

hour. Take them out and thicken the sauce with yolk of egg. Keep
hot till required.

Miss Hampton had not wanted to open wine, so only stock was used.

Priscilla added that Miss Hampton had told her to put the snails to
crawl over oatmeal for an hour or two before they were wanted to get rid
of their slime. She had found a cardboard dress-box and scattered oatmeal
over the bottom of that and put the glass over it, as she vas always afraid
of the creatures escaping again. The police inspected the dress-box, containing a gruesome mess, and the snails' original box, in which there now
remained only some dry stalks. They did not look much the wiser.

One funny thing came out in connection with the lunch preparations,
about a pin having been found sticking in one of the onions that were cut
up for soup. It did not seem as if this could have any bearing on the poisoning, but it meant something to the sergeant. It was easy enough to tell
when that man had an idea from a kind of grunt it produced. The superintendent, on the other hand, might have more ideas than he let on. He took
no notice of the sergeant, and no explanation was forthcoming.

The superintendent wanted to know if the kitchen had been left empty
at any time, and Priscilla said she had left it for short intervals, to see that
the table was laid, and to offer Mrs. De Vigne a paper and so on. She had
never been out of it for long at a time after she had begun the cooking, and
she and Miss Hampton had both been there together preparing the snails.
So far as she knew nobody else had been near the place except Mary and
Mrs. De Vigne when she hovered on the threshold. Most of the men had
been far away in the park, turning the hay that had been cut on Monday.
McVittie was in the kitchen garden patching up a bit of netting for putting
over the strawberries. If any outsider had approached the house the dogs
would have drawn attention to the fact.

The superintendent was inclined to cast doubts on the mushrooms.
He had a look at the peels and stalks, which seemed just like those of the
ordinary field mushroom. Billy McGuirk had brought them in from a place
where he had gathered quantities since the hot weather.

"Even if they were poisonous ones," said Tim, "it wouldn't be
atropine."

"Well, well," said the superintendent politely. "You'd know more
about that than I would, I expect."

"If you think it wasn't the ABC Liniment," said Tim, "What about
Belladonna atropa itself? Deadly nightshade, you know. Hadn't you better ask if there's any of that growing about?"

"There's plenty up by the old church," said the sergeant. He referred to an old ruin some miles away.

"My mother grows it," said Tim offhandedly. "She's interested in it as a commercial proposition. I don't think my cousin cultivated it herself, but there might be some growing around the place."

But when they applied to McGuirk he was most definite that there was no plant of deadly nightshade, cultivated or wild, anywhere about Hampton Court. A few years ago, on Miss Hampton's instructions, he had made a special search for it, because of a news item about a child having poisoned itself by eating the berries. There was no fear that Priscilla or Mary or Mrs. McGuirk could possibly in a fit of absent-mindedness have substituted belladonna for any other vegetable out of the garden.

The superintendent took out his watch and compared it with the kitchen clock, but the clock had stopped. They had covered a good deal of ground. He was wondering now what time the ambulance would arrive to take away the body.

Before it did, however, Liam appeared, having come across the fields by a shortcut. He walked into the kitchen with the dogs at his heels, apparently recognized by them as master.

Liam shook hands with the superintendent, hoped he had everything he wanted, and mentioned that he was expecting Mr. Counsel later on. Priscilla Hoyle was looking agitated; Tim guessed she was reckoning up how many there would be to dinner.

Liam went out to give the men in the yard their orders. It was not at all his idea that the occasion called for a holiday.

Tim seized his opportunity to ask the superintendent if he had a theory. The superintendent smiled and said he was not interested in theories, only facts.

"Time enough for theories when we've collected all the information," he said.

"But you have to have some sort of theory so as to know what questions to ask. For instance, you don't think she committed suicide."

"I never said I didn't. That's always on the cards. It's apt to be a painful matter for the family."

"You needn't be afraid of that in this case, because I don't mind telling you it's not a bit likely. There never has been a suicide in our family as far as I know, and Cousin Rebecca wasn't that sort at all. I mean, she'd absolutely nothing on her mind," said Tim, with the confidence of care-free youth.

"Had she not?" The superintendent turned to Priscilla and asked, with his rather attractive smile, what she thought.

Priscilla considered. "I don't think she would have wanted to die before her new flowers came out. She had some special ones that were due to flower any day. She went to look at them every morning.

"Irises she'd hybridized herself, if you want to know," said Tim. "But, listen here. There's a better argument against suicide than that. She'd never have done herself in without first settling about her will."

"Died intestate, did she?" asked the superintendent.

"Oh no, she didn't, luckily. But she only signed her will just in time."

Tim then artlessly described his dash for Mr. Counsel. It had never occurred to him that anybody might think he had anything at stake in the result. The superintendent did not point it out to him. He merely asked, "And who gets the place? Captain Hampton?"

"Oh yes," said Tim. Priscilla said nothing. Tim added as an afterthought, "Mother and I might get something left us too."

"Was Miss Hampton well off?" asked the superintendent. "Of course it's a fine old place, but—"

"Oh rather!" Tim assured him. "She must have had thousands and thousands. She never spent any of it on the house, and lately she was even getting stingier about the garden, but it wasn't that she hadn't got it. She just got a bit mean in her old age. Besides, she got a complex about the war. She used to say it was no good doing anything to the house or garden when we might any day all have to fly."

The superintendent accepted everything that was told him. "Glad to hear there's some money to spend on the place," he said. "Not so many people who come in to old places nowadays can afford to keep them up. Your cousin is to be congratulated."

A motor horn sounded faintly from the south gate. They all went out on the front steps, and presently two cars came out of the drive. The first was Dr. Claffey's. The second, brushing the evergreens on either side, was the ambulance from the county hospital. For a while everybody stood about on the gravel holding conferences. Then they divided into two parties: Dr. Claffey, the superintendent and the ambulance men went upstairs, and the sergeant shepherded Priscilla, Tim and Mary into the back parlor to take down statements from them, and incidentally to keep them out of the way while the body was being removed.

The parlor was still shuttered when they entered it, and Priscilla Hoyle apologized for it not having been dusted yet that morning. To Tim it did not look any different from usual. It was funny how Cousin Rebecca, with the whole huge house to choose from, spent practically all her time in this cluttered little den. She had piles of old plant catalogs on the floor behind the desk, seeds germinating on damp flannel on the mantelpiece, and cuttings rooting in a beer bottle hung up on the window catch. There were books and papers everywhere. Uncle Albert's stamp collection was piled on the seat of Cousin Rebecca's own straight-backed chair; it suddenly occurred to Tim that he had left it there himself, and only yesterday afternoon at that. Nobody would be wanting to sit in that chair anyway. He saw a handkerchief dropped near the window, and an empty spectacles case left open on top of the wireless. It seemed as if Cousin Rebecca ought to come in any minute to look for them. At that instant a trampling of footsteps on the landing above brought it home to him that his cousin was even then leaving her house for ever.

Taking the statements was a laborious business; the sergeant wrote so slowly and asked so many questions twice over. They had about two hours of it and were left hungry and exhausted. Even then the sergeant might not have released them if the superintendent had not come back. He had with him Liam Hampton and Mr. Counsel.

The little solicitor dodged round Liam to tell Tim, in a discreet murmur that blew out his straggly gray moustache, that he was hoping to call on Mrs. Linacre in the course of the afternoon.

Tim had been worrying because he felt he ought to say something to Liam appropriate to the mournful occasion, but he got no opportunity. Lam was standoffish at all times, and today, it seemed to Tim, there was a stony look in his eye. He seemed to be taking charge of everything. He settled Mr. Counsel in a chair at the table, and he himself moved the stamp albums and took Cousin Rebecca's own. The others turned out gladly. As they left, the superintendent was saying to Liam, "I think you last saw the deceased on Tuesday morning, Captain Hampton. I wonder would you give us an account of your conversation."

Tim heard Priscilla Hoyle catch her breath.

CHAPTER NINE
Condolences

MRS. LINACRE had felt too upset to come down till lunch time. By then she had achieved a successful little frock to wear as mourning out of an old black chiffon evening dress. When Tim came home he gave her Mr. Counsel's message, and an account of happenings at the Court.

"And is Liam taking charge of everything then, for the moment?" she asked. Tim said it certainly looked as if he was.

After lunch Tim had to do chores which he had scamped that morning, chopping kindlings for the kitchen fire and pumping water into the cistern. When he was at home his mother economized on an odd job man. Tim resented being distracted by domestic details from following his true vocation. He escaped as soon as he possibly could and returned to the scene of action.

Mrs. Linacre, with a firmer grasp of essentials, waited at home, in some impatience, for Mr. Counsel to come and tell her just what Cousin Rebecca really had left them in the last edition of her will.

Mrs. Linacre would have been hurt if anybody had called her mercenary. It seemed natural to her that Cousin Rebecca should interest herself in Tim's future, but people do not always do the natural thing unless it is pointed out to them. Family feeling was Mrs. Linacre's dominating impulse, and she even hoped that Liam had not been excluded from the will altogether, because that would create an awkward situation. There ought to be enough for both of them, and Liam's advice would be useful to Tim in running Hampton Court.

As it turned out she need not have worried. The last act of old Miss Hampton's life had been perfectly in character, and in case Mrs. Linacre had not fully appreciated her in the past, she was now to have a demonstration of her gift for exasperating her relations. The will left everything— house, land and fortune—entirely to Liam. A codicil left it all to Tim instead, but only in the event of Liam's marrying a Roman Catholic.

Mr. Counsel gave Mrs. Linacre these particulars as pleasantly as possible, as they both sat in Mrs. Linacre's bright, pretty drawing room in comfortable chintzy chairs. It was a charming, well-kept room, with all her nicest things in it, and only just enough of them, in contrast to the overcrowded room in which the solicitor had just been going over the same business with Liam. It was an awkward business from everybody's point of view. Mr. Counsel had hoped to persuade his late client out of that codicil, but Mrs. Linacre had forced his hand. He had wondered at the time just what she thought she was up to. However, he had spent more than fifty years smoothing over the seamy side of family life, and he was able to sympathize with both parties. He smiled blindly towards Mrs. Linacre through the two pairs of glasses he wore for reading, and the silvery strands of his moustache fluttered as he dealt her a final blow.

"Apart from the codicil, there are two small bequests to yourself and your son. Bequests of the kind intended more as remembrances than for their intrinsic value. 'I further bequeath to Timothy Linacre, son of my—er—etc.—er—my father's library of scientific books which is contained in the locked bookcase on the back stairs landing and all the contents of the said bookcase but not the bookcase itself and I bequeath to Mrs. Ethelwyn Linacre widow of—er—h'm, etc., etc.—the giltwood conversational seat at present in the hall at Hampton Court which I have heard her admire.' "

Mrs. Linacre looked blank. "But what is it?"

"A conversational seat? It is the name given to that curious round piece of furniture like a sofa, but I have never understood the reason, because people can only sit on it back to back."

"That thing! But I never admired that! Oh dear, I believe I did once say that it was an interesting period piece."

"Indeed it is," said Mr. Counsel. "I remember to have seen three others like it in the State Apartments at Dublin Castle."

But this was insufficient to console Mrs. Linacre. She knew the upholstery was moth eaten, and she thought the wood probably had worms in it.

Mr. Counsel folded up his copy of the will again and took off one pair of spectacles and put them away in his little dark brown attaché case But he still had something to say, and he began it with a gentle cough to clear the ground.

"On my way here," he said, "I passed—er—Tim, if I may call him that, on his bicycle. He seemed to be making for the Court."

"Oh dear, has he gone back again? He was there the whole of this morning. It is the police, you know, that are the attraction. Tim thinks he wants to study police methods, but I don't like it," said Mrs. Linacre. "It seems to me rather morbid."

Mr. Counsel shook his head, looking serious. "I am inclined to agree with you. This modern fashion for trifling with crime is regrettable, and it is a pity that a boy like Tim should become infected with it. I suppose he reads these detective stories." The old solicitor shook his head again. He evidently agreed with Sir Anthony Absolute that "they who are so fond of handling the leaves, will long for the fruit at last."

"Crime?" Mrs. Linacre repeated. "But you don't mean to imply—?"

"Oh dear me no, good gracious no!" cried Mr. Counsel, his voice quite sharp. "That is the very last thing I intended. I merely wanted to utter a word of warning. Not that I am suggesting for a moment that anybody has anything to conceal. But it is so easy for a careless remark to give a totally wrong impression. I think you should advise Tim to be on his guard against—er—idle chatter."

Mrs. Linacre had turned rather white. Mr. Counsel, having got everything said at last, did rise to go. Mrs. Linacre took him to the door herself.
Before they came within hearing of the taxi driver she murmured that she
did hope there was not going to be anything of that sort. Mr. Counsel
assured her he had every hope there would not. Neither of them cared to
put into words exactly what sort of thing they meant.

II

When Tim walked into the kitchen at Hampton Court he found the
police hard at work. More of them had arrived. Two plainclothes men had
come down from Dublin, along with the state pathologist, who had gone
on to the hospital. These two were trained searchers, and they had started
turning out the house for anything that could possibly have contained
belladonna. Beginning in the kitchen these intrepid fellows were explor-
ing the highest shelves and the deepest recesses. On the kitchen table,
dresser and floor were ranged neat rows of ill-assorted odds and ends.
There were old tins and jars and bottles and broken jugs and teacups and
teapots and lamp chimneys. There were dry bits of soap and candle ends
and spent matches and corks. There were withered orange peels and ba-
con rinds gone moldy, a large box of moldy bread crusts, and various
saucers on which flourished rich cultures akin to penicillin. There were
gadgets with unknown uses and substitutes for this and that in half-empty
packages. There was half a stone of sugar and three half-pound packets of
tea. There was a pair of stays and somebody's dental plate. There was just
about everything you could think of except belladonna.

Priscilla Hoyle had obtained permission to throw away rubbish, and
was joyfully piling things on trays and carrying them off to the dump
behind the shrubbery. This activity had acted on her as a tonic. She had
been looking miserable in the morning, but now, with her gray coat and
skirt exchanged for a shirt and slacks, she was in her element. She pressed
Tim into service.

They were coming back from a journey to the dump, cheerful for the
time being and making rather a noise—Tim had an iron tray and he liked
the way it reverberated when he banged it—when they heard voices on
the drive, and, peering through the bushes, they saw Mrs. De Vigne accompanied by Miss Tench.

"Visitors," said Tim. "You'll have to do the polite. Come on, I'll
stand by you." He was curious to know what brought Mrs. De Vigne so
soon again to the Court.

They slipped round by the back and found the two ladies sitting in the hall with the fixed expressions of two china dogs on a mantelpiece. They were not a pair, however, for if Mrs. De Vigne was an old maidish widow, Miss Tench was a matronly old maid. Mrs. De Vigne was in black, even to her gloves. Miss Tench wore one of her two washing frocks, which seemed to get tighter every summer. They both carried baskets.

Mrs. De Vigne apologized for intruding so soon. She had come to offer herself to Priscilla as a chaperone. She said, "I could not bear to think of you all alone, dear, in such a big house, where someone has just passed on. 'Think of Miss Hoyle there all alone!' I said to Eily as soon as I heard. I can easily arrange to come and stay with you for company. It's just a case of locking the door of Prospect View, and I can leave Molly the key to go in everyday and feed my pussycats, and I can pop over myself every now and then just to see things are safe. It wouldn't be any trouble. You see, I'm quite used to gadding."

Tim could tell by the earnest way Priscilla thanked her that she was glad she hadn't got to accept. She said her mother was coming, might even arrive that evening on the bus (which would be clever of her because Tim knew the telegram had not been sent till after the bus would have left). But there was no need to go into details, the great thing was to avert Mrs. De Vigne's visit. Mrs. De Vigne said of course there was nobody like your own mother, but she looked hurt and disappointed.

Both the ladies then described their feelings on hearing of Miss Hampton's death. Mrs. De Vigne especially bewailed the passing of "one of the old sort, a real lady, and a real good Protestant. There are so few of us old families left now." Miss Tench rounded her eyes as she asked, "And have you actually got *police* in the house?"

"Practically the whole Garda Siochana," said Tim cheerfully.

Mrs. De Vigne murmured, "Desecration!"

"They'll be coming to you too," Tim told her. "They're taking statements from everybody who was here yesterday."

"Were you here yesterday, Aggie?" asked Miss Tench. "You never told me."

"I had a small matter to discuss privately with Miss Hampton," said Mrs. De Vigne in a repressive voice. Miss Tench looked at her expectantly. Tim said, "That's what the police want to know about."

"Oh dear, do you think so?" said Mrs. De Vigne. "I hope they will not insist on my telling them. They may find out for themselves if they like, but I prefer to act on my dear husband's advice, *de mortuis nil nisi bonum*."

This was hardly going to satisfy Miss Tench's curiosity. She and Mrs.

De Vigne were bosom friends and spent their whole lives worming secrets out of each other. But Miss Tench could wait till she got Mrs. De Vigne to herself, and to Tim's disgust she changed the subject. She asked if, now that they had recovered from their walk, they might have a look round the garden. The baskets they were carrying came into evidence, and they hoped perhaps they might be allowed to take a few "bits." As Mrs. De Vigne neatly said, it would help them to keep Miss Hampton's memory green.

Priscilla would have gone to keep an eye on them, but at the garden gate she had to turn back to receive another caller. They all recognized the rector's car nosing its way out of the evergreens. Priscilla went to greet him while his other three parishioners vanished.

Mr. Owler was genuinely saddened by the loss of Miss Hampton. He cared for his flock with something of a collector's spirit, and the Hampton dynasty had been one of the gems of the collection. He feared it might not be the same in future. He had tried to keep on friendly terms with William Hampton. He had not shared Miss Hampton's disapproval of his joining the national army, in which, he understood, there were other Protestants.

Since Liam's return, he had done his best to extend a welcome, meeting him on his own ground and chatting about strategy, or crops, rather than on spiritual matters. But he was conscious of being up against some inner resistance. William was not an easy young man to know. There might be some unsoundness. Lately Mr. Owler had been very grieved by certain rumors.

Though looking despondent, the rector said nothing of his worries to Priscilla Hoyle. It was not as if she could help. She was only a bird of passage, and her spiritual condition was of no particular interest to him. Long practice enabled him to condole with her while his mind was occupied with other matters. He informed her of the funeral arrangements, which he had settled with Mr. Counsel and Captain Hampton. The whole interview took about ten minutes, and a final warm handshake was designed to make up for any chance omissions.

As he drove off, the rector was further saddened by meeting Meriel Booley Browne. She was riding up the drive on a showy chestnut mare. The mare played up at sight of the car, but Meriel managed it well and looked most victoriously lovely. If only Providence had seen fit to bestow such beauty on a Protestant!

Meriel called Tim to hold her horse while she dismounted and went in to talk to Priscilla. She had brought a note from her mother and backed it up verbally, pressing Priscilla to come and stay at Spangle Hill. It would be so much less lonely for her, and she could come over in the daytime to do anything that had to be done at the Court. It was such a kind invitation that it made Priscilla cry, and Meriel cried too and kissed her. Then they drew back and looked at each other, and Priscilla thought: "She's got everything I just miss; her hair's wavy and mine's only wiry, and I'm too thin, but she's just right." And Meriel thought she would like to tell Priscilla that she ought to use a deeper shade of face powder. Being at a loss for words they kissed each other again.

Priscilla went in to write a reply to Mrs. Booley Browne, thanking her for her kindness and explaining about her mother. Meanwhile Meriel was entertained by Tim.

"What are you doing here?" she asked.

"Oh, just keeping in touch," said Tim airily. "I suppose you know we have policemen on the job."

"Policemen?"

"Detectives. Guards. Practically the whole Garda Siochana."

"But what's it got to do with them?"

"Got to have an inquest in all cases of unnatural death. I'm a witness. So's Ma."

"How awful for her!"

"Oh, she'll be all right. I'll be there to hold her hand. I should have gone in any case. It's a great chance to study police methods."

"I never heard anything so revolting," said Meriel. "I think it's awful of you to be playing at detectives on your own cousin's grave."

Tim indignantly repudiated the accusation of heartlessness.

"If anybody did murder Cousin Rebecca," he declared, "I ought to help get them. Oh, I know you think I'm young and haven't any experience. Nobody would ever do anything if they listened to all the people who didn't think they could bring it off. As it happens I've been studying crime for longer than I can remember. I've got a whole shelf of books on it at home."

"This isn't crime," said Meriel. "Who would want to murder your cousin?"

"Naturally we don't know yet. But there may have been somebody who hated her. Because it's a queer thing they don't seem able to find any traces of poison about like there would have been if it had got into the food by accident. Mind you, we don't want it talked about all over the village, but it's no good pretending to hush up a thing like this in these days."

Meriel's big gray eyes widened as she stared at him. Tim had produced his impression and he let it sink in. Presently Meriel said in an awed voice, "Did you hear how old Mrs. Shegog cursed her? She cursed her on her knees. It happened in the Main street only last Tuesday, the day before she died."

"Couldn't have had anything to do with it," said Tim. "Pure coincidence."

"How do you know?"

"Be your age—how could it? I suppose you can't help being superstitious, being an R.C."

"How dare you!" said Meriel. Luckily at that moment Priscilla came out with her letter. Meriel swung herself up on the mare, disdaining Tim's assistance, and rode away.

III

The afternoon dragged on. What had been glorious weather was turning into a trying heat wave. The rhododendrons had all turned dingy, with dead flowers hanging on them like rags. The evergreens were half old leaves and half new, which made them look as if they were molting. Young birds squabbled in and out of the shrubbery, and the yard cats prowled watchfully below.

Priscilla had been to look for Mrs. De Vigne and Miss Tench in the garden and seen them disappear unobtrusively with loaded baskets. The police had finished in the kitchen and turned to Miss Hampton's bedroom and the bathroom. The kitchen now looked very clean and unreal, like an ancient monument after restoration. Tim and Priscilla and Mary had tea there. Then Tim went and dogged the footsteps of the searchers till they knocked off without having found anything of interest except two pounds of tea in the drawer of Miss Hampton's washstand, another four pounds on top of the canopy over the bed, and two pounds of pepper and four half-pound tins of mustard inside the wooden casing of the bath pipes.

Late in the afternoon Priscilla picked up a cushion worked with red parrots and dropped it on the front steps. A cloud of dust and two clothes moths flew out. Priscilla reflected that the job of spring cleaning this mansion was one she would not grudge to either Mrs. Linacre or Meriel Booley Browne.

It had been a tedious day, cluttered with oddments like the house. Nor was there much hope of subsequent days being any better. Tomorrow the inquest, Saturday the funeral, and thereafter whatever trials the police might have in store for them. All the more reason to enjoy a peaceful moment, basking on the sunny end of the portico, watching the evening light warm up the old stonework, and taking in the dignity of the house exterior, which was more enduring, after all, than the litter within. But the shadows of the Wellingtonias had now crept across all the portico, and only a stray beam of sun here and there managed to find the gaps in their straggly branches. Priscilla could not shake off a feeling of depression. She wondered if there was rain overhead.

She was just wondering whether Liam Hampton meant to look in again that evening when he appeared from the direction of the drive, talking to McGuirk. They had been discussing arrangements for the funeral and came to tell her about them. It was a more complex business than she had understood from Mr. Owler. There were traditions to be observed. The coffin would be sent back from the hospital to the house so that everything could take place as usual. An ancient farm cart that had served generations in this way would be used as a bier to carry the coffin to the church, and it must go by an old avenue that was now disused. McGuirk would see to getting the gates opened and the brambles cut back. McGuirk obviously relished all the details, and reminded Liam of several small things that might be forgotten. He seemed to feel it his duty to keep Liam up to the mark. Not only Liam either. The head gardener looked severely at Priscilla's slacks and remarked

"It's easy seen the old mistress is gone."

"That's enough, McGuirk," said Liam. "You have your instructions now. Good evening to you." McGuirk withdrew.

Liam still had instructions for Priscilla. He went on ticking off points in his well-ordered mind. "You'd better have some sherry or port or something handy to offer people. Some of them will have come a long way. One or two may stay to lunch. My mother is so sorry she can't come and help you. She's very much an invalid, you know." It was the first time Priscilla had heard him mention his mother, who had had a stroke and was partly paralyzed.

"I don't know how you were intending to get to the inquest tomorrow," Liam continued, "but I've booked Shankey, and we may as well pick up you and Mary and save you an early start. McVittie can drive in later and meet your mother at the station and bring you all back. It'll do the pony good to be exercised. Well, I think that's everything. Any developments here?"

"They haven't found what they were looking for," said Priscilla. "There doesn't seem to be anything anywhere that ever could have had belladonna in it."

Liam frowned. "That's bad. Old Counsel will be in a flat spin. Ever been mixed up in a murder case before?"

Priscilla stared at him.

"Don't look so frightened," said Liam. "It's nothing to do with you anyway. We'll keep it in the family."

"But—but what will happen? I mean, what will the police do next?"

"I haven't an idea. Never mind, it's all experience."

They were both silent for a spell, considering possible implications and complications. Then Liam caught Priscilla's eye and smiled.

"Don't let it get you down," he said, "and don't start thinking things more than you can help. Leave it to the experts. It's a nasty situation, but, as I said, it's not your affair. You did all anyone could for my cousin. Dr. Claffey told me all about it. He couldn't say enough for you."

"I wish I'd been a trained nurse, for her sake," said Priscilla. "Oh, I was forgetting to tell you, Mrs. De Vigne and Miss Tench came today. They took plants out of the garden while I was talking to Mr. Owler."

"Oh, let 'em come," said Liam. "Mrs. De Vigne seems fond of this place lately. Mind she doesn't pinch the antiques."

"Tim Linacre has been here all day too."

"What's he want here?"

"I think he thinks he's being a detective."

"Oh, is that all?"

Liam had looked dour at the mention of Tim, but his face cleared when Priscilla went on, "Miss Booley Browne was here too. It was so kind of them, they asked me to go there to stay."

"Did they indeed? Just like them. You couldn't want kinder hearted people than they are at Spangle Hill. Well, now, you're looking tired and I won't keep you. Are you all clear about tomorrow? Well, mind you get a good night's rest. I'll shut the dogs up on my way out."

He walked off to the yard, whistling the dogs after him. Later Priscilla watched him cross the lawn to his own shortcut. He looked graceful, tall and handsome. He and Meriel would make an outstanding pair.

Priscilla went up to her room and looked in her glass. The spot Mrs. Shegog had prescribed for had gone away, and country life was giving her a nice suntan, but she certainly looked tired, and she still felt depressed.

She had telegraphed to her mother: "Miss Hampton dead do come here," and the reply had come: "My poor child meet me morning train." So the awful breach in the Hoyle family was healed, and it would be unnecessary for either of them to apologize. As Priscilla was never going to apologize, that was probably all to the good. But she could not help wondering what on earth her mother would do with herself at Hampton Court. It was unsettling when two separate phases of one's existence impinged on each other.

She went to bed haunted by a sense of foreboding. Or perhaps there was rain overhead.

CHAPTER TEN
Conjectures

THE inquest was adjourned immediately after the hearing of the medical evidence. The post mortem could not go far to confirm Dr. Claffey's diagnosis of atropine poisoning until a report on the organs was received from the analyst. The distinctive symptoms exhibited by the patient—dryness of the mouth, flush, dilated pupils and so on—did not leave much doubt about the cause of death, but there was no knowing whether the belladonna was in chemical or natural form. The state pathologist, however, was skeptical as to its having come out of the bottle of ABC Liniment, on the grounds that this liniment contains camphor, which could easily have been detected by the smell, had it been present in the stomach.

No other witnesses were called, except Liam, who gave evidence of identification. The proceedings were all over before the general public in Brainborough realized that any had begun.

Only one incident took place of any dramatic interest, and the inner significance of that was concealed from the general public. It was the first meeting since the catastrophe of Liam Hampton and Mrs. Linacre. Mrs. Linacre went up to Liam and took his hand, as one grasps a nettle.

"How are you, Liam?" said she. "What a shock this must have been to you! So unexpected."

"I suppose it was to be expected any time at her age," was Liam's reply. He eyed the clean lace-edged handkerchief that fluttered in Mrs. Linacre's hand. She touched her eyes with it.

"I shall always be glad that I happened to be with her."

"Lucky, wasn't it?" said Liam.

Mrs. Linacre did not quite like his tone. She removed the handkerchief to look at him and said, "I hope you think I was right to send for Mr. Counsel."

"Oh, quite," said Liam. "I suppose it didn't occur to you to send for the rector."

"Well, you see, she never asked for Mr. Owler," said Mrs. Linacre.

Liam looked at her, and she met his eyes candidly. It wasn't that Cousin Rebecca had exactly asked to see Mr. Counsel either, but the two things were hardly the same. She hoped she was not going to have to explain it to Liam in so many words.

Liam laughed, or it might have been a snort.

"Well, I hope you're satisfied," he said. Then his attention was claimed by the superintendent, who wanted him to know they had decided it was a case for calling in the detective branch, and an inspector from Dublin was expected to arrive on that morning's train.

Tim had been told about the terms of the will. He was as disappointed as his mother at not being left any ready money, but he felt the codicil was overdoing matters. He could not see himself turning Liam out of the Court. Perhaps they could make a bargain, and Liam and Meriel could live there as his tenants, and he wouldn't be too hard on them over the rent. The details remained to be worked out, and his mother would have to be talked round, but everything was sure to turn out all right in the end, and Tim felt able to greet Liam with a smile of pure benevolence.

What interested him more at the moment was his own career in detection. He had heard what the superintendent said about the inspector coming down from Dublin, and he meant to be there to greet him on his first arrival.

The inquest had finished so early that there was more than an hour to wait before the train was due, and very likely another half hour after that, owing to the engine running on emergency fuel. The village shops were just beginning to show stirrings of life. Tim went to the "Brainborough Supermarket," otherwise known as Meegan's, which was the place to buy anything from haberdashery to pills. There he acquired a beautiful fat notebook with stiff covers, a survival from prewar stock. It was to be dedicated to writing up the case.

Liam and the superintendent had gone off together. Tim saw them disappear through the gilt-lettered door of the South Western Bank. The sergeant was on some other errand; he could be seen discoursing confidentially across the counter of Geraghty's, the grocer's. Mrs. Linacre had also gone into Geraghty's in the hopes of selling them her crop of green gooseberries for jam or bottling. She spent a good deal of energy on a trade in garden produce that brought in several pounds a year.

The sergeant's conversation with Geraghty was holding up the deal. Priscilla Hoyle was shopping too. She was buying another bottle of ABC Liniment, because the police had gone off with the first one, and it did seem to have done Mrs. McGuirk good. Mary the housemaid, the one person thoroughly enjoying the outing, was telling the whole inside story of the case to her elder sister in Meegan's drapery, a good way of ensuring that it would be all over the village before evening.

Seeing them all thus innocently occupied, and nothing likely to break at the moment, Tim took his notebook to the station, and there, sitting on an empty hen coop in a retired corner behind a weighing machine, he began to tabulate his information. He wrote "Facts" at the top of the first page, then reversed the book, and headed the first page at the other end, "Theories." At the "Facts" end, he wrote on one side of the paper only, and the blank pages opposite were headed, "Deductions." This seemed to Tim a model of compact method.

He had already drawn some deductions from yesterday's crop of facts. He considered that both suicide and accident were ruled out, and therefore what they had to deal with was murder.

Who might have wanted to murder Cousin Rebecca?

Not the Linacres anyway. Tim thought that must be obvious to everybody who knew the facts. Even if he and his mother had known positively that Cousin Rebecca's will was to be in their favor (which you really could not say it was), it would have suited them better to put off poisoning her until the document was signed in a regular way. It was only a chance that Mr. Counsel had arrived in time to fix things up. So although they had both been there at a time when they might have slipped belladonna into the food, they were the last people likely to do so under the circumstances.

Liam, on the other hand, had everything to gain by bumping off Cousin Rebecca before she had time to disinherit him. Knowing the house and its ways, he might have come and gone without being noticed. But Liam had been making silage that morning, and half a dozen farmhands had been with him all morning up to the dinner hour.

There was at least one other person with a motive: Mrs. Shegog. This idea had come to Tim as a by-product of his talk with Meriel. Putting aside with rationalistic scorn any idea that Mrs. Shegog's curse could have had any physical effect, he still had the fact that she must have hated Cousin Rebecca pretty badly. Might she have seen to it personally that her curse came home to roost? Mrs. Shegog was just the one to know all about the uses of deadly nightshade. Moreover, she was in the habit of slipping in and out of the kitchen, and the dogs might have let her pass without giving warning. Tim wrote, "N.B. Find out if anybody saw Mrs. Shegog on Wednesday morning."

Then again, what had Mrs. De Vigne been up to? Mrs. De Vigne was just about the last person anybody would suspect of murder. You'd say she would not hurt a fly. But why all this mystery about her visit, and had it really been only from motives of propriety that she had wanted to foist herself on Priscilla? She knew something against Cousin Rebecca, or she wouldn't have said that about *de mortuis nil nisi bonum.* Whatever it was, it surely ought to throw some light on the problem.

The last two people on his list were Priscilla Hoyle and the house-maid, Mary. They had both had opportunities of poisoning the food that morning, but there was no apparent motive for either of them. Mary came of a very respectable local family; she did not have much chance to go to the cinema, and Tim thought she had hardly the imagination to murder anybody even if she was likely to get anything out of it. Priscilla Hoyle was an outsider and, in a way, a dark horse, but there did not seem to be much point in her murdering her employer; it only meant she was out of a job and had got mixed up in a case that would not recommend her to another family. It might, however, be worth inquiring into Priscilla's background; there was always the hope that she had had some neurosis-forming experience in her childhood, or an ancestor who was a homicidal maniac. With these cheerful possibilities in mind, Tim looked forward to meeting Priscilla's mother.

These cogitations passed the time so well that when Tim next looked at his watch the train was twenty minutes overdue. The station had filled up with the usual oddly assorted collection: two nuns, five soldiers, a man who looked horsey; a man with fishing rods, and several women with baskets. Priscilla was down at the far end of the platform, standing apart and looking different from everybody else, with her neat hair and her townish coat and skirt. Over the low wall Tim could see McVittie and the trap in the station yard. He looked about for the superintendent, but could not see him anywhere; perhaps he had private information that the train would be later yet. All the same it looked as if something was expected to happen soon, because the station master's wife was shooing her chickens in off the line.

Tim put away his notebook and strolled along to join Priscilla. Before he could lead her on to the subject of her past life the train actually did arrive. It labored up to the platform, panting heavily under the weight of all the passengers in the carriages and corridors.

The station staff, banging doors and milk cans, did their best to provide effects appropriate to the arrival of the down express, and to work up the proper degree of panic. Ten of the waiting travelers fought their way in, and six of the train load were squeezed out. All the six were very ordinary homely bodies. Tim looked at Priscilla.

"Your mother hasn't come," he said. "She must have missed it."

Priscilla thought she might be still on the train, not realizing that she had arrived at Brainborough (the name of the station had not yet been painted up again after the war emergency precautions). The train needed several minutes rest before it pulled out again, so they had time to run along, looking in all the carriages. Mrs. Hoyle certainly was not on board.

"Damn!" said Priscilla. "That's just like Mother. I suppose she'll come tomorrow, or on the bus. I suppose I'll have to go on meeting everything till she turns up."

"Bad luck," said Tim. "It's funny the detective hasn't come either. I didn't see anybody that looked a bit like one, did you?"

Priscilla said she wasn't looking. She expected to see quite enough of him when he did come. She went off to join McVittie and the pony, which had had quite enough of waiting.

Tim thought he would go and find the superintendent and see how he felt about the detective letting him down. On the way he met his mother carrying an empty basket and looking pleased with herself. She had both secured an order for gooseberries and bought some cigarettes under the counter.

"I thought I'd never catch Geraghty's eye," said Mrs. Linacre. "He and the sergeant were having *such* a conversation. All about pins in onions or something."

"*What* about pins in onions?" Tim demanded.

"I don't know. I didn't listen. I very nearly gave it up in despair because they looked as if they'd never be done talking. However, all's well that ends well."

Tim was vexed at hating missed something interesting. He had forgotten that particular small point. He flipped open his notebook and scribbled "pins in onions?" on the inside of the cover. Should he go and talk to Geraghty or keep on after the superintendent? The question was settled for him by meeting the superintendent in the market square.

With the superintendent was a shabby little man dressed in rather an odd mixture of city and country clothes, for he began with a stiff white collar and tie and dwindled down to an old pair of flannel bags. He was a mild little man whom you would never notice in a crowd, or pick out from among half a dozen travelers at a railway station.

The superintendent introduced him to Tim as Inspector Devlin of the detective branch.

CHAPTER ELEVEN
Archives

ALTHOUGH the superintendent was most civil in introducing Tim to the detective—his first real life detective—it was a case of "How do you do? Good-bye!"; he was not invited to join the party. The two policemen walked on and left Tim gazing after them. They disappeared into the South Western Bank, where the superintendent had already spent most of the morning. Now what were they up to in the bank? They must be going into Cousin' Rebecca's money affairs, and from the time it was taking it looked as if something unexpected had cropped up.

Tim was finding that detecting what the detectives were doing was quite as hard work as detecting the criminal.

He went on to Geraghty's, but he had no luck there either. There was nobody in the shop but the stupidest of Geraghty's daughters, who was never told anything about anything, and had no idea what the sergeant wanted. Geraghty himself had slipped over to Devine's for his midmorning "jar." Tim was not quite man of the world enough to pursue him thither. He quailed at the thought that he might have to cultivate a taste for porter in the interests of his career.

It seemed as if one might as well go home, and Private Investigator Linacre spent the next couple of hours pumping bath water, filling up the kitchen wood basket, and helping his mother pick more gooseberries. This virtuous labor refreshed him, and by tea time he was strengthened to renew the siege of Hampton Court.

He walked into Mary's kitchen and asked her for the key of the bookcase on the landing. It had occurred to him that even if his legacy of books was no other use to him, it provided an excuse for hanging about.

Mary had not got the key, and Priscilla Hoyle had gone to meet the bus in case her mother was on it. Tim thought for an awful moment that he was baffled again, but then Mary suddenly thought that the captain might have it, and he was in the back parlor having tea with the detective. Tim's hopes rose, and he suggested that he might bring a cup for himself and join them.

But when he presented himself at the door with his teacup in his hand, nobody showed any disposition to invite him in. Things looked busy. The table was covered with bundles of papers, neatly tied and docketed, which must have been done by the police and not Cousin Rebecca. All the drawers in tables and bookcases were open and empty. Miscellaneous objects were scattered about the floor, among them two or three more packets of tea. The papers on the table mostly seemed to be lists; Tim's eye fell on one headed: "Things to take in case of Evacuation, 1. Nail scissors, 2. Keating's . . ." He took in all he could at a glance, but what interested him most was that the picture over the mantelpiece had been taken down, and behind it there was a safe built into the wall, a thing he had never known about before.

Liam and the inspector both had their backs to him. Liam was sitting at the writing desk having tea, and the inspector was standing on tiptoe over against the mantelpiece, turning over a bundle of documents out of the wall safe, and checking them against a list.

"I'm afraid it's not among these," he said. Tim saw that the documents were share certificates.

"That's a pity," said Liam.

"Oh, it may be some place else," said the detective. "If not, well, even if it is another five thousand gone west, the way you have to look at it is that it may put us on the right track. I shouldn't be at all surprised—" he broke off short, noticing that Private Investigator Linacre had joined them.

Liam turned round too. Before they could throw him out, Tim hastily said his piece about the key of the bookcase.

"Might be any of these," said Liam, picking up four jangling bunches. "You can try them all."

"It's not locked," said Inspector Devlin. "I tried it."

"Oh, thanks," said Tim. "Er, anything left in that teapot?"

"Not a drop," said Liam, pouring himself out a second cup.

"Shall I get you some more?"

"Thanks, don't bother."

"Well, can I help in any way?"

"If you can," said the small detective kindly, "we'll certainly let you know."

"I thought I heard you say you'd lost, something."

"Oh no, nothing to signify."

Tim looked at them reproachfully. He knew quite well they had missed a certificate worth five thousand pounds, and as the inspector had said *"another* five thousand," there must be other money gone too. Well, however used a professional detective might be to large-scale robberies, he need not talk as if that was a mere flea bite. It looked to Tim as if Cousin Rebecca had found out somebody was stealing from her and perhaps it was them murdered her. But nobody seemed to want his opinion. He sighed.

"Tim," said Liam sternly, "scram."

It was heartbreaking to be turned out of the room where the first real detective you had ever met was just getting down to work. Tim believed he might have got round the inspector, who looked a decent little fellow enough. But there was no arguing with Liam, who could barely be civil these days. Tim had a good mind not to rent the Court to him and Meriel after all.

He reluctantly withdrew, and for the look of the thing he went straight upstairs to the bookcase. He was glad he had done so, for a minute later Inspector Devlin put his head out of the back parlor, glanced left and right, and drew it in again. Indignation surged in the breast of Private Investigator Linacre to think he was suspected of listening at the door.

But Tim was not admitting defeat. He sat down on the floor by the bookcase, on the landing between the front and back stairs, as if establishing a squatter's right at the center of events. The old house slumbered round him. No sound of the activities in the back parlor or kitchen came through the thick walls and doors. One of the dogs was snoring on a chair in the hall, and houseflies hummed high up under the ceiling. Tim pulled a book out of the bookcase and a spider came walking out after it.

Presently Liam came out of the back parlor and sauntered out through the hall, a movement which was accompanied by an upheaval in the shadows as the fat springer flopped off its chair and followed him. A little later Inspector Devlin came upstairs and passed Tim and went into Miss Hampton's bedroom. Tim affected to be absorbed in his book. It was the first that had met his hand, but it turned out so appropriate to his present preoccupations that by degrees he became genuinely absorbed. It was a *Textbook of Forensic Medicine and Toxicology* by R.J.M. Buchanan.

Tim was reading all about "the injurious effects produced in some persons who had partaken of Canadian partridges," when the door down the passage opened and Inspector Devlin called his name.

"Mr. Linacre! Just a moment."

Hardly able to believe his ears, Tim stuffed the book back on the shelf and made two strides to the door. The bedroom was by now in much the same state as the back parlor, snowed under with papers. The inspector seemed to have turned everything out of the drawers first, and was now doing some preliminary sorting. He held out to Tim a large sealed envelope, saying, "Isn't this addressed to you?"

The envelope was addressed in Miss Hampton's own writing:

> "For Timothy Linacre, Esq.,
> October 28th, 1945"

Tim said excitedly, "That's my birthday. Twenty-first. That's why she put 'Esquire.' She always used to put 'Master Tim Linacre,' though nobody else does now."

"Well, although the great day hasn't come yet," said the inspector, "I daresay Captain Hampton would not object to your opening it."

Tim could see he was keen to know what was in it, and he thought how it would have served the man right if he had just gone off home when they turned him out, instead of sitting there all that time, waiting to give valuable help. He pried up the flap of the envelope with his thumb and took out an ornate card, all scrolls and flourishes: five thousand pounds worth of a shipping company's six percent debenture stock.

He showed it to the inspector, saying casually: "Jolly nice birthday present." He worked out six percent of five thousand in his head. Suddenly he felt sad about Cousin Rebecca having died before her grand surprise matured. It was a shame that he should not have been able to thank her.

The inspector's next words rather altered his point of view.

"Pity it's no use to you," he said. "She ought to have had it properly transferred into your own name. These old ladies! None of them seem to know anything about business. She didn't will it to you, so, the way it is, you've no legal claim to the money. Of course Captain Hampton might like to carry out her intentions"—his tone showed he thought this would be a lot to expect of Liam—"but he's under no obligation."

"I shan't go on my knees to him," said Tim haughtily. He reflected that anything whatever Cousin Rebecca ever did for you was sure to have a catch in it.

"Never mind," said the inspector, "you know she had the kind thought.. You might as well give me back the certificate. It's a good job the money's turned up."

The inspector liked to look on the bright side of things. So did Tim, and he thought at any rate here was his opportunity to ask questions. He asked, "Is everything accounted for now?"

"Well, no," said the inspector. "No, I can't say it is. This is all right as far as it goes, but there are still some queer things in the books. Looks to me like the old lady might have been paying blackmail."

Tim whistled. "Cousin Rebecca! Blackmail! Nobody would have the nerve."

"Well, it looks like it anyway." Inspector Devlin sat down on a curious piece of furniture with three steps, up which Miss Hampton used to climb into her big bed. He felt in his pocket for cigarettes and took out two, but Tim shook his head; he had promised not to smoke or drink till he was twenty-one. "Quite right too," said the inspector. Tim sat astride a cane bedroom chair, and fixed his eyes on the detective like a dog waiting for a biscuit, for it looked as if biscuits were now going to be handed out. No doubt the inspector had reasons of his own.

Outside, the country was stirring to life after a languid day. Dandelion seed drifted by the window on a light evening breeze. Inside, the room grew hotter and stuffier, and clouds of cigarette smoke hung in the air. But Tim would not have been anywhere else for the world. He felt he was now "inside" in the best sense of the word, settling down to be buddies with the inspector.

"I was saying to the captain," said Devlin, "that maybe your mother might be able to help us. She seems to have known the old lady as well as anybody, and she might have heard something sometime. It was Mr. Gahan, the bank manager, who first smelt the rat. He's had it on his mind for some time, apparently, whether he ought to say anything to Miss Hampton about the habit she was getting into of drawing out large sums of money. She wasn't spending anything on herself, and this place didn't cost all that much the way she ran it. But every now and then she would instruct him to sell out an investment (she did all her business through the South Western), and when she got the money she drew it out right away, or most of it, by checks payable to 'Self'. It was a thousand here and two thousand there. Not big money in itself, you know, but it went on for three or four years, and she'd dipped into her capital to the amount of about twenty thousand pounds:"

"Twenty thousand! How much is there left?"

"She should have left an estate of about eighty thousand. Now, sixty's nearer the mark. One thing," said the inspector cheerfully, "it's that much less to pay death duties on."

"Even sixty sounds quite a lot," said Tim, "but I suppose it isn't if you've a place like this. Poor Cousin Rebecca! There must have been some reason then why she got so stingy."

"Old ladies have their secrets. But it seems none of you ever suspected anything?"

"Well, I didn't," said Tim. "I never even thought of such a thing. No reason why I should have. I'll ask Ma if she has any ideas on the subject."

"Yes, you talk it over with your mother." The inspector tidied up his cigarette ash into the grate. "And tell your mother this," he added. "If there's any family trouble or secret at the bottom of it, she needn't be afraid to come to us. Remember, everything's safe with the police."

Tim said, "Oh yes," but he went home rather thoughtful. It seemed to him it would have to be a pretty guilty secret that was worth twenty thousand pounds.

CHAPTER TWELVE
Obsequies

"FUNERALS can be enjoyable when they're not your own," said Tim.

"How do you know you won't enjoy your own?" said Meriel Booley Browne.

"Oh, I mean not from your own house. Not your dearly loved father or mother or anybody like that. I think I enjoy funerals more than weddings really."

"I hope I'll enjoy my own wedding," said Meriel, and Tim wondered if it was any nearer taking place; but she did not enlarge on the subject.

They were walking back from the graveyard to Hampton Court, where everybody had been obliged to leave the vehicles they had come in to follow the funeral procession down the old avenue on foot. As Tim said, the funeral had been a great success. Ever so many people came, out of respect for such a feature of the neighborhood as the Hampton family, and for an old lady who had managed not only to live so long but to find an original way of dying in the end.

It was fortunate that many of the attenders were Roman Catholics who waited outside in the graveyard, otherwise the little church might have been unwholesomely crowded. The day was hotter than any that had gone before, with that utter stillness that often comes before a break in the weather. The smell of the flowers in the church was oppressive, especially the all-pervading scent of a massive sheaf of Madonna lilies from Spangle Hill.

The coffin was carried down into the family vault, an exclusive railed enclosure where the Hamptons slept till the last trump. There was the usual general feeling of relief and sense of tidying up that comes when dust has been returned to dust. People moved off chatting in twos and threes. It was natural for the talk to be in low voices. Yet one did not have to be hypersensitive to be aware of undercurrents in it, not of suspicion yet perhaps, but of speculation. Conversations broke off when Liam or the Linacres approached. People had Priscilla Hoyle pointed out to them, but did not go and talk to her. People glanced curiously at anyone they did not know, wondering if it was a detective in disguise.

"And is Miss Hoyle's mother here?" Mrs. De Vigne asked Miss Tench. Miss Tench had learned that Mrs. Hoyle had still not come down from Dublin. They both agreed that it was very strange.

One incident struck a sinister note in the proceedings. Mrs. Shegog set up a kind of keen over the grave, and went on and on, making a weird discordant wailing noise till Liam bought her off with half a crown.

"What do you suppose she meant by that?" Tim asked Meriel. Meriel thought Mrs. Shegog meant it as a compliment. "I daresay by now she's sorry about the time she cursed her."

"I wonder," said Tim, and told Meriel his theory of Mrs. Shegog as a suspect. But Meriel said it would not work. It so happened that she was able to give Mrs. Shegog an alibi.

"She was over at our house on Wednesday morning, about eleven. She doesn't often honor us with a visit." Spangle Hill was about eight miles away on the far side of Brainborough. "As she was in the village on Tuesday, she probably slept there somewhere and came straight on. She couldn't possibly have got back to Hampton Court."

Tim thought that over. Though the old woman was a good walker she was slow moving, and it would take her at least three hours to cover the distance between the two houses. She might have got a lift, but there were no cars on the roads that were likely to stop for the likes of her, and the country carts went as slow as she did. If Meriel was wrong about her not having returned home on Tuesday night, she might have been at Hampton Court a little after eight, but she would not have been able to get in so early in the morning. He asked how long she had stayed at Spangle Hill, and was told she got her dinner there. The alibi was not absolutely watertight, but it was fairly convincing.

"Cuddy was raging," Meriel remarked. "He said the last time Mrs. Shegog was there she put a spell on his onions and they all got mildew."

"I thought he had marvelous onions," said Tim. "Everybody was talking about them at the flower show,"

"He did have good ones in the show," said Meriel, "wherever he got them. He hasn't one if you want them for soup."

Tim was not much interested in Caddy's onions at the time, but a few minutes later everybody was talking about them, and a small scandal broke in which the greater mystery was momentarily forgotten.

The funeral gathering was a clearing house for all the clack of the countryside. The McGuirks were in the thick of it. Mrs. McGuirk had refused to be done out of the ceremony, though barely able to hobble. Her husband parked her in the kitchen while he himself came to mingle with the crowd, and there was about him an air of superiority, a kind of "holier than thou" attitude, which was something more than what seemed due to the solemnity of the occasion.

"Look at McGuirk allegating himself among the gentry," said McVittie, and spat into the rhododendrons.

McGuirk was asking Mrs. Linacre if she'd heard about Cuddy, and whether the flower show committee would now consider reversing the judge's decision in the class for Assorted Vegetables.

For Cuddy had cheated in the competition by exhibiting onions that were not of his growing. And not only had he cheated, but he had stolen the onions in order to do so. A Guard was on his way to serve him with a summons to the District Court. Cuddy had brought disgrace on Spangle Hill.

The sergeant had seen it all practically in a flash, the moment he heard about Miss Hoyle finding a pin stuck into an onion that had been bought in the flower show auction. He had heard of vegetables being marked that way, and when he made inquiries at Geraghty's, the only Brainborough shop that sold vegetables, he found as he expected, that Geraghty was on the lookout for onions with pins in them being offered to him. Any such onions must have been stolen from a local gardener who grew vegetables for the Dublin market and who had made the arrangement about the pins with Geraghty to lay a trap for garden robbers. The market gardener confirmed that six of his best onions of the variety in Cuddy's exhibit had been taken about three days before the show.

"But this is dreadful!" said Mrs. Linacre. "I should never have thought it of Cuddy. He always seemed such a nice man."

"Ay, it's a bad business. I pity the man's family," said McGuirk, with the utmost satisfaction.

When Mrs. Booley Browne heard about it she was horrified and went straight to Liam to say that of course there must be a committee meeting immediately, and McGuirk must have Cuddy's prize, and if there was any other way they could possibly make it up to him they would do so. "Only I do hope," she said, "that my husband won't insist on giving Cuddy the sack. It's not so much that he's a good gardener, but his wife is always ready to give extra help in the house."

"He won't if Liam puts in a word for him," said Meriel, who had rallied to the support of her mother. Liam said of course he would.

Meriel was looking "smashing" that morning (Tim's word). A frantic search for something to wear that was right for both the funeral and the heat wave had ended in a little black afternoon frock and a small, sophisticated black hat, in which she looked like somebody else, but somebody even more glamorous than her usual attractive self. Moreover, shrewd observers like Mrs. Linacre fancied there was a supercharged air about her, such as is sometimes observable in girls who are about to announce their engagements. Mrs. Linacre began to plan what flowering shrubs she would put in place of all those *ponticum* rhododendrons, and to calculate the supply of firewood to be obtained by cutting down the Wellingtonias. She was surprised when Liam came up to her and offered, with unusual civility, to send over her conversational seat and Tim's books as soon as he had a cart to spare. She thanked him and said there was no hurry. She rather wondered he thought it worth the bother.

The police did not intrude on the funeral, though yet another of them had arrived, a subordinate who was helping Inspector Devlin. Sergeant Carty had been freed to resume his own duties at the barracks, so the investigation was now in the hands of the detective branch, with the superintendent distantly superintending from county headquarters. Devlin and his junior had shut themselves up somewhere with masses of Miss Hampton's papers and were reading steadily through them all in the hope of uncovering a guilty secret. As Miss Hampton had always thrown papers into drawers in preference to wastepaper baskets, they were faced with the accumulation of years.

Priscilla Hoyle had had to provide accommodation for the detectives, and it had been something of a task to air their bedding, as the Hampton Court spare rooms had not been much in use. In fact, as they were occupying the only two habitable spare beds, it was lucky on the whole that Mrs. Hoyle had not turned up. Priscilla was getting anxious about her. She sent another telegram: "Impossible meet Saturday train. Wire me when to expect you." So far there was no reply.

But just when people were at last beginning to leave, the procession of wartime vehicles—governess carts, inside and outside cars, taxis, gas-producer cars and bicycles—was held up on the drive by something coming in the other direction. There was no room to pass so, after a frantic amount of backing and pushing at the expense of the evergreens, a number of the funeral guests returned on their tracks. In their wake there emerged a little donkey cart led by an apparently half-witted driver. Sitting in the cart was a lady of commanding appearance. She wore a plain, sensible felt hat and mackintosh, and she was clutching two magazines, a large handbag, a paper parcel and an umbrella. There was really no reason, apart from the donkey cart, why she should have reminded Tim of the Dame making her entrance in a Christmas pantomime.

"I'm afraid I have arrived just at the wrong moment," said the lady, addressing the world in general, and remaining seated in the donkey cart, from which, indeed, it was going to be difficult to descend with dignity. She had a calm, clear voice like a lecturer or a schoolteacher. She looked inquiringly round, hesitating between Mrs. Booley Browne and Mrs. Linacre, who both seemed more at home than the rest of the bystanders. Then her face cleared as Priscilla Hoyle came forward.

"Oh, there you are!" she cried. "When you didn't meet me at the station I was afraid something had happened."

She jumped to her feet in the cart, and the donkey, in surprise, took a step forward, then stopped short at a frightful curse from its owner. The lady tottered. Several people leapt to her assistance. The donkey started forward again, and the lady fell overboard. Luckily she saved herself from damage by flinging her arms round Liam Hampton's neck.

"I beg your pardon! I do hope I didn't hurt you. No, no, I'm quite all right. Oh, thank you, thanks so much!" said the lady, releasing Liam and collecting her magazines and handbag from helpful hands. She straightened her hat, drew a deep breath, and looked round for Priscilla. "Well, darling, here I am at last!"

"Oh, Mother!" said Priscilla. Tim Linacre thought she only sounded half pleased.

CHAPTER THIRTEEN
Things Come To Light

ABOUT an hour and a half later an informal conference on the blackmail problem was held on the lawn.

Having it on the lawn was Mrs. Hoyle's doing. People who live an open-air country life of farming or gardening are generally content to stay inside their houses if they want to sit down. But Mrs. Hoyle had a townswoman's enthusiasm for getting out into the fresh air, and after lunch she insisted that coffee should be taken outside, everybody carrying their own chairs and Mary bringing a table and the tray.

One or two funeral guests had stayed to lunch, and Mrs. Linacre had acted as hostess; but Mrs. Hoyle had taken much of that responsibility off her shoulders. Over lunch the talk ran on the reasons why Mrs. Hoyle had missed her train the day before, her dislike of traveling by bus, the inefficiency of the post office in not having been in time to catch her with Priscilla's second telegram, the scarcity of vehicles at the station (everything had been hired for the funeral) which had compelled her to arrive in the donkey cart. In this way conversation was kept going without any reference to awkward subjects.

Mrs. Hoyle had come down to look after Priscilla, and as Priscilla was looking after the house her mother was quite prepared to take that on too. Already she had made several minor improvements in the arrangements, culminating in the transfer of the lunch party to the garden. They found themselves, after a commotion that was bad for digestion, sitting on mahogany dining-room chairs in the long grass around the Wellingtonias, where the midges hovered. Somebody said it must be a sign of rain that the midges were beginning to bite. The funeral guests left almost at once, but the others sat on; they could not face another upheaval so soon after a meal on such a sultry day.

Mrs. Hoyle, however, arose to tackle the problem of her own accommodation. Inspector Devlin was in the bed that was kept for the Bishop, and his assistant had the one allotted to the Bishop's chauffeur. In all the other unoccupied suites of rooms at Hampton Court there was not one in which you could expect a middle-aged lady to sleep. There were beds and bedding; but the damp was more than could be dried out in an afternoon. There was only one thing to be done, and that was to install Mrs. Hoyle in Miss Hampton's own room.

Priscilla took her up to it and introduced her to the glories of the carved oak and the valance and the featherbed; the flowery toilet set on the marble-topped washstand; the two mahogany wardrobes; the commode (for such was the inner nature of the contrivance with three steps up to the bed, on which Inspector Devlin had sat while chatting to Tim). Mrs. Hoyle surveyed it all from the doorway and observed that it was lucky she was not the sort of woman to let things get on her nerves.

If she had been a nervous woman the weather would have encouraged her to give way; it was a stupefying afternoon. There are days when Irish air seems to become impregnated with some narcotic that makes the slightest action an effort and thinking too much far all but the strongest. Loaded clouds were now piled up like bales all round the horizon, and a little hill which all the week had been misty in the distance had suddenly thrust up a truculent blue shoulder just behind the shrubbery. Nothing else dared move; the dark green pointed fingers of the Wellingtonias hardly quivered in the stillness.

At the foot of the largest Wellingtonia, the two detectives, Liam and the Linacres sat on. They felt that the time had come to hold a family council on the difficult situation in which they were placed so long as mystery obscured the reason for and the cause of Miss Hampton's death. But they were not making any progress. The blackmail theory had introduced a new complication with all sorts of unpleasant possibilities.

Inspector Devlin thought Mrs. Linacre ought to have been able to remember something helpful. He handed her the list of dates on which the large withdrawals from the bank had taken place, in the hope that she would be reminded of some happening that might indicate a blackmailer at work. Mrs. Linacre glanced vaguely down it and had no suggestions to make. She said, "It's so unlike Cousin Rebecca."

"People are often different from what we think," said the little inspector. "I don't go much for all this psychoanalysis, but there's this much truth in it: we all have a lower nature. Even a fine old lady like the deceased might at some time or other have given way."

"Really, Inspector! We have never had that type of vulgar scandal in our family."

"I wouldn't say that," remarked Liam, through cigarette smoke. "At least, if not precisely the kind of scandal you seem to think the inspector is thinking of, we have had our scandalous episodes. The police have heard of Great-Aunt Hebe. The stolen Nepenthe, Inspector."

"What, Mrs. Hebe Hampton Jones?" said the inspector. "Was she a relation of yours?"

"Many old families have produced cases of kleptomania," said Mrs. Linacre.

"Call it what you like," said Liam, "but to steal a rare Nepenthe from the Botanic Gardens—well, it was like pinching the Mona Lisa from the Louvre. Then there was that poisoning case."

The inspector sat up. "What, another one?"

"Be quiet, Liam," said Mrs. Linacre crossly. It was not like her to be so flustered. Tim could see she was hating all this. Liam was in a funny mood. He seemed to be amusing himself, if nobody else.

"Never conceal anything from the police," said Liam. "Especially when they already have it on the record. It wasn't homicide, Inspector. I was talking about the case of Chaffinch v. Hampton and the poisoning of a tree. My old cousin Augustus and a Mrs. Chaffinch lived next door to one another in Dublin in Ailesbury Road. Mrs. Chaffinch had a fine copper beech in her garden which kept the sun from reaching Cousin Augustus in his bath. Augustus asked her to cut it down and she refused. A year later the tree was dead. Cousin Augustus had gone out at dead of night and bored holes deep into its trunk and filled them up with paraffin. At least, that's what Mrs. Chaffinch said he did, and I should think it's likely. She couldn't prove it against him and he got off without paying any damages."

"Yes, but," said Tim, "no sense in Cousin Rebecca paying money to hush up anything like that. I mean, everybody knew all about it."

"That is the difficulty," Liam admitted. "You see, Inspector, in our family we don't hush up scandals. We feel a good scandal is something everybody can enjoy."

"Cousin Rebecca particularly," said Tim.

Inspector Devlin mopped his forehead. The younger detective apologetically scratched his ankle. Tim kindly informed him that there were ticks in the long grass which would burrow in and lay eggs under his skin. Mrs. Linacre put her feet up on the rung of another chair and took a little phial of oil of lavender from her handbag to keep off the midges.

"I suppose you haven't found anything interesting in Cousin Rebecca's papers?" Tim asked the inspector.

The inspector was literal-minded. "I wouldn't say that," he replied. "They're full of useful hints and receipts. There were some tips on growing strawberries and a way of doing spiced beef that I'd like to copy out for my wife, and several receipts for homemade insecticides and some for wine and beer."

"You can count those in with the insecticides, Inspector," said Liam. "I've had some."

"Ha, ha," said the inspector politely. "But I'm sorry to say we haven't come across anything the old lady would have minded us seeing, not in the very least. There was one bunch of stuff though, I'd like to get your views on. George," he turned to his junior, "would you get me that little brown attaché case?"

George loped off across the lawn, and there was a drowsy interval, during which the inspector mopped his brow again, Liam smoked, Tim scratched himself, and Mrs. Linacre dabbed more oil of lavender on her wrist. From far away, somewhere behind the little blue hill, sounded a disapproving mutter.

"Thunder," said Mrs. Linacre. "We ought to go in."

Nobody moved, however, and presently George came back with the attaché case. Inspector Devlin took out of it a number of sheets of paper in Miss Hampton's writing and passed a few to each of them.

"Know any of these people?" he asked.

They knew nearly all, at any rate by name. The papers were the family trees of almost everybody who had ever intermarried with the Hamptons, and also a few who hadn't yet, like the British royal family. Miss

Hampton had enjoyed unraveling complicated interrelationships, just as some people enjoy working out equations and others read detective stories. Her relations knew all about this hobby.

"She was starting one for Miss Hoyle; she hadn't got far with that," said Tim, turning over a blank sheet. "Here's Mrs. De Vigne, I mean her husband. They're no connection of ours, are they?" He pored over the tables. "What do you know about this? Cousin Rebecca makes Mrs. De Vigne a third cousin by marriage of Devine's at the pub!"

"No!" said Mrs. Linacre, interested. "How does she make that out?"

Tim went on deciphering. "There's a note scribbled here in pencil at the side. 'James Devine, grocer, joined C. of I. in 1800 and took Protestant trade from his brother, Kevin. James did well through gaining county connection and sent son, Thomas, to Trinity. Son turned lawyer, and spelled name De Vigne to be different, from R.C. relations still in trade.' That's what she says, and Thomas was our Mrs. De Vigne's husband's grandfather. Isn't that funny?"

"Not particularly," said Liam.

Mrs. Linacre suddenly remembered that the detectives were sure to be Roman Catholics.

"Do forgive my son, Inspector," she said sweetly. "It isn't funny at all, really, unless you know the lady. She's a very strong Protestant and rather a snob. Besides, she's strictly T.T. and would hate to be related to publicans even more than sinners."

"Do you tell me so?" said the inspector. "You think she might object to this being known?"

"I'll say she would," said Tim. "She's always made a great point of the De Vignes being descended from the Huguenots and having French blood. But you don't think Cousin Rebecca was blackmailing her?"

"Don't be an ass, Tim," said Liam. "You've got blackmail on the brain."

"Oh, I don't mean blackmailing her, exactly, at least, not for money. But she might have been going to tell everybody, or Mrs. De Vigne thought she might and poisoned her to stop it."

"Well, do go and tell her you've found out, and see if she poisons you."

"You needn't get so cross, Liam," said Tim, injured. "I don't want to do anything to upset her, poor old dear. I'm only wondering if it was anything to do with this, the frightfully confidential business she had with Cousin Rebecca on Wednesday."

"But I don't believe Mrs. De Vigne knows herself," said Mrs. Linacre.

"What, not know about her own husband's grandfather?"

"My dear Tim," said his mother, "although we, of course, do know our family history, there are plenty of people who are quite in the dark even about their grandparents."

"Then you don't think she deliberately invented the Huguenots?"

"I'm sure she didn't. She's transparently honest and quite lacking in imagination. Her husband may have, but more likely the idea just grew up. It was natural, after they'd frenchified their name. I think it would be kindest not to say anything about it."

"Yes, but Mother, we ought to find out what she wanted with Cousin Rebecca."

"I think you might leave that to the inspector."

At that moment the thunder made itself heard much louder, and a big drop splashed on the inspector's head where there was a thin place in his hair. Another hit Mrs. Linacre's nose. They leapt to their feet and seized their chairs for a dash to the house. Halfway across the lawn they met Mrs. Hoyle running out with an armful of umbrellas, but as the heavy chairs were enough to carry, the best she could do for them was to run between the inspector and Mrs. Linacre with an open umbrella in each hand. The storm broke on them promptly, but their speed saved them from more than a sprinkle, and they clustered on the portico like pictures of survivors from the Biblical deluge.

"This will freshen the atmosphere," said the inspector, looking on the bright side as usual.

"Indeed, I'm sure you are glad of it," said Mrs. Hoyle. "Priscilla has been telling me all your problems, and I do sympathize with you. But so often when one can't think, it's really just the weather, and I shouldn't be at all surprised if now when it clears up after this you find that all the time there's been some perfectly simple solution."

CHAPTER FOURTEEN
More Things Come To Light

THE shower was a short sharp one. They watched it from the portico, and as it began to show signs of clearing up, the inspector said he thought he would go over at once and interview Mrs. De Vigne.

"Do you know the way?" asked Tim eagerly. "It's next to the churchyard. If you don't mind climbing walls, I can take you there by a shortcut."

But when he had pointed out the direction of the shortcut, the inspector said he could manage by himself, and Tim's hopes of being present when Mrs. De Vigne was interviewed were disappointed.

Mrs. Linacre thought before going home she would just take the measurements of her conversational seat, and Tim could show her his books. Tim asked Mrs. Hoyle what had become of Priscilla, as he wanted a word with her before he left.

Mrs. Hoyle called, "Priscilla! Priscilla! Where are you, darling? Captain Hampton wants you." Priscilla came out of the dining room. "Oh, there you are, darling," said Mrs. Hoyle. "Have you been in there all the time? What are you doing? Putting away the silver? Why didn't you ask me to help you? Here I am doing absolutely nothing. Darling, Captain Hampton wants to speak to you before he goes."

"Oh, Miss Hoyle, I wonder might I bother you for a tape measure?" said Mrs. Linacre.

Liam secured Priscilla's attention by gripping her arm. He drew her out on to the portico. "I just wanted to thank you for the way everything went. Lunch was excellent. I'm afraid it made a lot of work for you without Mrs. McGuirk."

Priscilla was surprised and pleased. In a conscientious feminine way she had gone to a great deal of trouble and had never expected anyone to notice.

"You're a blessing," said Liam, smiling at her. "So detached. The rest of us are fit to bite each other."

"Oh, so are Mother and I," said Priscilla. "It's the weather."

"Partly, perhaps. But some people"—was he thinking of Mrs. Linacre?—"have the capacity to annoy me in any weather. What's more, I believe it's mutual. Now I'm going to do a good deed, and that'll shake them." They went back into the hall, and Liam said to Tim, "Oh, by the way, the inspector told me about that share certificate. I'll have the shares transferred to you when we've got probate."

"I say!" said Tim, greatly surprised. "I say, thanks most awfully. But Liam, you know you needn't if you don't want to. I mean, there's all the other money gone too. I mean, are you sure you can afford it?"

Mrs. Linacre had reeled and recovered. She said hastily, "That's generous of you, and like you, Liam. I knew you would want to do that, and I feel sure you won't regret it."

Liam said coldly that he felt bound to carry out Miss Hampton's intentions. Then, telling Priscilla he would look in again tomorrow, he walked off without any further good-byes.

II

It was about half an hour after the inspector had left when Mrs. De Vigne came diffidently up to the door.

Mrs. Hoyle and Priscilla had finished the silver and were upstairs in Miss Hampton's bedroom. Tim was looking through his books, and Mrs. Linacre, having got Tim to turn the sofa right over for her and borrowed some paraffin oil from Mary, was carefully going over the wormholes one by one. The barking dogs disturbed them all. Priscilla put her head out of the bedroom door. Tim said, "I'll see them, whoever it is," and she went in again.

Mrs. De Vigne, standing on the threshold, took off her gloves and put them on again, and asked Tim if he happened to know where she could find the police inspector.

"Oh, bad luck," said Tim. "He's just gone looking for you."

"Looking for me? Oh dear! Then I'm sure he'll say I ought to have gone to him before."

"Well, you've come now, anyway," said Tim, to reassure her. "It's just bad luck that you didn't find him here. You must have crossed each other. He went across the fields and I suppose you came by the road."

"The other man is still here somewhere, isn't he?" said Mrs. Linacre. "This thing is simply riddled with wood worm. I shall have to treat every one of these little holes with paraffin."

"Oh yes, I forgot him," said Tim. "What's his name? George? Will George do, Mrs. De Vigne?"

Mrs. De Vigne looked doubtful. She looked very much inclined to turn and fly, but Tim could not allow that.

"If you go back home now," he pointed out, "you'll only miss the inspector again. When you're not there he's sure to come straight back."

"I suppose he will. Oh dear! I wonder what he wants."

"I can tell you that," said Tim. "He wants you to tell him what you went to see Cousin Rebecca about on Wednesday."

"Yes. I was afraid it must be that. I ought to have told him at once; only one does not want to make trouble."

"Do sit down, Mrs. De Vigne," said Mrs. Linacre, looking up again from her furniture restoration problem. "I am sure the inspector will be back in a few minutes."

"If you'd rather not wait," said Tim, "you could tell me, and I'll explain matters to him when he comes."

"I think I had better see a responsible person," said Mrs. De Vigne. "Yes, I think the best thing will be to wait. That is, if I am not in anybody's way. At least, I suppose I couldn't see Captain Hampton? I know he's very busy."

"He's just gone off somewhere too."

"Oh dear, how unlucky!"

Seeing that there was nothing for it but patience, Mrs. De Vigne at last made up her mind to cross the threshold. She even took off her gloves and her mackintosh. If it had not been for the heavy shower, she said, she would have come sooner, but Tim said that if it had not been for the shower the inspector would have started sooner too, so that it made no difference.

They all sat down round one of the potted ferns. Mrs. De Vigne and Mrs. Linacre agreed that it had been a beautiful service, and that it was nice to see so many people present of every way of thinking. They agreed that it was nice that the rain had held off till after the funeral, and that it was a good thing it had come now, as it was badly wanted for the garden, if not for the hay. Mrs. Linacre hoped the weather was not really going to break, as she wanted a fine day for her herb-gathering picnic. Tim knew they were capable of going on like this for hours.

Tim asked if Mrs. De Vigne had heard about Cuddy and the onions. To his surprise she started and turned red. She *had* heard, but not till after her midday dinner (living next door to the churchyard, she had not come along to the house with the majority of the attenders at the service). Mrs. De Vigne seemed to think she had been very backward, and entered into a long explanation of how her maid was a niece of Mrs. McGuirk's, and had gone to help her aunt home and stayed to get her uncle his dinner, so that it was only when she got back after Mrs. De Vigne had had her own dinner that she heard the whole story. "And then there was that heavy shower, but as soon as it stopped I put my hat on and came here as fast as I could."

The Linacres did not quite see the connection of ideas, but before they could pursue the subject, which was beginning to interest Tim very much, there came two interruptions. The first was the return of the inspector, looking tired and muddy. Tim's shortcut had been the laborious kind, by gaps in brambles at muddy crossings where cows drank. The ditches had been softened by the thunder shower, and the inspector had slipped in one of them. After failing in his errand he had come back the longer way by road. When he saw Mrs. De Vigne sitting in the hall, he must have felt like the storybook child who set out to search for the four-leaved shamrock, and went all round the world, and came home to find it growing at his own front door.

But before they had even begun to explain to the inspector how Mrs. De Vigne had set out simultaneously to interview him, the second, and more dramatic, interruption occurred. There was a burst of excited conversation upstairs. Miss Hampton's bedroom door had opened, and all of a sudden Priscilla and her mother came running downstairs to the hall. They were each carrying a number of small packages, and they were both covered from head to foot with curly white feathers and soft feathery fluff.

III

The Hoyles had gone up to Miss Hampton's room to make the bed, which had not been done earlier because the sheets were still having their final airing at the kitchen fire. Priscilla prodded the mattress and remarked that she was afraid Mary did not turn it regularly, as it felt lumpy.

"Let's turn it now," said Mrs. Hoyle. "I know these old featherbeds; they're really too much for one to handle." She pulled off the old counterpane that was being used as a dust cover, and put aside the eiderdown and pillows stacked underneath. "It *is* lumpy!" she exclaimed, taking hold of the mattress. "How could she sleep on it like that?"

"She always used to lie over on this side," said Priscilla. "I don't believe this mattress has been turned for a year at least. I must speak to Mary. Let's give it a good shake-up now between us."

Mrs. Hoyle prodded again, and said she believed there was something inside. Priscilla, used to her mother's flights of fancy, said, "Oh, nonsense, how could there be? It's only old lumps of feathers."

But Mrs. Hoyle insisted: She examined the seam of the mattress and declared that it had been stitched up with new thread, probably quite lately. Priscilla sighed, because she saw there would be no peace now till they looked inside. She did not take to the idea, because she knew what happened when you made holes in pillows or cushions, let alone a whole featherbed. But her mother, enthusiastic by nature, was picking away at a seam with her fingernails. The ancient ticking gave unexpectedly; it tore along, and clouds of feathers filled the air, like a snowstorm out of a picture in Mother Goose. Feathers flew out of the window, and the house martins swooped for them and carried them up to their nests. Feathers tickled the Hoyles' cheeks and hands, and caught in their hair. Fluff went up their noses, and they both started sneezing. Between one paroxysm and the next, Mrs. Hoyle thrust her arm into the featherbed up to the shoulder, and triumphantly pulled out, with another cloud of feathers, a small flattish package stitched up in a gray linen cover.

"There!" she cried. "Who was right this time? And this isn't the only one." With more burrowing, five more small parcels came to light. Priscilla gave up trying to catch feathers and sat down. She thought it was a great pity Mrs. Hoyle had been right. She had too strong an imagination anyway, and after this her wildest ideas would have to be followed up by her reluctant daughter. Mrs. Hoyle exclaimed, "Open them quick! I can't bear being kept in suspense. I must know what's inside them."

"No, wait a minute," said Priscilla, coming to life. "I think we ought to give them to the inspector."

Mrs. Hoyle took a poor view of this idea. She would not put it past the inspector to take charge of the packages and never tell them anything. But Priscilla insisted that it was important to behave very correctly towards the police. She might not have carried her point if the inspector had not happened to come back at that moment. She saw him crossing the gravel, so they ran down, just as they were with feathers all over them, to meet him in the hall.

"Oh, Inspector, there you are!" cried Mrs. Hoyle. "We've just made a discovery and we want you to tell us what it is. Do open these little parcels because they might be very important. We've just found them in Miss Hampton's bed."

They dumped the packages on the table by the potted fern, under the noses of Tim, Mrs. Linacre and Mrs. De Vigne. The inspector stepped forward quickly with his hand out, and it looked for an awful moment as if he was going to be too official to open them in the presence of so many outsiders. If so, Mrs. Hoyle, who was bigger than he was, might have torn them from him. But even the inspector could feel human curiosity. .He took the first package and slit the wrapping. Inside was chamois leather, also stitched, and when he had slit that up too he shook out the contents. Something like hailstones rattled on the table, and draped itself over the potted fern like a Christmas tree bauble. The inspector picked up the necklace and dangled it across his hand. They all said it together:

"Diamonds!"

CHAPTER FIFTEEN
End of a Theory

THE inspector refused to open any more of the packages except in the presence of Liam Hampton. He took them all away and locked them up in the safe in the back parlor. Then he called his assistant and went to investigate the mattress himself. He found one more small parcel, which spurred him on to tremendous burrowings. Before he gave up, the room was thick with feathers, and he and George looked as fluffy as newborn chickens. They came out sneezing and requested Mrs. Hoyle to remove her belongings from the room, as it would have to be sealed up until the police searchers had gone over it a second time.

One thing at least was beyond argument: Mrs. Hoyle could not sleep on that mattress. The inspector locked the door and fastened up a crisscross arrangement of sticking plaster. He had just completed this when Mrs. Hoyle had to ask him to undo it all again, as she had forgotten her toothbrush.

Tim had undertaken to fetch Liam. He found him in his yard with his head cowman, discussing the case of a sick calf, which they had decided must be shot. Liam was in a bad humor. He said he had wasted enough time at the Court that day. But he came, sulkily, with Tim worrying him along like a zealous young collie dog.

They found the Hoyles, George, and the inspector, still picking feathers out of each other's hair, while Mrs. De Vigne hovered timidly round making dabs at them with a clothes brush. The inspector and Mrs. Hoyle both made for Tim and told him what had happened, as Tim had already done on the way over. When they were all satisfied that he was clear on the scenario they led him into the back parlor. The inspector made a heartless attempt to exclude the general public, but just when Tim was prepared to lead an ugly rush, Liam said carelessly: "Let 'em all come." So even Mary came from the kitchen, leaving her kettle to boil over on the range. At last they got down to opening the safe and undoing the packages, and then everybody stopped chattering and stared in amazement at the growing heap of treasure.

It was all diamonds, and the first necklace was not the finest. The first had forty-five stones and a silver clasp; another had fifty-seven stones, and there was yet another with forty-five stones and twelve more stones in a cross. There were also rings, earrings, brooches and buckles. In one package there was a box containing a set of three star brooches and a necklet. Mrs. Linacre picked them up and showed, to the fascination of all the women, how part of the necklet was detachable and could be combined with the stars to form a tiara. But the inspector said, "Excuse me, better not touch anything, ma'am, till we have an inventory made of them." Mrs. Linacre put down the tiara, looking deeply offended.

"But are they real diamonds?" asked Tim. The inspector said he was no expert, but he'd seen some precious stones in his time and these looked like the real McKay. Mrs. Linacre said, "Tim, dear, Cousin Rebecca wouldn't have had sham jewelry." Tim, ignoring the warning about not touching, picked up a ring and tried scratching with it on the window, till Liam took it from him and told him to stop destroying the glass.

On further investigation of the wrappings, they found that inside each little bag of chamois leather was a folded receipt, made out to Miss Hampton by one or other of the principal Dublin firms of auctioneers. Inspector Devlin studied these. He arranged them in date order, noted down the separate amounts, did a sum in his head, and said to Liam, "Well, now we know where the money went."

He was comparing the dates and figures with those on his list of Miss Hampton's large withdrawals from the bank. They tallied fairly exactly, although the sums of money on the receipts were usually a few pounds smaller, and the dates a few days later, than those on the inspector's list. The total of the receipts was only a hundred or two short of twenty thousand pounds.

"She must have carried the money on her in cash," said the inspector. "She'd draw out rather more than she expected to spend, a day or two earlier than she wanted it, and go off up to Dublin and lay it all out at auctions. I suppose she might go to Dublin any time without any of you thinking much about it."

"Every two months or so," said Mrs. Linacre. "We understood she was having some kind of treatment. It never occurred to me to connect that with your list of dates."

"Good job nobody knew the old lady was carrying around thousands of pounds in cash," said the inspector in a very disapproving voice. "Suppose some fellow grabbed her handbag! People run these risks, and then when they only get what they're asking for it's all the fault of the police."

"But nobody looking at Cousin Rebecca would ever have thought she was rich," said Tim. "She used to go around looking exactly like old Mrs. Shegog or somebody. There was one time she'd just come out of the Shelbourne, and she was standing there and somebody gave her a penny. She was highly delighted and told everybody."

"But good gracious," said Mrs. Hoyle, and everybody realized that she had been silent for a long time, "she must have had a passion for diamonds!"

"Women get like that about jewelry, don't they?" said Tim knowledgeably. "They go quite dotty over it sometimes."

The inspector said, "There might be method in her madness," and looked rather hard at Liam, who resented the look and replied, "If you mean, was she trying to dodge taxation, it was a damn silly way of doing it, and if you mean, did I know anything about it, I didn't."

"I never said so, did I?" said the inspector. "You needn't be so ready to put ideas into our heads. You're right to say it was a risky investment. Those things won't likely fetch the same price again, and there'll be the dealers to get a rake off."

"I believe I can guess why Miss Hampton did it," said Priscilla Hoyle slowly, raising her eyes from the pile of splendid ornaments to the shabby little inspector. "She used to talk to me sometimes about politics and the future outlook, you know, and she worried a lot over what the world was coming to. What she used to say was 'the banks won't be safe.' She seemed to look on that as the very worst possible thing that could happen. So I daresay she thought if she turned some of her money into precious stones and kept it here in the house, that then whatever happened she'd have something to fall back on."

"That's right," said George (whose real name nobody ever found out). "There's a lot of that sort of thing in her papers. Press cuttings of discussions about separating Irish currency from sterling, and all that. I daresay too, the old lady looked on jewels as something she could carry about with her. She made lists of things she might want if she had to evacuate. Same as she made lists of what she'd lay in if there was another war and she had the chance."

"What sort of things?" asked Mrs. Hoyle, interested. George did not reply; the one he was thinking of began with toilet paper.

"Poor old thing!" said Mrs. Linacre. She was sincerely touched, and a little hurt that Cousin Rebecca had never said anything to her.

Tim tried to imagine Cousin Rebecca without money. In the course of her life wealth had spun itself round her like a cocoon. Without it, would she have been a miserable larva, or a hardy insect like Mrs. Shegog?

Mrs. Hoyle said, echoing his mother, "Ah yes, poor old lady! They get like that, you know. Terrified of change."

"She might be right too," remarked George,

"We should try to keep our reactions fluid," Mrs. Hoyle told him severely. Inspector Devlin frowned at his junior for talking too much, and told him to make an inventory of the jewelry and then lock it up again in the safe.

Tim said in a flat voice: "Then there never was a blackmailer, and you needn't bother looking for a guilty secret any more."

"I told you it was ridiculous," said his mother. "Well, Liam, this is very satisfactory for you, not being so poor after all."

Mrs. Hoyle glanced at her wristwatch. "Isn't it time for tea?" she said. Tea was to Mrs. Hoyle what a straight rye is to Mr. Lemmy Caution. Luckily it flowed freely nowadays at Hampton Court. There had been a momentary danger of the police seizing all Miss Hampton's little hoards as suspected produce of the black market, but the wrappings showed that it had all come innocently from South Africa in small presents from a kindhearted friend. Miss Hampton had been delighted to get it and had never touched any of it, preferring to scrape along on her rations and secrete her reserve supplies all over the house. That very afternoon Tim had found two pounds in among his books and was pleased to reflect that under the terms of the will he was entitled to "the whole contents of the bookcase," so that now they could have an odd cup of tea at Glenwood too.

Liam said if nobody wanted him for anything else he had better get back to the farm. It was only then that a mouselike scuffing noise reminded them all of Mrs. De Vigne.

II

As Mrs. De Vigne laid such stress on the delicate and confidential nature of her business, everybody had to withdraw from the back parlor and leave her with the inspector, George, and Liam.

It was not very long, however, before the dark secret became public property to the confusion of McGuirk. For it turned out to be just one more revelation of the seamy side of the flower show. If McGuirk, that pillar of righteousness, had had less to say about the misdeeds of Cuddy, less might have been said about him. As it was, Liam decided there could be no question of hushing the story up. Yet McGuirk always thought it unjust that he should be classed with Cuddy. *He* had never come down to stealing. Among the twelve vases of hardy cut flowers, in the exhibit that won first prize for Hampton Court, was a *Verbascum,* or mullein, that caught Mrs. De Vigne's eye. It was attracting everybody's attention as a new variety with unusual dark red florets on a fine strong spike. But Mrs.

De Vigne was less concerned with its horticultural virtues than with trying to remember where she had seen it before, and it came back to her that Shankey, who was a keen amateur gardener as well as Brainborough's taxi driver, motor expert and auctioneer, had the very same plant. She remembered the dark red spikes standing out against Shankey's drab concrete house. She had been particularly struck with them, and it was curious that she did not remember noticing them in the garden at Hampton Court.

The *Verbascum* was in Shankey's back garden, out of the public eye. Mrs. De Vigne happened to have an errand to the back door about some paraffin oil. So she went to fetch it on her way home from the flower show, and naturally she looked out for the red spikes again. To her disappointment she found they had been cut down.

Now detective instinct was latent even in Mrs. De Vigne, and she began to wonder. On the following Monday she arrived early at Hampton Court for the Work Depot and made an opportunity to go round the garden alone. She could not find any kind of *Verbascum* there at all. She had now gone too far to stop. She had to have certainty. So she went back to the garage and entered into an artless conversation with the youngest Master Shankey, who told her that his Dadda had given the dark red flowers to Mr. McGuirk, and Mr. McGuirk had given his Daddy half a crown.

Mrs. De Vigne was deeply shocked, and all the more so that such a thing should happen in connection with Hampton Court and McGuirk. "Such a good man! Such a good Protestant!" she said, almost in tears. "I can understand the temptation," said Mrs. De Vigne, wringing her gloves round and round till they were reduced to pulp. "Any gardener would know how he felt when he had eleven such good exhibits and was only one short. But he shouldn't have let everybody think the flowers were his own growing. It was acting a lie. And I can't understand," said Mrs. De Vigne with her eyes quite round, "what pleasure there is for anybody in winning a prize that you have not deserved."

When she had found out the truth, Mrs. De Vigne wished she hadn't. It is a mistake to detect things; you may have to do something about them. It was not thinkable for a person of her scrupulous conscience to let the matter rest, but it took another sleepless night before she nerved herself to tackle Miss Hampton.

Mrs. De Vigne did not tell the inspector or anyone else, but Miss Hampton's reception of her story had been the most disconcerting part of all. The old lady did not seem nearly as much taken aback as she ought to have done. She laughed heartily, and seemed to think it was clever of

McGuirk. Mrs. De Vigne even formed a dreadful suspicion that Miss Hampton had *known*.

Miss Hampton promised to "take steps," but Mrs. De Vigne was left in doubt whether the steps would go as far as confessing to the flower show committee. She was hustled out of the house before she could pin Miss Hampton down to any definite course of action. She was not even sure whether she had undertaken to go to the committee herself, or promised Miss Hampton not to.

She was still dithering when Miss Hampton died, and at first it seemed to her that the best thing was to let the shameful episode of the *Verbascum* be buried with her. But then there came the detectives, asking for statements, and though she put them off at first, when she heard how poor Cuddy had been exposed for doing almost the same thing as McGuirk, she felt that it was time to tell all.

The poor lady told even more than she intended, for in her nervousness she let slip the mention of her paraffin oil transaction. There was still such a shortage of paraffin oil that rations for domestic purposes were only issued in the winter months. Prospect View, like every house round Brainborough, depended on oil lamps for light, and obtained oil illegally through Shankey, who was entitled to draw a special ration for motor trade purposes. This was what brought so many foolish virgins to Shankey's back door.

The moment she had spoken, Mrs. De Vigne's hand flew to her mouth and her eyes mutely beseeched the inspector to overlook it. He said nothing at the time, but he reported Shankey later to the department of supplies, and the department cut off Shankey's ration, and the whole of Brainborough suffered in consequence. Inspector Devlin looked a harmless little man and was civility itself in all his dealings, but sooner or later you discovered that neither in large matters nor small would he allow personal considerations to deflect him from his professional duty.

CHAPTER SIXTEEN
Fresh Start

"So now where are we?" Tim Linacre asked himself on the following afternoon.

After Sunday dinner he had shut himself up in his bedroom with his notebook. It had gone on raining, and a flicker like you get in an old film

reel ran across his view of his mother's garden and a big field of sugar
beets and another field full of cows lying down. He could see the rain
splashing off the cows' backs. There was no sound from outside except
an occasional trickle of bird song, as liquid as the weather. Indoors, the
house had sunk into Sunday plethora.

Tim felt depressed. He could not think what to do. Yesterday had
been a day of discoveries, but today was a blank. He did not know whether
the police were progressing. They could always keep on reading through
Miss Hampton's papers and interviewing everybody for miles round. He,
Tim, had to rely on his unaided powers of deduction, and at present he
was deducing so little that he almost wondered if Providence intended
him for a detective after all.

Yet it was Tim himself who ultimately cleared up the mystery of
Miss Hampton's death. Already he knew all the relevant facts,* though
he had so far failed to assemble them. But if, in the course of that wet
afternoon's stock taking, he had seen who really was responsible, it might
not have done much to relieve his depression.

He was strongly tempted to give it up, but he could not quite bring
himself to let the problem alone without making one more effort to clear
his mind by putting everything down on paper.

The blackmail theory was ruled out. Tim had never thought much of
it, though he could understand its appeal for the police. Anybody who
had ever known Cousin Rebecca when she was alive could not help thinking she cared a lot more for her money than for anything anybody might
think of her. Either she had no secrets to be ashamed of, or she would not
have been ashamed of them.

At first Tim had thought that, if the hypothesis of a nasty lurking
scandal had to be abandoned, it was all to the good. But when he thought
about it more, he began to wonder. Because the blackmail theory had
allowed everybody to hope that the murder would be traced to some shadowy unknown outsider, you did not have to worry about the feelings of a
fellow like that; hunting him down would be just wholesome fun. But if
there was no such person, it began to look as if the murderer must be
somebody you knew. It might even be somebody you liked.

The field had narrowed alarmingly since yesterday. Meriel had given
Mrs. Shegog an alibi, and Mrs. De Vigne had explained her own movements, so that was two names he could cross off his list of suspects. He
did so regretfully, for either of them would have done for a poisoner, in
theory. He would have been shocked to hear that either of them had really

* And so does the reader.

done anybody in—Mrs. Shegog was a harmless old faggot when she had
no drink in her, and Mrs. De Vigne was a well-meaning old dear, though
completely batty—but once everybody had said they would never have
thought it of them, it would be possible to reconcile oneself to the idea.

But what about the three names left on his list? Either he could shut
his notebook and go away and do something else till the police fixed on
one of them, or he could detach himself from personal considerations and
think out the case against each of them as it stood.

He began with the easiest, the housemaid, Mary.

Why on earth should Mary commit a murder? She was a decent, reli-
able girl, who went on quietly doing her job regardless of funerals, inquests, visitors and the collapse of the cook. If she had cherished a secret
hate against her employer she could always have given notice. Finan-
cially she only gained a legacy of a few pounds.

Mary might have known about the diamonds. She ought to have, of
course, if she had been the kind of girl to turn a featherbed regularly. But
what good would diamonds be to the likes of her? She wouldn't have a
notion how to dispose of them.

Lots of these country girls had insanity in their families, but Tim
knew all about Mary's people, who were quite as much respected as the
Hamptons in their different sphere. Her father was a local small farmer,
her brothers were in the British Army, and her mother had been in Miss
Hampton's service before she married. Not even any of her aunts and
uncles had ever dreamed of taking a hatchet to their relations, or firing a
shot across their neighbors' land, or putting strychnine in their rivals' tea.

But Mary's name remained on the list because of her opportunities.
Though she had been sent off to Brainborough before the cooking started,
she would have had the kitchen to herself for several minutes afterwards
when she was dishing up lunch alone. Tim remembered the look of the
Escargots à la roulette. They were served in the Pyrex glass dish in which
they must have been cooked. Cousin Rebecca would have arranged them,
and left Mary nothing to do but take them out of the oven. If Mary, or
anybody else, had stirred or sprinkled or poked poison in among them
after they were cooked, would Cousin Rebecca have noticed that the dish
had been tampered with?

Tim thought Mary could, just conceivably, have poisoned the *Escargots*, but there was somebody else who had a much better chance at it, and
that was Priscilla Hoyle.

The only trouble about Priscilla Hoyle as a suspect was that she was
too obvious. Tim considered a murderer ought to take the elementary

precaution of having somebody else about on whom to throw suspicion. Priscilla could surely have chosen a better day to poison the dinner, some day when Mrs. McGuirk and Mary were about, instead of choosing the one time when all the cooking was left to her. But even the most efficient people slip up sometimes.

At first Tim had been put off Priscilla by thinking she had no motive, but the discovery of the diamonds suggested a different view. For, like Mary, Priscilla might have known about the diamonds all the time, and she would have had a much better chance than Mary of cashing in on them. She could have taken a few at a time to any jeweler and said they were family jewels of her own, and nobody would have questioned the fact. For there would be no fear of the police being on the lookout for the jewels, because nobody knew Cousin Rebecca had them, and so they need never have been missed. They might as well have been handed to Priscilla on a plate. Twenty thousand pounds worth of diamonds might tempt anybody to commit murder, even if they were not naturally inclined that way, and as nobody knew anything about the Hoyles, there was always the hope that homicide might run in the family.

It was a slight drawback to this theory that Priscilla herself had been the one to bring the diamonds to light. But had she? From Tim's recollection of their conversation, it was really Mrs. Hoyle who had made the find, with Priscilla trying to choke her off. But even if he was wrong about that, Priscilla's nerve might have broken when she saw the thoroughness of the police search. She might have thought it tactful to make the discovery before they did.

Tim sighed, because he rather liked Priscilla. But that was what he had resolved to forget about. He did not like the last name any better: Liam. Goodness knew, they did not want a murderer in the family. Liam was a deviation from the family type. There was all this nationalism of his; Tim could never decide if it was sincere or only done to be different. Liam did not really know Irish (he had been to an English public school and Oxford), but he always pretended that "Dun Laoghaire"' came natural to him, and when he wrote to the flower show committee he began "A chara." You would not think anything of that from a fellow like Proinnsias Hopkinson, Biddy Gahan's fiancé, but in Liam it was upsetting to all one's preconceived ideas. He was peculiar in other ways too; he did not hunt or shoot or fish and so lacked natural outlets for blood lust. But it was not solely on general grounds that Tim thought his cousin capable of murder. The point about him was his outstanding motive. For it mattered so much to Liam that Cousin Rebecca's death should happen just then, before she had time to alter her will. The thing came so pat for him that it seemed more than a coincidence.

There had been times that Wednesday morning when anyone from outside could have gone into the kitchen unobserved, but Liam did seem to have a complete alibi. Tim had talked to at least half a dozen of his farmhands who had been with him all morning. They had been cutting silage and filling up Liam's new silo, a job which required his presence and his very particular instructions. On any average morning he would have been out making a round of his fields, and lost to sight for long spells at a time, but on that particular Wednesday he had suddenly decided to cut the silage. It was a lucky decision for him.

It did not seem as if Liam could possibly have been at Hampton Court that morning. But could he have acted through an accomplice? That brought Tim back to Mary or Priscilla Hoyle. If they did not do murder for diamonds, would they do it for Liam? Tim pondered about Women, a subject of which he did not know a great deal. Liam's manner annoyed Tim's own mother, but he did that on purpose. In general, he was considered attractive. Meriel had once informed Tim that Liam had plenty of S.A. So perhaps if he worked on a woman he might get her to do murder for him, but if she guessed that the main object of the murder was to enable him to marry Meriel, she'd hardly be so apt to oblige.

It was certainly not easy to see how Liam could have put any evil intentions into practice, yet the feeling persisted that, of the three suspects, it was he who best fitted the part. And as Tim sat and stared at his notebook, there started in his mind yet another disagreeable train of thought. He had been wondering if there was any reason for selecting the snail dish as a vehicle for the poison. Was it, for instance, because it might be expected to taste peculiar? But then it occurred to him that perhaps it was not a case of choosing the snails, but of choosing whatever they were having on Wednesday, and what was there special about Wednesday, except that he and his mother were coming to lunch? Who would have an interest in wiping out the whole family? Liam again.

Of course, they might have to do with an undiscriminating lunatic. Tim suddenly thought how extraordinary it was that nobody had made any fuss about the danger of having an unknown poisoner in their midst. People went on eating lunches and teas at Hampton Court just as if nobody had ever been the worse for it. Yet poisoners, of all homicidal types, were notoriously in the habit of trying again.

He decided to be careful what he ate at Hampton Court in the future and to warn his mother. It was difficult to get Mrs. Linacre to talk about the mystery; she pretended to be much more interested in the herb picnic and the flower show committee and the future of the Work Depot. For two days she had talked about nothing but putting off the herb picnic on account of Cousin Rebecca's death, and Tim was all in favor of it. But then she had decided that private grief ought not to interfere with public service and had fixed a day and issued a general invitation to everybody she met at the funeral. As well as this she was fussing about the transfer of the Work Depot from Hampton Court to Spangle Hill.

Tim knew it was her way when she was worried about anything to take refuge in being extra busy, and all this excitement over nothing only showed that she was taking the murder to heart. He thought he had better go and talk to her, and, flipping over the pages of his notebook, he mentally rehearsed a summary of the present position. Rereading what he had written about Liam, he suddenly saw the flaw in his cousin's alibi.

II

Tim found his mother sitting at her writing bureau in the drawing room, using up a stock of black-edged notepaper that had been on her hands since Tim's father died. She leaned her forehead on her hand as if her head ached, and her hair had been pushed all untidy.

"Oh, Tim," she said, before he could start talking, "I do wish you'd go over on your bicycle for me with this note to Mrs. Double-B., I've just found I can't get Shankey's lorry for the Work Depot things on Tuesday, and I wonder if tomorrow would be too soon."

"What's your hurry?" asked Tim.

"Well, darling, we're very busy sewing for Europe, and the sooner we can get on with it the better."

"Can't the Work Depot stay where it is for the present? We don't know what's going to happen."

"Tim dear, for all we know, Liam is going to occupy the Court. It would never do for us to look as if we thought anything else."

Tim agreed. "You certainly would think so, the way he's going on. But then, what about Meriel?"

"I'm very, very sorry for Meriel."

"Do you suppose she knows how things stand?"

Mrs. Linacre shrugged her shoulders.

"Couldn't you drop a hint to Mrs. Double-B?" said Tim. "Tell her about Cousin Rebecca's will. You'd think they must be wondering."

"Oh no, Tim, I couldn't. That would look terribly bad. It would look like trying to intrigue against Liam. It would be different if they had actually got engaged, but you see, we're not supposed to know there ever was anything between them at all."

"Yes, that's awkward." Tim wandered round the room picking up ornaments and putting them down again, till Mrs. Linacre asked him not to fidget. She went on writing her note, but her attention was divided, and presently she said, "Liam's a funny person. He's very secretive. He hates to tell anyone what he means to do before he does it, and I expect that's at the bottom of the way he's behaving about the Court. It's all very embarrassing, and one can't very well ask him his intentions, but somehow I can't believe he would jilt Meriel after all. I believe he's deliberately keeping us in suspense. He's capable of it."

Tim thought it was time to bring into the conversation the matter that was on his own mind. He hesitated how to put it, and finally said bluntly, "Suppose it was Liam who poisoned Cousin Rebecca."

His mother jumped down his throat as he expected. She said he must not say things like that, exactly as if he had remarked on Inspector Devlin having false teeth, or Mrs. De Vigne spitting when she talked.

"That's all very well," said Tim. "You needn't think I'm going off to tell it to the police. I only said 'suppose,' didn't I? But I would just like to point out that if things haven't turned out as well for Liam as he might have expected, the logical thing would be for him to go on and poison us. Then he could marry Meriel and live at the Court as well."

He was prepared to back up this argument by close reasoning out of his notebook, but Mrs. Linacre short-circuited him by beginning to cry. A tear ran down her nose and dropped on the letter to Mrs. Booley-Browne.

"Try not to think things, Tim," she begged him. "Try to fill your mind with something else, like I do. Once you start suspecting people, there's no end to it. It's like some dreadful creeping venom."

Tears unnerved Tim always. "No need to go off the deep end," he said crossly. "I only thought I'd better say it, once I'd thought of it. We might try to be a bit careful perhaps."

Mrs. Linacre blew her nose and sat up.

"All we can do is to carry on," she said. "That's what your father would have said, 'Carry on, like good soldiers.' We won't say any more about it, dear boy, till the police are able to tell us something definite. And now, do take this letter for me to Spangle Hill."

Tim took the letter. He wanted to go to Spangle Hill now, because it seemed to him that an explanation was indicated. Meriel, poor girl, probably expected Liam to propose any day, and it seemed to Tim that in a case like this tactfulness could be overdone. He knew it was no good arguing with his mother about what might be diplomatic or proper, so he decided to rush in where angels feared to tread and tell Meriel all about the will, and his suspicions, and exactly how things stood.

CHAPTER SEVENTEEN
Mother Instinct

"I SHOULDN'T be surprised if it was that Mrs. Linacre," said Mrs. Hoyle.

She was looking out at another aspect of the same wet Sunday afternoon. At Hampton Court the rain was pitting the surfaces of the puddles at the edge of the drive, streaking down the oil silk leaves of the rhododendrons, and soaking into the Wellingtonias till all their branches drooped. It drifted mistily across the dark green shrubbery, and the little hill beyond was smudged out. The weather weighed on Mrs. Hoyle's spirits, and she confessed to herself, not for the first time, that she did get bored in the country.

At home she was never bored. She had the two great resources of charity and culture. Never a day without some lecture to attend or some sad case to visit: a busy, happy life. Sometimes she was afraid she had too many interests. If their home life had suffered, if Priscilla had got entangled with an undesirable man, perhaps it was partly her fault. But at least she had shown her devotion by coming down here at a moment's notice, with her hair newly waved for a dinner she would not be able to attend, and her brain likewise full of waves for her pet committee, which would languish without her.

Priscilla had had a disappointment, and a merciful escape, so she had taken it into her head to go off and live a life of her own, all prickly with independence. Mrs. Hoyle smiled indulgently. And the next thing was, here she had got involved in a murder mystery, in a set of complete strangers, in an old mausoleum of a house that would give anybody the willies (Mrs. Hoyle did not usually affect slang, it was a reaction against the atmosphere of Hampton Court). So her poor old mother had to come along and look after her, and save her from being bothered by detectives and put upon by employers, and generally taken advantage of in her youth and innocence.

As nobody happened to be trying to take advantage of Priscilla at the moment (the detectives had gone off in the police car to confer with the superintendent), Mrs. Hoyle had time on her hands. Since morning she had made several small improvements in the routine of the housework, been to church, and planned out the meals for the next three days. Now, her everactive brain turned to the mystery.

"You only say it's Mrs. Linacre because you don't like her," said Priscilla.

"Yes, I *am* inclined to trust my instinct about people. As you know, I'm very often right." This was an oblique reference to Hugo Everard. Priscilla let it go. She said, "Most people would say Mrs. Linacre was charming."

"Most people would take her at her own valuation. The charm is all on the surface, and underneath she's both selfish and shallow. Look at that boy of hers! The way she's brought him up! Twenty-one, and hasn't a notion what he wants to do with himself."

"Yes, he has. He's going to be a detective."

"I don't call that a serious occupation. He ought to make up his mind how he's to earn his living. Did Miss Hampton leave them a lot of money?"

"I've no idea."

Priscilla yawned. The night before she had slept badly. In the end she and her mother had had to share a bed, and though Mrs. Hoyle did not talk in her sleep she went on to the last minute before it. They ought to have exhausted some subjects by now, Priscilla thought.

She said, "It couldn't have been Mrs. Linacre. I was with her all the time, and she never went into the kitchen at all."

"Well, darling, I know you keep on telling the police and everybody else that nobody but you went into the kitchen, but as somebody must have gone there to put poison in that dish, I can't help thinking you must be mistaken."

"I never said nobody but me went into the kitchen. Mary did, and so did Mrs. De Vigne. And someone else might have when I ran out to the garden for parsley. But Mrs. Linacre never had a chance. We stood talking in the hall till we all went into the dining room."

"H'm. I suppose she couldn't have got at the dish in there."

"No, she couldn't."

"Darling, that sounded rather cross. These questions have to be asked, by the police if not by us, and I think we all ought to try and help. Now tell me, have they considered McGuirk?"

Priscilla looked blank. "McGuirk?"

"He has a very hangdog face. And we know he had something to conceal."

"What, you mean that business over the flower show? Then he, ought to have poisoned Mrs. De Vigne."

"Oh yes, so most people would say. But he couldn't get at Mrs. De Vigne, and he may have hoped that if he prevented her from telling Miss Hampton that would do as well. Or he may have thought that he'd be safer with Captain Hampton, who doesn't seem to be inclined to sack him, and he had his legacy too. And you see, he took good care that his wife couldn't be implicated."

"He didn't know she was going to get lumbago."

"How do we know she ever had it? Oh yes, darling, I know she took you in all right, but after all, you're not a person of vast experience."

If Mrs. Hoyle had been looking at Priscilla instead of out of one of the hall windows, she might have noticed on her daughter's face an expression of exasperation merging into despair.

When Priscilla left home it had seemed to her that she was not doing at all badly. She knew she was useful to Miss Hampton. The old lady was not given to gushing, and the fact that she had let fall a word or two of praise from time to time almost suggested that she found her new companion a treasure. Then, on the dreadful night when Miss Hampton died, the doctor had relied on Priscilla rather than on Mrs. Linacre. Mrs. Linacre had hovered round the patient's pillow till she was sent away, but Priscilla had been useful with basins and bedpans. Dr. Claffey had said she would make a good nurse. After that—Priscilla's thoughts slid hastily over that time when she cried—apart from one slight fit of hysteria due to shock, she had kept the house in order and had meals for all who came and felt and behaved like a responsible person. Liam had noticed. He had thanked her after the funeral. And Priscilla had been looking forward to having her mother come down, because it would be lovely to have somebody she knew was for her in the midst of all these strangers. But ever since Mrs. Hoyle had arrived Priscilla had felt her own importance shrinking and shrinking till soon there would be nothing left of her but an inferiority complex.

It was like that at home. Her mother couldn't help it. She must have been born with her dominating personality. But what was so bad for her was the way she kept turning out to be right. She'd been right about Hugo, and about the diamonds, and Priscilla supposed she would also claim to be right about her daughter not being able to look after herself, considering what a spot of bother she was landed into.

Despair was near getting the upper hand. Meanwhile Mrs. Hoyle went on talking, and after proving to her own satisfaction that the guilt lay almost certainly with McGuirk, she suddenly tried a new tack and said, "But of course, from the police point of view, the most obvious possibility is Captain Hampton."

Priscilla said sharply: "He wasn't anywhere near the house that morning. He was making silage."

"Oh indeed! And how long does that take? Naturally he would provide himself with an alibi."

"What do you mean 'provide himself'? He has an alibi. If it's good enough for the police it ought to be good enough for you."

"Ah, but is it? Surely you realize, darling, that that inspector man is not telling any of us what he really thinks."

"Mummy, how you do let yourself run on. You don't really think he did it. You can't."

"Excuse me, Priscilla, I did not say he did it. I only pointed out that he was one of the people who might have done it. And murders are just as likely to be committed by good-looking young men as by anybody else." Mrs. Hoyle turned on her daughter a smile of superior penetration which was one of the most aggravating smiles in her range and somehow invoked the shade of Hugo again. Priscilla jumped up.

"Where are you going, darling?" her mother asked.

"I don't know. Out."

"But it's raining harder than ever. Listen, darling, I know I'm only your old mother, but I do rather understand you. You're so imaginative and impressionable, and really, any young girl might be dazzled by a man like Captain Hampton. But you know, just because you find him a considerate employer, you need not assume that he has all the virtues."

Priscilla stamped her foot. "And just because I say he didn't commit murder, you needn't assume I'm in love with him."

"Darling, I never said—"

"Yes, you did. And anyhow, you get carried away by your imagination once you start talking, till you make yourself believe nearly anything. So I'm not going to stay here and encourage you. If you want to know, Captain Hampton's practically engaged to Miss Booley Browne."

"Well, you needn't shout, dear."

"I didn't. I may have just raised my voice—"

The hall door, which was closed against the rain, but was always kept on the latch, swung ponderously open, and Liam, in a dripping mackintosh, stood on the threshold.

The door was solid mahogany, and the windows on each side of it were shut tight as they had been for years past, so Liam could hardly have heard the discussion, but his appearance was a shock. The two Hoyles reacted differently: Mrs. Hoyle greeted him with the dissimulating serenity of the practiced hostess; Priscilla gave him the scowl of one who is determined not to have her sentiments misinterpreted.

Liam's mackintosh was too wet to bring into the house. There was a chair on the porch and he draped it over that. Mrs. Hoyle observed that the rain was keeping on. Priscilla said, "The inspector's out."

"But you're in," said Liam. "How do you like it here on a wet afternoon? I thought one might take advantage of it to have a look round the house."

"What a good idea!" said Mrs. Hoyle. "Of course you won't know what you may have in all these rooms and rooms. I suppose there are all sorts of family treasures hidden away under dust sheets. It's so romantic, not knowing what you may find, and after yesterday!"

"I hope we shan't find dry rot," said Liam.

"I'll get you the keys," said Priscilla.

"You're coming too," said Liam. "There'll be fellows coming down to take an inventory for probate and you'll have to show them round."

No apology for disturbing Priscilla's Sunday afternoon. And no suggestion that her mother, who was dying to see over the house, should accompany them. Just business as usual, that was Liam Hampton all over, and Meriel Booley Browne was welcome to it if she liked it.

Mrs. Hoyle gave Priscilla a look which said, "I know I can trust my daughter," and sat down and opened a book. Priscilla fetched the keys and tagged along.

II

Meanwhile, in a dreary little room of the barracks at the county town, the superintendent, Inspector Devlin and George were in conference.

The inspector reported the discovery of the diamonds. The superintendent commented that it did not get them anywhere. The inspector dissented, pointing out that, besides saving them the trouble of looking for a blackmailer, it suggested a further motive for the crime.

The analyst's report had been received from Dublin. That did not get them very far, either, but in confirming previous deductions it was satisfactory. When the organs were tested for atropine, enough alkaloid was found present in the tissue extract to corroborate the diagnosis already made of the cause of death. Atropine was also present in the mangled remains of snails and sauce that had been salvaged from Tim Linacre's pocket, but not in the stock or any other ingredients for the making of the dish. No vegetable remains of belladonna leaves or seeds could be identified either the in snail mixture or in the stomach, but apart from this negative evidence there was nothing to indicate whether the atropine had been in natural or in chemical form.

"We're limiting the time factor," said the inspector. "The poison was put in the snail dish after it was made up. That was after Miss Hampton herself came downstairs and after Mrs. De Vigne had left."

"On the evidence of Miss Hoyle," said the superintendent.

"Mrs. De Vigne confirms it. She happened to have taken notice of the preparations in the kitchen, and saw the Pyrex glass dish standing empty and everything else put ready to make the sauce. She's what you might call quaint, that old lady, but she doesn't miss much."

"So her evidence checks Hoyle's and vice versa. It lets her out, if she was ever in, but it's not so good for Hoyle. What do you think of the chances of an outsider?"

"Fair enough," said the inspector judicially. "We've only Hoyle's word, of course, from now on, but what she says sounds plausible. After the snail dish went into the oven there wasn't a great deal more to do. Miss Hampton went down to the cellar for a bottle of port. Hoyle herself went upstairs to tidy. They both looked in at the dining room to see that the table was laid right. They were in and out of the kitchen during that three quarters of an hour, but there were several times it was left empty for minutes together."

"That doesn't make it so easy to narrow it down."

But the inspector spoke with confidence.

"The way I see it, we have it already narrowed down to two. We've eliminated all the unlikelies. Trouble is, there are two with a good case against each of them, and we could hardly arrest either one in the face of the evidence against the other."

"Two only, do you say?"

"Hoyle or Hampton."

"Hampton or Hoyle," repeated the superintendent, frowning. "But Hampton has an alibi."

"No. He never had. We thought so at first. It looked right enough that he was with his men and they didn't knock off for their dinner till one o'clock, the time lunch was starting at Hampton Court. But you see, the day we came all the clocks in the house had stopped, and we didn't realize at the first go off that the deceased always kept old time."

"Did she, by damn? And the captain doesn't?"

"He does not. With the captain everything has to be the latest. His whole farm works by machinery, and he wouldn't give in to having a different time from Dublin at all. So the old lady sat down to her lunch at two instead of one, and that gave the captain plenty of time to slip across to the Court in his dinner hour. The only thing is, we can't find any evidence that he did."

"You're checking up on that still?"

"We are, but it's slow work. These country people have so little idea of time it's enough to break your heart. But there seems to be about twenty minutes of his dinner hour unaccounted for. We're trying round for anyone who saw him near the Court. Oh, if he was there, we'll get him yet."

"They're working on Hoyle at the Dublin end," said the superintendent. "We should get a report this evening or tomorrow, but there's nothing come in yet."

"I was thinking," said Inspector Devlin, "that I might do a bit of work at that end myself. I'll have to go up anyway over this business of the diamonds. I'll get the expert valuation and have a talk with the auctioneers whose names appear on the receipts. While I'm in town I could make one or two inquiries about Hoyle. I might hit on something."

"No harm in trying," said the superintendent. "By the way, there's one line you haven't done much work on. We're no nearer knowing where this belladonna stuff came from."

"We know where it didn't come from," said the inspector, referring to the analyst's report. "It definitely wasn't the ABC Liniment."

"None of the chemists here or in Brainborough can trace selling anything with belladonna in to any of the suspects in the last six months. Apart from the one bottle of liniment, of course. Not that that means much; it might have been bought in Dublin or anywhere. What do you think about this deadly nightshade that grows round here? It might be worth having a look round some of the places where it grows and seeing if anyone's been picking it."

The inspector grunted. He thought it was very nice to be a superintendent and invent impossible tasks that you didn't have to tackle yourself.

"I'll put George on to it," he said. It was George's turn to grunt.

"This case may be tougher than it looks," the superintendent warned them. "I wonder, ought we to have fixed the inquest so soon as Thursday? Would you ask for another adjournment?"

The inspector did not think so. "We should be all clear by then, but if not it may help things on. Something might break."

"Or somebody," remarked the superintendent dryly. "If the murderer is in court and hears all the evidence set out he'll need all his nerve."

The two detectives rose to go. There was still plenty to do at Hampton Court, sorting through papers and correspondence. The superintendent promised to send over the report on Miss Hoyle as soon as it came in.

The two men in the blue police car drove back through the rain, which was coming down harder than ever. Steam rose from the backs of the cows, and of Mrs. Shegog's goat, which they encountered in the drive. They herded it before the car through the narrow defile of evergreens till it slithered sideways into the greenery and disappeared. Though they might consider themselves guardians of public property, the two policemen did not feel inclined to get out and round up the animal at the moment.

Mrs. Hoyle came out of the kitchen to greet them. Being a great believer in the policy of "feed the brute," she had been making a cake for tea. She informed them of Liam's arrival, which they had already deduced from seeing his mackintosh drying outside.

Liam and Priscilla had been absent nearly two hours, but it might take far longer than that to make a complete tour of the house. Beyond the inhabited rooms near the hall and staircase, long corridors stretched away right and left, giving vistas of shut doors, undecipherable pictures and busts or aspidistras on pedestals. There were three stories between the attics and the basement, and there must be fifty or sixty rooms in all.

"I wonder where those two have got to," said Mrs. Hoyle. "I do wish they'd come down. I'm sure we all want our tea."

In immediate answer came a shriek from upstairs, followed by a heavy thud and a splintering crash overhead.

CHAPTER EIGHTEEN
Family Skeletons

THE shriek had come from the room called the music room, the one above the Work Depot. Mrs. Hoyle and the two detectives rushed upstairs. They flung open the door, and there stood Liam, with Priscilla clutching his arm. They were gazing at a hole in the floor.

It was rather a fine room, with the usual handsome carved mantelpiece and a gray wallpaper representing an entire landscape with everything from ships to shepherdesses. There was no furniture except the grand piano and a couple of chairs and music stands. The piano stood between the two windows, and the floorboards there had perhaps weakened under the weight of performers on the music stool.

Liam had been trying to open the shutters. The fastening was high up; he had climbed on a rickety chair; the shutters had yielded suddenly; the chair gave way, and he had crashed down on to a rotten board below.

It was not the damage to the floor that held them fascinated, it was something underneath. As Mrs. Hoyle entered with the detectives, Priscilla drew away from Liam, turned startled eyes on her mother, and whispered "Bones!"

That brought Inspector Devlin forward as eager as a terrier. He squatted down by the hole, peered in, put his hand down and, working cautiously, extracted a long white object. He said disappointedly, "Not human. Horse."

Priscilla gasped with relief, but Mrs. Hoyle said in a tone of mild annoyance: "Horse? Horse? Why on earth should anybody bury a *horse* there?" As if a human skeleton would have been all in the day's work.

"Well, they have," replied Devlin. He groped again and lifted out an unmistakably equine skull. "What's more, it's not just one horse, it's dozens. The whole floor seems to be packed with them. That's a queer thing if you like. Doesn't seem to be anything in our line, though."

Priscilla said, "Thank goodness for that!"

"But you'll have to investigate it, won't you?" said Mrs. Hoyle. "I should have thought you'd feel responsible for any kind of strange skeleton. Surely you aren't just going to leave it at that."

"We'd better have a look, I suppose," said the inspector, being aggravatingly casual. "There's probably some simple explanation. Can't afford to waste too much time on side issues."

Liam said he would have the rest of the floorboards up tomorrow.

Mrs. Hoyle said if that was all they could do now, they might as well go down and have tea.

So Mrs. Hoyle and the two policemen and their unsuspecting suspects sat politely about in the hall, where tea was laid on the silver tray in honor of Liam. There were soda bread and strawberries and Mrs. Hoyle's sponge cake, beautifully baked. But it was not a very cheerful meal as everybody had too much to think about.

The tour of exploration had not unearthed any more treasures. Mrs. Hoyle had imagined the unused rooms to be full of antiques and fine art, but Priscilla had found instead the big game trophies left by several military Hamptons; the Oriental bric-a-brac brought home by one or two who were missionaries; the natural history collections made by the uncle who owned the stamp albums and the same uncle's photographic output. He had had a darkroom in the basement, and his family groups, meets, shoots, hockey teams and tombstones competed for wall space with his wife's oil paintings of bridges, churches, tombstones, ruins and bends in roads. These were treasures which neither moth nor rust could corrupt. Moth had, however, got into some nice old brocade hangings and most of the wool embroideries, and had riddled a brown velvet suit that some gentlemanly Hampton had worn at levees at Dublin Castle and that still hung in his bedroom cupboard.

Liam Hampton had no veneration for the relics of his ancestors. He said the moth-eaten court suit was symbolical.

"The captain likes to move with the times," said Inspector Devlin.

"Well, so do I," said Mrs. Hoyle, "but one does miss the old pageantry. A handsome man like you, Captain Hampton, would look so well in those clothes. I'm sure if you could only see yourself. Have you never tried them on?" She was ready to make Liam dress up then and there. He got up to go, in alarm.

When the big hall door swung back to let him out, there on the top step of the portico was Mrs. Shegog's goat. Its eyes glinted; its beard wagged aggressively; it smelt like a goat with no best friends. The belt of Liam's mackintosh was dangling from its mouth.

Liam addressed the goat in what sounded like Irish and selected the largest of several sticks in the hall stand.

"Oh, don't beat him!" cried Mrs. Hoyle. "Look, it's only the belt. He hasn't chewed it much at all. Very annoying, I know, but it isn't any use losing one's temper, is it? Especially with dumb animals."

Priscilla regrettably said, "Shut up, Mother!" Liam said: "I am not losing my temper. This is the only thing it understands." And the goat certainly did understand from a whack on the flank that Liam wished it to be absolutely elsewhere. It disgorged his property and staggered off down the steps.

"There now, you've only sent it into the garden," said Mrs. Hoyle. "It will be wandering all over the place. We ought to catch it and restore it to its owner."

"You can attend to it," said Liam, shrugging himself disgustedly into his mackintosh. He dropped the stick back into the stand with an angry rattle and stalked away.

Mrs. Hoyle remarked that she had no respect for a man who could not control his temper. Then she took down her own mackintosh from a peg where it hung on top of Miss Hampton's, buttoned herself into it, took an oil-silk bonnet from the pocket and tied it under her chin. Priscilla saw that there would be no stopping her from giving chase to the goat.

The two detectives emptied their teacups and said they must be getting back to work on Miss Hampton's papers. They did not want to help chase goats.

"I'm not coming out," said Priscilla. "Not in all this rain." Mrs. Hoyle replied sweetly: "No, don't get wet, dear. I can manage by myself."

Priscilla stood on the portico, watching and blaming herself for being so cross. She had been in a bad humor all afternoon. First she had been irritated by the nonsense her mother talked about Liam, and then she had gone on being self-conscious and sulky with Liam himself. Now he had gone away angry too, and she only hoped she was not going to worry about that for the rest of the evening. For she had lately got into a habit of thinking far too much about Liam, especially if she was at all tired. When other people were being tiresome—the police keeping on and on with their questions, her mother criticizing, Tim Linacre fidgeting about, or Mrs. Linacre making conversation whatever happened—the thought of Liam was Priscilla's refuge, and he alone seemed quite real. Apart from the police, nobody else seemed to have anything to do but footle round. Liam had his farm and attended to it, and found time to smooth out difficulties for her as well. The fact that he was always kind where she was concerned disposed her all the more to sympathize when he could not suffer fools gladly.

It was not that Priscilla attributed any importance to her feelings about Liam. She knew she was too susceptible, as her mother said. That being the case, it was a great pity she had ever let him put his arm round her, because apparently even that was enough to leave a weak-minded girl feeling like something out of Aldous Huxley.

She blamed this hypersensitiveness on Hugo Everard. Hugo had been the first man in Priscilla's life, and she had all but vowed he would be the last. He began so promisingly as a companion on an intellectual plane. The discovery that they both appreciated not only Blake but Mozart and Cezanne seemed to single them out for each other. She had discovered him through joining a society; he persuaded her to join two or three more. They walked home together from the meetings, continuing the discussions. On New Year's Eve he took her to a Watch Night service, which so exalted them both that she hardly noticed when he kissed her good night, though subsequently she noticed when he didn't. About this time Mrs. Hoyle discovered a book he had given Priscilla, with an inscription, and expressed a wish to meet this Mr. Everard. Hugo had a masculine impatience of invitations to tea, but Priscilla eventually brought them together by introducing her mother as a guest at one of their meetings. Mrs. Hoyle disliked Hugo Everard at sight. She said he had shifty eyes. So she was less surprised than Priscilla when, shortly after, Priscilla received a reproachful letter from a Mrs. Everard, Hugo's wife, whose existence he had never happened to mention.

Mrs. Everard's letter caused Priscilla to break off relations with Hugo at once. She was both unhappy and ashamed, and had time on her hands to be miserable in, as she had resigned from all the societies she had joined to please him. All the intellectual interests she had shared with him now went bad on her. Blake, or Mozart, or Cezanne, who might have helped, only made her wince. But she had heard that work for others took you out of yourself, and the healing powers of nature were well spoken of, so she hoped that to bury herself in the country with Miss Hampton would be a solution.

The experience had put Priscilla on her guard against her own weakness. She was suspicious of her own attitude towards Liam. Was it reasonable to spend quite so much time thinking about him? She would control her mind and think about something else.

In this she was assisted by the goat, which broke away from Mrs. Hoyle's blandishments and, doubling back from the drive, came charging towards the steps. Priscilla had no wish to be butted again. Luckily the steps broke the charge. Priscilla shooed the goat and it turned about and went off into the rhododendrons, with Mrs. Hoyle in pursuit. Priscilla saw her mother looking flushed and thought this could not be good for her. Blood is thicker than water, and it is not for a gentle-hearted person to stand on a portico watching her mother panting after goats in the rain. For the thousandth time Priscilla gave in to the blackmail of affection, and she put on her own mackintosh and went to help.

Priscilla had learned something of the technique of goat herding by now. She brought the big stick with her, and when at last she succeeded in catching the end of the animal's halter rope, she handed the stick to her mother, who by this time was past raising any humanitarian objections. One pulling and the other prodding, they assisted the animal to move in the desired direction. Between their they maneuvered the creature the whole way back to Mrs. Shegog's.

Mrs. Shegog's house looked like a witch's dwelling. Two elder trees, source of many country remedies, leaned confidentially towards each other across the gate. The garden was all brambles, hung with rags like votive offerings. One boarded-up window gave the facade of the house an expression like a knowing leer.

Priscilla did not half like the place and would have been content to tie the goat to one of the elder trees and edge away quietly. But Mrs. Hoyle was immune from superstition and only saw the establishment as a sad case that ought to be visited.

In any case, Mrs. Shegog had seen them coming. She tottered out to welcome them with smiles and curtseys, interspersing civilities to the ladies with abuse for the goat. She invited them in out of the rain and ushered them into her drawing room, or what might have been that by her manner, while she sized the goat's halter and dragged it right through the cottage to some place of penitence at the back.

The Hoyles found themselves standing on a stone-flagged floor, blinking in the cloud of smoke that rushed out to meet them. The smoke, though it pricked their eyes and nostrils, was some help to counteract the smell of goat. There was a lot more smoke than fire, but over the hearth hung a cauldron very appropriate to a witch. Mrs. Shegog's bed was in one corner of the room, and in another a pile of rags that looked as if it might be the goat's. There was a wooden bench, and one chair by the fire. On the chair lay a grubby paperbound book, and Priscilla picked it up, inquisitive to see what Mrs. Shegog had been reading. She was amused to see what it was and put it down before Mrs. Shegog rejoined them.

"He's a bad old fella', I'm moidered with him," remarked the goat's mistress. "Whatever I do he'd stray away from me. I had him tied with a rope I got from Mr. McVittie. It was an odd bit of an old rope that had some weakness in it, but if it had been a new rope it's all one to that one and he'd give himself no trouble to break it. To think I of you coming out in the rain for the like of that! 'Deed you shouldn't have bothered now. But it's an honor to have a visit from the ladies from Dublin. And are you Miss Hoyle's mother, Ma'am? Sure, who'd believe it?"

As she talked, she wiped some drips from the roof off the wooden bench, moved it back a few inches, and indicated that it might be sat upon. Mrs. Hoyle sat down, gathering her mackintosh under her:

"That's very kind of you, Mrs. Shegog," she said, "but we ought to tell you that Captain Hampton is very much annoyed."

"Is he now?" said Mrs. Shegog, looking stricken.

"Yes, he is. And you really must prevent your goat from straying all over the place. It's becoming a nuisance. Why don't you sell it?"

This seemed to strike Mrs. Shegog as a completely new idea, and instead of being hurt at the callousness of the suggestion she put on a great appearance of gratitude, and said that was what she must do at the first opportunity. Perhaps Mrs. Hoyle might hear of somebody who would make her an offer? Mrs. Hoyle encouraged her to hope that this was quite likely. Goat dealing had not been in her line hitherto, but she had an infallible system, whenever she wanted anything or had anything to dispose of, which was to ask everybody she met about it till sooner or later someone turned up to make the other side of the bargain.

"I think that's a very wise decision of yours," she told Mrs. Shegog, "though I do know how one feels at parting with animal friends. But you really have no room here to keep pets, and after it has gone you'll be able to tidy up a bit."

Mrs. Shegog curtseyed, and thanked her.

The Hoyles were both coughing and wiping their eyes, and not being able to stand the smoke any longer, Mrs. Hoyle rose to go. Mrs. Shegog saw them to the gate with old-fashioned politeness. In her bramble patch she suddenly stooped and picked some leaves.

"Do you suffer with rheumatism, my lady?" she asked.

Mrs. Hoyle did not really, but being interested, pretended to an occasional twinge.

"There you are then," said Mrs. Shegog. "There's for you now. Boil those and let them stand till they're cold and take a teaspoonful in the name of the Blessed Virgin, three times in the day."

"Dear me, how kind of you."

"You're welcome, my lady. There's those'll tell you I done more for them than the doctor, though they had to pay him and I never charged them anything. There's some would give me whatever they'd think themselves, when they were grateful like, but I wouldn't ask a penny whether it was a poor person or a lady the like of you. Sure it wouldn't be right."

"I wonder if that was a hint," said Mrs. Hoyle to Priscilla as they walked home. "I hadn't my purse with me anyway. These leaves are white horehound, I think. I must press them and look them up when we get back. Most interesting, these old remedies the country people know. Some of them are well worth recording. I must have some more talks with Mrs. Shegog and see what I can learn from her."

"I don't think you need to," said Priscilla. "That book she had that I was looking at, that was *Mrs. Lavender's Herbal Book.* I expect she gets it all out of that, and you could buy a copy for yourself in Woolworth's."

Mrs. Hoyle sighed.

"Another disappointment. I did think while I was down here I might collect material for a talk to the Culture Club on Old Remedies and Recipes. I asked Mary to let me have her mother's recipe for real Irish soda bread, and she lent me *The Daily Mail Cookery Book*."

They went up to their bedroom, and at once Priscilla had an uneasy feeling. She knew somebody had been in there, although everything seemed to be just as she had left it. She had a sense of some things being just slightly out of place: a heap of torn lingerie, left out on the bed for mending, looked tossed, and her suspender belt, discarded because she had no stockings on, was hanging the wrong way round on the chair. She was sure that somebody had been going through her things, but it had been done so skillfully that when she told her mother about it she could not point to anything definite in support of her impression.

She was right, nevertheless. The detectives, seeing the Hoyles go out together, had seized their opportunity. But they had not found anything of interest to them.

A Guard on a bicycle had delivered the superintendent's notes on a telephoned report from Dublin. It said that Priscilla's father had been a much esteemed schoolmaster; that he had died of appendicitis, leaving their house and his life insurance; that Priscilla and her mother lived economically but not meanly, paid their bills and subscribed to charities. Nothing was known against them in Rathgar. No connection could be traced between them and the Hampton family before Priscilla answered Miss Hampton's advertisement.

Inspector Devlin was no nearer and no farther from making an arrest. It would not do to act without certainty. On his last assignment he had got into his superiors' bad graces for arresting a man whose lawyers got him out again. This time he wanted a cast-iron case.

As for the bones, he was mainly interested in those because he fancied they might be a red herring to distract him from following up a more important trail.

CHAPTER NINETEEN
Telling Meriel

As Tim bicycled through the rain to Spangle Hill he planned what he would say to Meriel about her prospects. As he saw it, there were two questions to be settled: did Liam want to marry Meriel, and would she be wise to let him? It might seem a delicate subject to most people, but Tim

had few inhibitions and felt quite competent to probe the secrets of a
young girl's heart.

The difficulty was to prise the young girl out of the bosom of her
family. Even Tim was not prepared to tackle her in public, and the Booley
Brownes were having a domestic and united Sunday afternoon. They were
all indoors because of the rain. Mr. Booley Browne was yawning over a
book; Mrs. Booley Browne was dozing over a magazine; Meriel's next
youngest brother and sister were playing the piano; a still younger brother
was playing patience; four dogs and three cats were disposed about the
rugs and furniture. They were all delighted to see Tim except the cats,
who were thrown out of an armchair for him.

Tim delivered his mother's note, and Mrs. Booley Browne said any
day that suited Mrs. Linacre would suit her for moving the Work Depot,
and what day was the herb picnic? Tim said, Wednesday. Two of the
children called out together that it couldn't be Wednesday, because that
was Beltane. Mrs. Linacre, aloof from the peasantry, had forgotten the
traditional celebrations Brainborough held on Midsummer Eve. Beltane
in Brainborough was a fair day, with customs attached to it that might,
some said, be lingering imitations of old pagan rites and that were observed all the more punctiliously because nobody had any idea what they
meant. It was a day for a good time to be had by all. The village would be
humming, and the four roads meeting at Puck's Cross, where the fair
centered, would be jammed from early morning.

An argument began as to whether it mattered, and whether, even if it
did, Mrs. Linacre could change the day now: She had broadcast a general
invitation and did not know whom she expected. But this conversation
was swamped by another which had sprung upon the subject of the diamonds.

The story of the discovery had spread all over the parish, with
many variations, and the Booley Brownes seized on Tim as one of the
few people who knew what had really happened. It was the kind of
news that was difficult to believe in. They told Tim as a great joke
that the story was going round of thousands of pounds worth of diamonds being found in Miss Hampton's bed. There was a sensation
when he said it was true.

"What a nice surprise for Liam," said Mrs. Booley. Browne. "I'm
sure he's delighted."

Tim explained how the diamonds were not really an extra, but merely
patched up what right have been a bad loss. Meriel wanted to know what
the jewels were like, so Tim described the necklet that could be turned

into a tiara. Meriel said she would love to see the things, and Tim said she must get Liam to show her them. He fancied this caused a slight constraint, but it might have been his imagination. That large and cheerful family could not keep up any constraint for long.

They were soon arguing again. Mr. Booley Browne's deep voice struck in among the shrill ones of his women and children to ask if the police thought Miss Hampton was murdered for the diamonds. Mrs. Booley Browne protested

"Don't speak of such a thing, Father! We don't know whether she was murdered at all."

All the children spoke at once.

"Of course she was, Mammy. It's what everybody thinks."

"When's this the inquest is?" asked Mr. Booley Browne. Tim told him it had been adjourned till Thursday. Mr. Booley Browne said with a shake of his head that it would be as well when they knew the worst whatever it was.

Tim was wondering how on earth to get Meriel to himself. In the end he did it by the crude method of winking at her and jerking his head towards the door. She was quick in the uptake, and promptly asked him to come on down to the stable and look at Punch. Punch was Meriel's mare.

They lounged in the stable doorway looking out at the weather. Meriel lit a cigarette. Gazing at the smoke, her expression became dreamy, and Tim wondered if she was thinking about Liam. He felt very indignant with his cousin. It was damn queer how he had changed since Cousin Rebecca died. Now that it had come to a plain choice between the Court and Meriel, it almost looked as if the Court was what he wanted most after all: After the way he had gone about with Meriel, it wasn't treating her fairly. If Liam could behave like that to her, mightn't he be capable of anything?

"I say, Meriel," Tim began, "I want to talk to you if you don't mind. Or even if you do. I mean, you'll probably think it's awful cheek, but it has to come up some time. It's about Liam."

"What about him?"

"Oh, well, I just wondered if by any chance you were thinking of marrying him."

Tim hoped that sounded casual. Meriel was looking cross and it was all rather more difficult than he had expected. He supposed now she would bite his head off. But she only said, after a second, "What makes you ask that?"

Tim waggled his hands inexpressively. "Well, you know, he did seem to be around rather a lot."

"You mean, people were talking?"

"'Well, you know Brainborough for gossip."

"Damn Brainborough!" said Meriel.

Tim said: "Cousin Rebecca didn't take to the idea of a mixed marriage."

"No, I suppose not. I knew she didn't like me anyway. But why can't people mind their own business?" said Meriel, echoing the cry of ever so many pretty girls since the world began.

Tim did not answer that; he had a weakness for other people's business himself. He watched Meriel's face anxiously as she drew hard on her cigarette and knitted what was left of her brows after stern work with the tweezers. She was a merry, not a sulky type of a beauty, and this frown she had put on was unusual enough to be worth watching. To look at her, anyone would say she was thinking.

She finished her cigarette and fired the end accurately into a puddle. Then she folded her arms and turned square on Tim.

"It's enough to make anyone furious," she said, "the way people make up stories about me. It'd try the patience of a saint. I suppose next thing you'll tell me it got round to Liam. I could die of shame, so I could. Did it get round to him, Tim? Answer me!"

Meriel stamped and Tin quailed before her, but he had to reply, "Well, it has sort of been in the air. Liam had trouble over it with Cousin Rebecca. She even tried to stop it by putting something in her will." He explained about the last-minute codicil which deprived Liam of the Court if he made a mixed marriage.

"What?" said Meriel. "When was this?"

"The day before she died."

"The Tuesday?" Tim nodded. "That's funny," said Meriel. She turned away and started pacing thoughtfully up and down. This unfortunately took her out in the yard in the rain, so she gave it up and lighted another cigarette. There seemed to be a good deal on her mind.

"I wanted to explain to you," said Tim. "Ma said I shouldn't, but I thought you ought to know, just in case you were wondering."

"Wondering what?"

"Well, why he didn't propose."

At that she went off into peals of laughter, that sounded to Tim a little forced. Then she gave him an odd look, as if wondering how far she could trust him.

"You've got it all wrong," she said. "If I tell you something, will you promise not to breathe it to a soul?"

Tim hesitated. He did not want to commit himself to hushing up anything that might affect the investigation. But Meriel changed her mind between one sentence and the next.

"No, I won't after all. I mean, I can't without asking somebody. But you can take it from me there's nothing whatever between me and Liam. That's definite."

Tim did just wonder if she was being proud and putting on an act for his benefit. She was in a rotten position, and if she liked to pretend that her relations with Liam had never been more than polite and distant, there was no call to argue over it. He still thought it was due to her to tell her his suspicions.

He told her frankly that he fancied the police must regard Liam as Suspect Number 1. Admittedly there was no definite evidence to connect him with the poisoned dish, but he had no genuine alibi. If he had really had no hope of marrying Meriel—and Tim had only her word for that—it weakened his motive, yet nobody else was so well in the picture. It was solely in Liam's interest that Miss Hampton should die before she altered her will, for he must have believed that she intended to cut him out of the property altogether.

Meriel stared at Tim in silence, and her eyes filled with tears. "Don't cry," said Tim uncomfortably. "It might not be him after all."

Meriel swallowed her emotion as well as she could. She said, "I can't believe it of Liam. He isn't cruel. He doesn't even hunt. He doesn't like killing things."

"Doesn't necessarily follow," said Tim. "Poisoning's different, you don't have to see it work. I expect that's why women so often go in for it."

"Do they?" Meriel looked at him. "Do you know, they're saying in the village it was Miss Hoyle."

"Well, it might have been her. She's suspect Number 2. Depends whether she knew about the diamonds beforehand. Apart from those she had no obvious motive, but nobody had a better opportunity."

"I shouldn't have thought she was like that," said Meriel. "I liked her."

"So did I," said Tim. "Of course, we don't know much about her."

"It isn't easy to believe in anybody doing a thing like that. One doesn't expect people to be murderers."

"Some of them are, I'm afraid. The fact remains that somebody poisoned the lunch that day. It couldn't come without hands."

"They've poisoned the atmosphere too," said Meriel. "All this suspicion—"

"Don't think about it more than you can help," said Tim, "and don't say anything about what I've told you. I only mentioned Liam because I was afraid you might be getting involved with him."

"Well, I'm not. I'm positive he didn't do it. I know he isn't that sort of person. But you needn't worry about me getting engaged to him because it's quite out of the question."

She fixed her large gray eyes on Tim so earnestly that he had to believe her, and it took a weight off his mind. It was like Tim not to consider till long afterwards that this was the end of the Linacres' hopes of inheriting Hampton Court.

CHAPTER TWENTY
Accident or—?

HAVING stayed away from Hampton Court a whole day, Tim was more than ready to accompany his mother there on Monday morning. Mrs. Linacre wanted to pack up the possessions of the Work Depot. Tim hoped to have a chance of talking to the inspector and finding out how the land lay.

Whether or not he would have got anything out of the inspector is doubtful, but he did not have a chance to try. Inspector Devlin had gone to Dublin, taking the diamonds with him. George was out too, looking for places where deadly nightshade grew and talking to people living round about their movements on Wednesday morning. Mrs. Hoyle and Priscilla had gone to Brainborough, shopping. So Tim had to make good his word and help his mother pack.

Organization with Mrs. Linacre meant making the most of a job. She had drawn up several lists and called on Tim to help her check them. They enumerated all the possessions of the Work Depot from reels of thread to the sewing machine. The fun came when raw materials that figured on the list had to be checked against finished articles, or against entries in the book in which finished articles were supposed to be entered when they were sent out. No one with any experience of organization will need to be told that the lists never tallied. Mrs. Linacre became absorbed in mental calculations while Tom yawned and fidgeted.

McVittie unexpectedly appeared in the doorway. He touched his hat (he never went so far as to take it off in the house) and hoped he would not be disturbing Mrs. Linacre if he took up the floor above.

"Whatever for?" Tim asked.

"Captain's orders," said McVittie, leaving Tim none the wiser.

Mrs. Linacre told McVittie to go on with whatever he wanted to do, but she was soon complaining that the hammering made it impossible to hear oneself think.

They saw Liam through the window and Mrs. Linacre sent Tim to ask him if all this was really necessary.

"Ma wants to know what McVittie's doing," said Tim to Liam as he passed through the hall. "It's giving her a headache."

"He's looking for bones," said Liam over his shoulder.

Tim thought he was being funny. He was about fed up with Liam getting at him for his detective efforts. Beastly superior of him. He might see that it was better to take an intelligent interest than just twiddle your thumbs. Unless he had his own reasons for discouraging anybody from inquiring into things too closely.

Tim had never felt at ease with Liam. Since his latest analysis of the situation he felt more uncomfortable with him than ever. Having jerked out his mother's message and been snubbed for it he was glad to fade away again.

The hammering upstairs ceased, however, and Mrs. Linacre, who had been struggling to decide whether fourteen babies' vests really accounted for two pounds of baby wool, had the brilliant idea of weighing them on the kitchen scales. She was moving towards the door with her hands full of tiny garments when an odd thing happened. There was a scurry as of snowflakes; plaster pattered down on the worktable, and they looked up, startled, to see a man's boot with a large hole in the sole of it, sticking down through the ceiling. A voice from above cried, "By the Holy powers!"

"Mind yourself, McVittie!" said another voice, Liam's, sharply. "Look out! You'll have the whole thing down in a minute."

The boot waved wildly and was withdrawn, with a heavier shower of plaster after it. Then came plunging sounds overhead, and a more ominous noise, a crescendo tearing and a shout that was echoed by the Linacres as the whole ceiling collapsed and the workroom vanished under a heap of rubble before their eyes. It was lucky that Tim and his mother had both been near the doorway, or they could hardly have escaped being hurt.

The Work Depot's hygienic American cloth-covered table was completely buried under dust, flakes of plaster, broken laths and—bones. It was those that held Tim fascinated. Amid the wreckage of the ceiling lay numerous long bones, the leg bones of animals, and twenty or thirty horses' skulls. Mrs. Linacre had screamed; and one more skull, dislodged by the vibration of her voice, rolled out from between the joists above and fell on top of the others. Afterwards they found fifty-five in all.

Looking up, Tim could see into the music room through a huge gap in the ceiling. He had a glimpse of the gray wallpaper with its peaceful pastoral scene, and the grand piano, at a drunken angle, with one leg through between the joists. The cut-glass chandelier, relic of the grander days of the workroom, still hung by a thread, with all its lusters quivering, and still tinkled faintly after the louder crash had died away.

Liam and McVittie had also escaped damage. They came hurrying downstairs. "You clumsy bosthoon!" said Liam to McVittie. "Look what you've done!"

McVittie gazed at the wreckage and gave way to his natural impulse to spit right into the center of the heap. Liam did not see him. He was asking Mrs. Linacre if she was hurt. She was looking rather white and shook her head without speaking.

"Luckily we were standing near the door," said Tim, "otherwise we'd be underneath all that. We'd have been interred with the bones, like Julius Caesar. So there really were bones after all."

"Bones? My God yes," said Liam. "McVittie, you'd better get busy and clear away this mess. Get a barrow and wheel all the stuff out to the yard. We can do with the plaster for lime rubbish."

McVittie touched his hat.

Liam looked at Mrs. Linacre again and said she'd better have a glass of sherry, which she refused. He was still pressing it on her when a diversion was caused by the return of the Hoyles from Brainborough. They had heard the crash while they were still away off down the drive. Five different explanations had occurred to Mrs. Hoyle, and she recounted all of them while they gazed at the ruins.

"But I don't understand about the bones," said Tim, sticking to it. "What were they doing there?" Liam said, "How the hell should I know?"

"Begging your pardon, sir," said McVittie, "I can tell you that."

They all stared at McVittie, and he seized the opportunity to restore himself to favor. He remembered hearing about the bones from his father's grandfather, who was a young lad about the place in the time of Miss Victoria and Miss Adelaide, great-aunts to poor Miss Rebecca, God rest her. The young ladies, as they were then, were mad keen on music. It was they who turned the upstairs room into a music room and imported the first grand piano ever heard in Brainborough. They used to play duets on it, and people came in evening dress to listen to them. Nothing else would do them but to have the floor rebuilt. It was to cut out noise, they said, from down below, and to improve the sound in the room itself. It was some gentleman from Dublin who started the idea of the bones. He wanted them to pack the spaces between the joists with shells, but shells were scarce round Brainborough, as people were not great on eating oysters in those parts. So then he thought of using horses' bones, for there were plenty of those to be had in the knacker's yard where the hounds' meat came from. The gentleman came down and saw to it all himself, and everybody thought he was courting Miss Victoria, except those who thought it was Miss Adelaide. People were laying bets on each of them. But perhaps he could not make up his mind between them, for he went away, without speaking for either, and Miss Victoria died and Miss Adelaide married a man who took her to India, and nobody had played on the piano since.*

The fall in McVittie's voice on the concluding words of his narrative showed that he relished the pathos of old romance. Nobody seemed able to produce an appropriate comment, and there was a slight pause. Then the chandelier, which all this tine had hung trembling and tinkling above the wreckage, suddenly tore away from its moorings in the last unbroken patch of plaster and came crashing down. All its pendants clinked and clashed together in a cascade of shivering glass.

Mrs. Linacre gave a wild peal of laughter and sank on to one unbroken chair by the wall. She rocked backwards and forwards, in uncontrolled abandon unlike her usual cool poise.

"Steady on, Ma," said Tim.

His mother's laughter ceased, and she clutched his arm and burst into tears.

"We might have been killed," she sobbed.

"Come now," said Mrs. Hoyle, "there's nothing to get excited about. It was a nasty accident, but all's well that ends well."

"Accident!" cried Mrs. Linacre. "Was it an accident?" She began to laugh again. "Or was the accident that we weren't killed? You know what the inspector would say if he was here? He'd say it was attempted murder."

* Some years ago there was a correspondence in the *Sunday Times* which mentioned several instances of horses' skulls in floors. There is an illustration of a floor packed in this way in a book called *Old Bungay* by Miss Ethen Mann. Shells are used in the floors of the Casino, Marino, Dublin, one of the showpieces of Irish eighteenth century architecture.

"Has she gone mad?" demanded Liam.

Indeed, it looked like it. Mrs. Linacre flung herself back in her chair, crying: "Don't touch me!" and drumming her heels on the floor. Her eyes opened and shut rapidly, and there was even a suspicion of foam at her mouth. It was an appalling sight, which left Tim sick and shaken. Priscilla glanced at Liam, who understood and put a hand on Tim's shoulder.

"Hysterics," said Mrs. Hoyle. "Seen it before in one of my club girls." She marched up to Mrs. Linacre and slapped her on both cheeks. "Pull yourself together, woman, and stop making an exhibition of yourself!" The shrieks stopped.

Liam took Tim out through the hall into the garden, where Priscilla joined them. McVittie had already effaced himself tactfully. "Don't worry, Tim," said Priscilla kindly. "She'll be all right in a few minutes. My mother knows just what to do." Tim was beyond words for the time; it had been a shattering experience for him. The other two left him sitting on the steps and strolled up and down together. There was peace and calm. Everything was fresh and sweet after the rain. The little hill behind the shrubbery had receded again and was today the color of a pigeon's breast. Liam and Priscilla paced about the gravel, and, white against the dark green Wellingtonias, two cabbage butterflies danced over their heads.

Mrs. Hoyle came out. She said Mrs. Linacre was lying down and would be quite fit to go home after half an hour or so. The best treatment was to leave her alone.

"Shouldn't she have the trap to go home in?" said Liam. "I'll tell McVittie. Extraordinary thing, hysterics. How far d'you think she's responsible? She accused me of murder."

"Don't pay any attention," said Mrs. Hoyle. "People say things they don't mean. You're all in a false position at present. Priscilla had an unpleasant experience this morning too."

Liam asked what happened. "Nothing," said Priscilla. "Oh, nothing to make a fuss about," said Mrs. Hoyle. "It was just something a little boy called out after us in the street. I couldn't really catch what he said, but he seemed to be accusing poor Priscilla. Some of the shop people were rather uncivil too."

"Who were?" demanded Liam indignantly, but Priscilla intervened. She was angry with her mother for mentioning it and refused to have names brought in. Liam said that the matter ought to be reported to the police. "It's up to them to prevent that kind of persecution."

"Well, I don't really see what they can do," said Mrs. Hoyle reasonably. "People are bound to think things, I'm afraid, until they really know what to think."

"It's about time that damn fool inspector got a move on," said Liam. "I don't know what he thinks he's paid for."

"I suppose he has his methods."

"He may think he has. We shouldn't have time for them in the army."

The army has a traditional contempt for the police. Scowling at his thoughts, Liam made one of his usual unceremonious departures.

Mrs. Hoyle invited the Linacres to stay for lunch, but Mrs. Linacre refused with a shudder. She looked washed out and was really glad to have the trap to drive home in.

She and Tim did not talk much over their own meal, but afterwards Mrs. Linacre said, "Tim, will you promise me not to go back to Hampton Court till everything has been cleared up? I simply can't bear the thought of entering that house again."

CHAPTER TWENTY-ONE
Romance

OF all the sensations that stirred Brainborough in connection with the Hampton case, the greatest broke on Wednesday morning. It was not the full story of the diamonds, though the police gave that to the Press to keep them quit, and the Press naturally made the most of it. Nor was it the solution of the mystery of Miss Hampton's death; when that came, a few days later, it proved rather an anticlimax. The news that started Brainborough talking harder than anything else between the end of war in Europe and the atomic bomb, was Meriel Booley Browne's engagement.

The notice caught Mrs. Linacre's eye as soon as she opened her *Irish Times*. Tim saw in her face there was big news, and went to read over her shoulder. The postman brought the paper, and they had both been attracted to the front door by his arrival.

The notice said:

MR. C.S. GREALISH—MISS M.A. BOOLEY BROWNE

The engagement is announced and the marriage will shortly take place between Captain The Hon. Charles Stuart Grealish, D.S.O. and bar, eldest son of Lord and Lady St. Enda, of Carrig, and 10 Charles

Street, Mayfair, W. I, and Meriel Anne, eldest daughter of Mr. and
Mrs. Bernard Booley Browne, of Spangle Hill, Brainborough.

"Well!" said Mrs. Linacre. "Of all the catches!"

"He sounds very posh," said Tim. "Who is he anyway? I never heard
of him."

"I've seen his photo in the *Tatler*. He's a war hero. He's very good-
looking too. Quite as handsome as Liam."

"But, I mean, I never heard the Booley Brownes mention him. Did
you?"

"Well, yes, I did, once," said Mrs. Linacre reflectively. "Mrs. Double-
B told me they met the St. Endas in the West last summer and had a
couple of days on their water, and Captain Grealish was home on sick
leave. I expect that was when it all started. Mrs. Double-B didn't say
much about him. She must have been holding her breath in case it came to
nothing. It's a wonderful match for Meriel. The St. Endas are R.C. too."

It was another lovely morning. A lovelier morning than ever. A day
to talk of weddings.

Tim picked a piece of long grass that had no business to be growing
out of the front steps and chewed it to help with thinking. He was thinking
how this affected the case against Liam. A few days ago that had made a
traceable pattern, but it had since had a couple of shake-ups, like a kalei-
doscope, and everything looked different.

He said, "Liam must have known all along."

Mrs. Linacre said, "I wonder."

"Surely Meriel would have told him. She's not the sort to keep string-
ing him along."

"That's a crude way of putting it. Perhaps she was hesitating between
the two of them, and this awful business sent her into the other man's arms."

"But that would mean she thought he did it."

Mrs. Linacre nodded. "If she doesn't, I can't think why she should choose
just this moment to jilt him. She must know he's under suspicion."

Tim saw that his mother, at any rate, had made up her mind about the
murderers. She had never liked Liam and had been quite prepared to believe he had gone the length of demolishing the ceiling of the workroom
just for the sake of interring her with the bones. But all the same, he felt
there was something that did not fit.

He said aloud, "If Liam knew he had a rival it might have driven him
to desperation. But if he knew he was out of the running altogether, there
wouldn't be any point in his annoying Cousin Rebecca at all."

"And we know he did defy her," said Mrs. Linacre.

"But Meriel said—" began Tim, and broke off, because he was not quite sure what exactly Meriel had said. Somehow, either he or she must have got a wrong impression.

"There's one good thing about this, anyway, Ma," he said, "Liam knows now he can stay at the Court forever and ever. No need for him to bump us off."

"Nothing would induce me to live there after this," said Mrs. Linacre, "and I had still rather you would stay away from the place. We know this dreadful wickedness is in the air, and that somebody capable of murder is still at large, and none of us is safe until the police find out what happened, and as far as I can see they never will."

Silence fell on this depressing statement of the position. Tim could hear, on the path outside the tap, tap, tap, of a thrush with a snail shell. The bird was an escargot fancier himself.

Tim started down the steps. "Where are you off to?" asked his mother.

"Spangle Hill," he told her. "I'm going to find Meriel and ask her what she means by it."

II

Mrs. Hoyle had outmaneuvered the inspector for the *Irish Times* and had taken it out to read on the portico steps. Suddenly she jumped to her feet.

"Such news!" she cried, and looked round for an audience. She had one handy. George was pumping the tires of the police car on the gravel sweep, and Priscilla was reading letters in the hall. Mrs. Hoyle stood in the hall doorway and announced to both of them

"Miss Booley Browne's engaged."

Priscilla said listlessly: "Oh, is it in the paper at last?" George said: "That all? I thought they'd found Hitler or something." Mrs. Hoyle enjoyed her scoop.

"It's not to Captain Hampton at all."

She spread the paper wide for the others to look.

"She's made a brilliant match," said Mrs. Hoyle with unselfish satisfaction. "I'm sure her parents are delighted. I've never heard anything but good of the St. Endas, and they've pots of money. Do you know Captain Grealish, Officer?"

George said the police had nothing against him so far.

Priscilla said, in a careless voice, "It's hard on Captain Hampton."

"I wonder if he knows," said Mrs. Hoyle. "I daresay Miss Booley Browne will have broken it to him beforehand. That is, if there really was anything between them, because I must say, I never saw any signs of it myself."

"There was, according to our information," said George. "Perhaps recent events made her change her mind. The chief will be interested."

"Hadn't you better go and tell him?" said Mrs. Hoyle.

III

Tim found Meriel playing singles with her next youngest brother. It was a halfhearted game and they broke off when they saw him. The Booley Brownes were a hospitable family, always delighted to abandon whatever they were doing and cluster round a visitor. Meriel shook the younger brother off and brought Tim up to her own room, saying she wanted to talk to him.

Tim had been in Meriel's room before. He at once spotted the new photograph in a silver frame on the table by the bed.

"That's Charlie," said Meriel. "I suppose you've seen the paper."

"You kept him very dark," said Tim.

Meriel laughed. "I was nearly telling you the other day, only I couldn't, Tim. Charlie and I had agreed it would have to be a secret till he had time to break it to his parents. Mummy and Daddy knew, of course, but nobody else. Do you think he's handsome?"'

It was just a photograph of a British officer in uniform with his hat on.

"Oh, you can't really tell from that," said Meriel. "That's only an enlargement of one that was in the *Tatler*. I'll make him have a better one taken."

"I think he's too, too marvelous," said Tim sarcastically. "Have you known him long?"

"Not very. Only since last summer. But I've been crazy about him since the first day I saw him. He was about me too. There really is such a thing as love at first, sight, Tim."

"I'll take your word for it," said Tim, feeling extremely mature and cynical, as people do who are obliged to listen to raptures. "Congratulations, and all that. By the way, how's Liam?"

"Now listen," said Meriel, "you needn't be throwing him up to me at all."

"All right," said Tim. "Have it your own way. Liam never dreamed of proposing to you. He only hung around to keep in practice."

Meriel took a rag and a bottle off the washstand and started whitening the tennis shoes she had been wearing. She was humming a little tune. She made a nice picture in her big round mirror, against the background of her nice pink and white bedroom.

"People will say," Tim told her, "that you chucked Liam because you thought he'd poisoned Cousin Rebecca."

She looked up, startled. "Oh, nonsense!"

"They will. It's what, I thought myself, soon as I heard."

"But I told you there wasn't anything between me and Liam. Anything there ever was, was over before ever your cousin was poisoned at all. If you want to know, he proposed on the night of that dance, and I refused him."

"He probably didn't believe you meant it."

"He couldn't. I told him all about Charlie. Charlie was in Dublin then, and that was really why I went up. The dance made a good excuse."

From Meriel's point of view, to have one young man in public and another in private, was only elementary common sense.

She may, however, have felt that some excuse was needed after all, for she added, "You know, I never felt Liam really meant it. And from what you told me, I do believe he only proposed because he'd heard people were talking. He thought he'd compromised me or something."

"Yes, that's all very well," said Tim, "but how do you explain that the day after that, when Cousin Rebecca threatened to disinherit him if he married you, he just dared her to get on with it?"

"Oh, but that's just like Liam," said Meriel, with superior feminine insight. "He was probably in a foul temper. He wouldn't give your old cousin the satisfaction of knowing she was to have her own way."

"What, chuck away all that money for nothing?"

"Liam honestly doesn't care about money."

Meriel spoke with conviction, and she knew Liam well. Tim thought she might be right. Liam had risked disinheritance once before, when he had the row with Cousin Rebecca over joining the Irish Army. He might not have changed much with the years.

A knob of Meriel's brass bedstead, which Tim had been twisting round and round, came off in his hands. He screwed it on and off again thoughtfully. Meriel finished her shoes and propped them on the windowsill to dry.

Tim said, "Can I tell the inspector all this?"

"What's it got to do with him?"

"Well, in case he was toying with the idea of arresting Liam, I think he ought to know that the tremendous motive we thought he had for murdering Cousin Rebecca seems to be a complete washout."

IV

The inspector, George, Mrs. Hoyle and Tim went on talking and talking. Priscilla left them and went out across the lawn. She wanted to intercept Liam; he might be coming any time now, and she dreaded his walking into the hall and finding everybody discussing the news.

Beyond the Wellingtonias, round the angle of the garden wall, where the shrubbery thinned out and the park began, there was a gate in an iron fence, and near it a pile of stones overgrown with scutch and small ferns, which somebody had once intended as a rockery. Sitting on one of the stones, Priscilla could drink in the peace of the morning. The sun was warm and kind, and there was a pleasant buzz of harmless insects. The thin crop of cut hay lay yellowing in the park; Liam's Jersey cows had been let in to eat it as it lay; they looked charming, like deer. The hay scent mingled with drifts of scent from the *Clematis montana* that covered the garden wall. Some young blackbirds, brought up in the clematis, were having their first flying lesson. The grass at Priscilla's feet was full of curious mosses, and on an old root sat a very clean butterfly, like a newborn hope, wondering at itself and at the chrysalis it had left in a crack of the wood.

"Hallo!" said Liam. "You sitting here all alone at this time of day?"

"I was waiting for you," said Priscilla. "They're all having committees about you up at the house."

"Oh, why?"

"Have you seen today's paper yet?"

"I glanced at it. Nothing special, was there?"

"Miss Booley Browne's engaged to a Captain Grealish."

Liam laughed. "So, that's official, is it? I wondered how much longer they'd be announcing it."

Priscilla said, "So long as you knew—"

"Oh yes, I've known for some time."

There was a short pause.

Liam said: "Am I expected to go and shoot lions in Africa or something?"

Priscilla glanced at him, up and sideways. "Not if you don't feel like it."

"Well, I don't," said Liam.

CHAPTER TWENTY-TWO
Mixum Gatherum

IT must not be forgotten that Wednesday was also Midsummer Eve, the day of Beltane and of Mrs. Linacre's herb-gathering picnic.

Inspector Devlin took no interest in either of these attractions, except that he found it a nuisance to have Sergeant Carty busy with the Beltane Fair when he wanted to talk over the arrangements for tomorrow's inquest. He drove off to confer with the superintendent and the coroner. George spent much of the lovely day indoors, getting papers together and writing a long report.

Priscilla was worried. She fancied she noticed a change in the manner of the police. They were always ready with civil conversation, but however much they talked, they never gave anything away. The feeling of police in the house was on everybody's nerves. Mrs. Hoyle complained of the way Inspector Devlin clicked his false teeth and of George's habit of saying, "Is that so?" whenever she told him anything. Mrs. McGuirk was scared stiff, and though back at work, was not much more use than if she had still had lumbago. Even Mary took a habit of bursting into tears for trivial reasons. And Priscilla could not reason herself out of a feeling of menace in their officially correct attitude. She could feel them always on the watch.

She knew now that instead of being a mere spectator, as she had anticipated, she herself was an object of suspicion. She had become conscious of it on her shopping expedition to Brainborough on Monday. Liam had said, "It's nothing to do with you, we'll keep it in the family," but on the contrary, it was she, as a stranger, who was automatically condemned by public opinion. She found she was both dreading and longing for the resumption of the inquest. It would be an ordeal, but it might clear the air.

She would gladly have avoided attending the herb picnic. Unfortunately the idea, even though it was Mrs. Linacre's, had greatly appealed to Mrs. Hoyle. It was the kind of thing Mrs. Hoyle organized herself if she got a chance. She said it was a splendid example of self-help and economy of national resources and might turn out to be a big thing for Brainborough, and even for the whole of Ireland. There the herbs were to be had for nothing. Nothing but the trouble of picking and marketing them, and with proper organization that was nothing at all. Another year, Mrs. Hoyle planned to bring down parties of Dublin factory girls to help with the picking. It would give them a wholesome open-air holiday and they could do the hard work.

So that afternoon, after an early lunch, McVittie drove Mrs. Hoyle and three homemade cakes and Priscilla and her bicycle to Brainborough. The day had grown brighter and hotter from hour to hour. The hedges all along the route were untidily hung with wisps of hay from passing carts. The dust, once laid by the rain, was now as thick as ever. Flies pestered the pony and McVittie kept flicking them off with his whip. McVittie had his own sufferings. On such a dry, dusty day, he felt an urgent need to spit out of the trap, but he dared not in front of Mrs. Hoyle. She had presented him with a little card, something like the texts given out in Sunday schools, on which was artistically printed:

DO NOT SPIT!
EVERY TIME YOU SPIT YOU ARE A
PUBLIC DANGER.
SPITTING SPREADS GERMS AND
CAUSES T.B.

McVittie had the card in his pocket, and there were half a dozen more in Mrs. Hoyle's handbag for distribution as need arose.

Only about ten minutes later than the time fixed for the meeting, they jogged into the village square and found it crowded. For a wild moment they thought the herb picnic had a record attendance, but this was not the kind of crowd to rally round Mrs. Linacre. It was interested in bargains: china, ironmongery, secondhand clothes and quack medicines. Also houpla, roulette, and boys or girls according. In fact the famous Beltane Fair of Brainborough, known all over the world and the United States and even the twenty-six counties, had once more spread out its attractions on the cobblestones, and along the pavement in front of Devine's, and even against the railings of Mr. Counsel's. Beltane was a day of affliction to Mr. Counsel, though it brought him business from wealthy farmers who combined a day's outing with making their wills or starting litigation against their neighbors.

To make it world-famous, Brainborough's fair had to have some in-
dividual feature to distinguish it from all the other fairs and sports and
races and patterns and carnivals held in other Irish towns and attended by
the same tinkers, quacks, three-card tricksters, traveling shops and traveling gambling wheels. Brainborough had all these and a goat too.

The goat is the king of the fair, nobody quite knows why. A note
about Brainborough, printed on the back of the tourist map of the county,
suggests that this is a survival of some ancient form of animal sacrifice or
possibly a form of totem worship. It adds to the interest of the subject for
the folklorist that this is the only instance of a goat in connection with
midsummer rites, though at Killorglin, in County Kerry, a goat plays its
part in the well-known September Puck Fair. There is room here for research. One writer on folklore, an Englishwoman, has suggested that the
antiquity of the Brainborough custom has been exaggerated, and that Brainborough, jealous of the publicity given to Killorglin's fair, borrowed the
idea of the goat in modern times. This unsupported opinion is perhaps
hardly worthy of mention.

McVittie edged the trap into the square between carts and hucksters'
stalls, with children dodging in and out. Mrs. Hoyle assisted with directions, and as they were both preoccupied, Priscilla was the first to recognize an old acquaintance. It was Mrs. Shegog's pet that now presided
over the fair from a position of eminence on a wooden staging about ten
feet high, erected in the middle of the square. (Or as near the middle as
possible, the exact center being taken up by a pink marble drinking foun-
tain in memory of one of the Hampton family.) Mrs. Shegog's goat owed
its position to influence. The diplomatic young Civic Guard, the one who
had rescued it from captivity at the Court, had made a suggestion to the
committee who were getting up the fair. The committee had thereupon
approached Mrs. Shegog and persuaded her to allow her goat to accept
the offer of a star part. In the end it would be sold by auction, after a
ceremonial procession to the place known as Puck's Cross. The excitement of the occasion would ensure a much better price than the goat would
fetch on its own merits, so its owner could look forward to consolation in
cash, besides the reflected glory of the goat's apotheosis.

The expression of the king of the fair, as it gazed out over its subjects,
was disillusioned. Now that the excitement of getting it up on the staging
was over, nobody was taking much interest in it. It fidgeted about in a
bored way, and ate the evergreens that decorated the staging in preference to the cabbages which had been supplied to it for nourishment.

The trap came to a standstill. Priscilla looked about for anybody who

might belong to the picnic. She became aware that other people were
looking at them, and she fancied she saw some of them nudge each other
and mutter together. Was it her imagination, or were they pointing her out
as the young lady who did the murder? A little boy shouted something at
the trap. She could not catch it and asked McVittie what he said, but
McVittie pretended not to have heard. She knew he was pretending; he
looked very dour and spat into the gutter, regardless of Mrs. Hoyle.

At this moment Mrs. Hoyle saw the goat, and immediately became
concerned for its comfort. Nobody, she said, would like to be stuck up
there on a tiny little platform in all that dust and noise. Priscilla had suffered much in her time from her mother's bouts of humanitarian impulse.
She waited in dread for Mrs. Hoyle to arise in the trap and lecture the
crowd on cruelty to animals. They were saved by the sudden appearance
of Tim Linacre, apparently from underneath the pony. Miss Counsel was
coming out of her front door, and Mrs. Owler and Ursula were pushing
their bicycles forwards along the footpath. Other elements of the herb
picnic separated themselves from the fair, and Tim marshalled them all to
the schoolhouse, where Mrs. Linacre had set up her G.H.Q.

There was not quite the assemblage that Mrs. Linacre had hoped for.
The schoolmistress had failed to furnish any child labor; it had all gone
off to the hobby horses at Pucks Cross. Father Lawrence had sent his
good wishes, but was sorry he could not be present, and Mr. Owler was
not coming with them, though he had turned up to see the start. He wore
an expression of guarded benignity, not being sure whether it was wise to
encourage activities that might divert people's energies from the annual
garden fete. The juvenile talent was supplied mainly by the Work Depot
helpers bringing their families

Miss Counsel's nieces and nephews, the two Gahan girls, all the young
Booley Brownes, Ursula Owler, and Mrs. De Vigne's little maid: Mrs.
Linacre said sadly that when, it came to doing anything useful, it was all
left to the same little band of people.

There was to have been a donkey cart to carry the picnic tea out and
the sacks of herbs home. So far it had not turned up, so Mrs. Linacre said
it would be better to borrow the Hampton Court trap. McVittie's chance
of an afternoon at the fair vanished. Priscilla took her bicycle off the trap;
and it was loaded up, under Mrs. Linacre's and Mrs. Hoyle's combined
instructions, with everybody's contributions of scones, cakes, butter and
so forth, as well as the empty sacks, the large red enamel teapot, and the
picnic kettle that left a black mark on Mrs. Hoyle's skirt. Mrs. Hoyle
remained in the trap. Mrs. Linacre got on her own bicycle and took the

lead, and the whole party streamed off.

Priscilla told herself she must be getting hysterical. When Mrs. Owler and Miss Tench had a conversation together in undertones, glancing in her direction, why did she have to think it was about the Hampton case? Was it just chance that, though Mrs. Linacre was effusively polite to Mrs. Hoyle, nobody came up to talk to her? Of course they were all busy congratulating Meriel Booley Browne on her engagement, and Meriel herself could not be expected to do more than wave and smile, but even funny old Miss Counsel, who was usually rather an odd man out, seemed to avoid Priscilla's eye. In the bicycle party she found herself riding alone. Then Ursula Owler rode up and started chatting brightly about wildflowers, and this only confirmed Priscilla in her misgivings. It was too obviously Christian of Ursula and not spontaneous.

The feeling that people were thinking about her as a possible murderess persisted throughout the afternoon, and the worst moment of all for Priscilla came during the picnic tea.

Before that the herb pickers had toiled for two hours in the hot sun till hands were sore, nails splitting, backs aching, legs scratched, frocks torn, necks sunburnt, faces red and shiny. Nobody liked to suggest stopping; the sacks took much longer to fill than had been anticipated.

They were picking deadly nightshade in the place called the old churchyard. It was not the churchyard where Miss Hampton was buried, but a place wilder and farther from Brainborough, where a tiny overgrown ruin in a rough stone enclosure, still in utter decay, retained an atmosphere of timeworn piety. The deadly nightshade might have been introduced there long ago by some cleric who was a bit of a herbalist. If so, no trace of him remained, not even the tradition of his name. But the plant nowadays grew inside the church as well as out, pushing the gravestones aside with its strong dark stems. The graves jostled each other in unseemly confusion, because people still set store on being buried in the holy place. There were always a few graves with dead flowers on them. People used to leave them in jampots of water, but the jampots had disappeared during the time when the shops put up notices "No jars, no jam," and some connected this with the fact that Mrs. Shegog had been hawking round jampots for twopence each.

Mrs. Linacre encouraged everyone to work by telling how she hoped to get a shilling a pound for the leaves and five pounds a hundredweight for the roots. Unfortunately the wholesalers would not deal in less than hundredweights.

"How much would you say we have now?" asked Miss Counsel,

straightening her back after a long spell of picking. Guesses ranged from
three to seven stone. Then Tim Linacre pointed out the catch in it,

"The leaves will come down to nothing when they're dried," he said.
"I've read somewhere that two stone of fresh leaves when they're stalked
and dried only weigh about five pounds."

His words were rapidly passed round, and the groan that arose from
the toilers warned Mrs. Linacre of rebellion threatening, so she let them
stop for tea.

All the various oddments that people had contributed to the meal
were unpacked from the trap: rather a surplus of oatmeal scones, some
biscuits, and one or two homemade cakes, among them a beautiful sponge
cake and two jam sandwich sponge mixtures baked by Mrs. Hoyle. Mrs.
Linacre simply could not thank Mrs. Hoyle enough for these. But Priscilla
saw her exchange glances with some of the other picnickers, and presently she whispered something to Tim. Tim put the three cakes down near
the mouth of a big fox hole under a furze bush, and sat down near them,
and somehow managed to push the cakes right down the fox hole, acci-
dentally on purpose. Nobody made any comment when all the eatables
were spread out and the Hampton Court cakes were not to be found. It
came to this: people were afraid to eat anything that came from Hampton
Court.

Priscilla was afraid her mother would fuss over the cakes being lost,
but Mrs. Hoyle showed unusual restraint and ate a good tea of other
people's inferior buns. Priscilla could not eat anything at all; she was too
hot and tired, and possessed with the longing to be not less than a hundred
miles away and absolutely alone.

Even after tea there was no immediate escape. The picking was intended to go on till all the sacks were filled. But people soon began to
drop out; Mrs. Gahan had to feed her hens; Mrs. Owler had some duty to
perform for the parish mothers, and Meriel Booley Browne said frankly
that it would take an hour's work on her nails to get them presentable
again for dinner. But staunch spirits like Ursula Owler and Mrs. De Vigne's
little maid remained in the field, and the Hoyles could not go before the
bitter end, because transport for the sacks depended on the Hampton Court
trap. At least, Priscilla could have ridden off home on her bicycle, as she
finally did, but in her state of supersensitized misery she could not allow
herself to leave her mother alone with the enemy.

It was after seven o'clock when she at last experienced the joy of
seeing the last limp herb pickers take the road to Brainborough, and of
turning herself in the opposite direction. She blessed Tim for telling her

of a shortcut back to Hampton Court, which made it absurd for her to ride round with the trap to Glenwood. She called out gaily that she would have dinner waiting by the time Mrs. Hoyle got back, and plunged thankfully into a deep boreen between hedges that almost met over her head. Here the dog-roses were still in flower, where they had had protection from Sunday's rain, and little pointed pink and purple orchises pushed up here and there in the soft banks.

As usual when she was overtired, Priscilla started thinking about Liam Hampton. It had improved as a form of mental relaxation since he had separated himself in her mind from Meriel Booley Browne. Nevertheless, Priscilla was ashamed of her obsession, for she could so well remember being just as silly over Hugo Everard, between whom and Liam there was simply no comparison. Two months ago, ridiculous as it seemed now, she had very nearly made herself ill over Hugo. She did not want to have to go through all that again.

> "Oh were you e'er in love, boys, and have you felt the
> pain?
> I'd sooner be in jail myself than be in love again,"

hummed Priscilla defiantly as she slipped through the green lane.

It was harder to keep up her spirits when she left the pleasant boreen and toiled along a straight stretch of tarmac. She tried to face the possibility that she might be accused of murder. Who else might be shown to have been in the kitchen that morning? Mary? McGuirk? Mrs. Shegog? Her brain churned the alternatives over and over. Two miles went by, and then she came to a place where the road forked and she found she could not remember whether Tim had said right or left. She took the right, and round the next bend found the evening sun shining down a long straight stretch into her eyes. It was impossible to recognize landmarks. After riding on for ten minutes and meeting nobody, she saw she must humble herself to ask the way at a house.

She turned in at an open gate without a name on it, and rode up to a pleasant two-storied, round-windowed, pink-washed old house that stood two fields back from the road. Liam Hampton opened the door.

For a moment Priscilla really thought her mental condition must be serious enough to cause hallucinations, and she gazed at him, speechless. Then it dawned on her that she had come to Hampton Lodge.

"What's the matter?" asked Liam. "Come in and sit down. You look all in."

CHAPTER TWENTY-THREE
Suspects Get Together

MUSIC sounded as Priscilla stepped into the hall. "Mother's listening to a symphony concert," said Liam. "If you don't mind, we'll come in here." He took her into the dining room, a cool and pleasant place after the glare on the road. The blinds had been half down all day, for it was an old-fashioned house. Large mahogany pieces loomed in the shadows, and Priscilla sat in a curly-backed, horsehair-padded armchair that felt stiff but agreeably cool.

Liam brought her a glass of milk and poured brandy into it from a Tantalus on the sideboard. He watched her seriously while she drank it. He had no small talk; he never had. He was accustomed to wait till people got out whatever they really wanted to say.

Priscilla explained how she had lost herself and began to describe the herb picnic. She intended to make this light and amusing, but she could feel that Liam saw through her. He was convinced that something was the matter. Priscilla's story tailed off, and she found herself abruptly asking, "Do you think I poisoned Miss Hampton?"

"You?" said Liam. "My God, no!"

He had spoken stoutly and without hesitation, and when she looked at him he was half smiling. Priscilla had to put down her glass because her hand was shaking.

"I don't see why you shouldn't, really," she said. "Other people do."

"They don't know you like I do," said Liam.

"Why," said Priscilla, "you haven't known me very long."

"Long enough for that. What's been happening to upset you? Is it the police?"

"Oh no, not them. I suppose they could arrest me if they wanted to. I wish they would. I'd rather be downright accused of something than go round all the time among people who aren't saying what they think. Because either nearly everybody thinks I'm a murderess, or else I'm imagining it and that means I'm getting persecution mania."

"Drink up your milk now, like a good girl," said Liam, putting her glass back into her hand. "Has anything special happened, or is it just the general atmosphere?"

"Atmosphere, mostly," Priscilla admitted, "but there was something happened this afternoon." She told him about Tim Linacre burying the cakes. This made Liam laugh, and for the first time it struck Priscilla as funny. She drank the last of the milk and began to feel better.

She was able to look round the room and take in her surroundings: the paintings of horses and photographs of prize pigs and cattle; the sideboard set out with challenge cups; the black mantelpiece with two heavy silver candlesticks; the leather screen to keep off draft from the door; Liam, in silhouette against the window, as handsome, solid and reassuring as his belongings.

Liam said, "I've been expecting them to come and arrest me. That gawk of a fellow, the younger one, is all day hanging round this place asking questions and keeping the men from their work. And Mrs. Linacre thought I meant to drop my great-aunts' grand piano on her. You needn't think you're the only one."

"But sometimes I almost think I must have done it," said Priscilla. "Only they seem to have proved that I couldn't have done it by accident. At least, they've turned the kitchen inside out, and it's an ill wind that blows no good, because the place is so tidy now compared to what it was, but they haven't found any remains of poison or any bottle of anything that it could have been in. It couldn't have come without hands."

"So what?"

"Well, as nobody else was there, I can't help seeing that from an outside point of view it looks as if it was me."

"But you can't be sure nobody else was there. I'm supposed to have slipped round in my dinner hour and tampered with the food when nobody was looking. Nobody saw me, and I never left any fingerprints or footprints, but that just shows my artfulness. And once they assume that anybody got into the kitchen without your knowing, it opens up lots of alternatives. So don't you go setting up to be Suspect Number One."

"But Liam, I don't think they could. The more I think about it the less likely it seems. You know the noise the dogs make when anybody comes. I'd have heard even if I was out getting the parsley, or upstairs changing. Besides, think of the risk they'd have run, when I or Mary or Miss Hampton herself might have come in any moment,"

"Yes, you arranged things rather badly. You ought to have taken care to provide some false clues for the detectives. I can't think why you made it so obvious that nobody but you had access to the cooking. It's not like you to be inefficient."

Priscilla had to laugh. "You do cheer one up. I'm glad you don't think I did it anyway."

"I haven't gone completely mad," said Liam. "Are you feeling better? Good ! Then let's talk about something else."

Priscilla said she ought to be getting home; her mother would be there by now.

"What's your hurry?" said Liam. "Tell me, what do you really think about Hampton Court as a place to live in? Could the old barracks ever be made habitable?"

"Oh yes!" said Priscilla. The question surprised her. "It's been let go, of course. I'm afraid it will want a good deal of money spent on it. I don't see how you'll ever catch up with the painting and repairs. But that doesn't matter so long as there's always some part of it you can live in. And it's a beautiful old house."

"Do you think so?"

"What I'd like to do," said Priscilla, warming to her subject, "is to cut down some of those trees that have grown much too big, and clear away some of the shrubbery and let people see the building properly. And inside, I'd scrap about two-thirds of the furniture, and keep it rather bare, with just the nicest things. It would make the housework easier too. If you had a lot of people staying you'd want another bathroom, and I *should* like to put in an airing cupboard and the hot-water system could be improved on, but I expect that's the same in most country houses."

"What about the winter, with no electric light?" Liam sounded amused.

"Yes, that must have been rather grim these last winters. But it's easier to get candles now, and perhaps by next winter there'll be more paraffin. After all, the war *is* over. And you've plenty of fuel here, which we hadn't in Dublin, so at least you can have fires. I shouldn't mind those things compared with the satisfaction of having space and dignity all round one. I'd like to make the house live up to itself again."

"I'm glad you feel like that about it," said Liam, "because you're liable to be taken at your word. Priscilla, will you marry me?"

Never had anything been so sudden. A moment before Priscilla had been regarding Liam's feet where they rested on the edge of the hearth rug (he was leaning against the dining-room table), and one corner of her mind was concerned with the pathos of a hole in his socks, and forming a daring project for knitting him a new pair. She had no idea that she was about to take on his socks for life.

She hung on to the arms of her chair (Liam was gripping the edge of the table) and they stared at each other, and it suddenly came over Priscilla that of course she had got to marry him, and that she had known that all along. She had known it since the time she cried, and even since the time when she told him he ought to apologize to Miss Hampton. That was just over a week ago but one does not argue about dates when it is a question of one's life's happiness.

"Yes," said Priscilla.

II

Before Priscilla left, Liam took her in to see his mother. Mrs. Hampton was not very like him. She looked kind, and tired with illness. Paralyzed on one side, she divided her time between two chairs, her armchair by the wireless and the wheelchair that enabled her to get out of doors. It would not do to tell her of her son's engagement without previous preparation, so Priscilla only stayed a few minutes during which they talked about the wireless concert and discovered a mutual enthusiasm for Mozart.

Liam then saw Priscilla back to Hampton Court. She abandoned her bicycle (she thought she might soon be coming that way again) and they walked back across the fields.

Looking over towards Brainborough from a rise in the ground, they could see the smoke of the first Beltane fire. All summer was in the hour. The woodquests cooed over them as they passed, and the low-angled light of the evening sun irradiated them with a golden glow.

Before they reached Hampton Court they came on Mrs. Hoyle. She was balanced unsteadily on top of a stone stile, scanning the horizon in all directions. "Where have you been? I thought you were lost!" was written in her expression, with a great many other questions from among which, when Liam and Priscilla walked up hand in hand, she selected, "Now, what have you two got to say for yourselves?"

"We're going to get married, Mummy," said Priscilla.

"Oh my dear child," said Mrs. Hoyle, "my dear children, in fact, now *are* you wise?"

She sat down on the stile and regarded them severely.

"I don't mean are you wise to get married," said Mrs. Hoyle, "because there are some risks in life that one simply has to take. I'm in favor of marriage on principle, at any rate for girls, and that naturally implicates men too. And I will say that under any other circumstances I should be delighted to welcome you, Liam Hampton, as my son-in-law to be. Priscilla might have done much worse. *Much* worse," repeated Priscilla's mother, and the shade of Hugo Everard gibbered just once more at them from the subconscious, before it vanished forever. "But don't you see, darlings," said Mrs. Hoyle, "that for you two to announce your engagement just now would be sheer madness? Don't you know you are both under suspicion of murder? Oh, Priscilla dear, did you see what happened about those cakes this afternoon?"

"But Mummy, we don't mind. We trust each other. Liam will eat all the cake you like to make for him."

"Darling, that is not the point. What you have to consider is the effect this will have on that inspector's mind. A mind like a sink if ever there was one. You can see what's bothering him at present. He thinks that you could have poisoned Miss Hampton, only why on earth *should* you? And that Liam probably wanted to poison her, only how on earth *could* he? Well, up to now there's been no hint of any connection between you, which would have been a help. But if it comes out that you've been in love with each other all the time, he will leap to the conclusion that Liam had the idea of killing his cousin off, and that you did it for him."

There was silence. Mrs. Hoyle's summing up of the situation had left her out of breath and the other two speechless. The woodquests went on cooing in a silly way, and a whole lot of rooks got up out of the trees and cawed. There was also an out-of-tune cuckoo.

Priscilla said, "Oh, Liam, we shall have to wait till everything is cleared up."

"This damned investigation's been dragging on far too long;" said Liam. "I wonder what the hell's going to happen at the inquest."

"Swearing won't help," said Mrs. Hoyle. Watching Liam's expression, Priscilla decided that it would be better if her mother did not come and stay with them too often after they were married.

They went on talking for several minutes longer, but in the end Mrs. Hoyle talked them round to her point of view. They agreed to keep the engagement a secret for the present.

"And do be careful how you look at each other," Mrs. Hole warned them. "You'd better avoid each other as much as possible, otherwise you're sure to give yourselves away."

Liam and Priscilla said good-bye there at the stile, kissing each other circumspectly under Mrs. Hoyle's maternal eye. Then Liam turned back and Priscilla went on with her mother.

The Beltane bonfires were burning more brightly as the day faded. Other couples would be jumping over them hand in hand, to make sure of being married before Beltane came round again.

CHAPTER TWENTY-FOUR
A Ray of Light

THE mystery of Miss Hampton's death might have been solved in the end by experts working overtime at the expense of the taxpayer, or they might have come to a false conclusion involving some innocent person, or it might have remained a mystery forever, casting a shadow over the lives of all who had been implicated, if it had not been for Tim Linacre's indefatigable energy.

Tim's indefatigable energy led him to set out again that evening. After he had carried in the sacks of herbs for his mother and helped her to spread the leaves out to dry in the two attics at Glenwood, he ate the scratch meal which Mrs. Linacre had managed to provide in the midst of her planning for the picnic, and then he set out again to see what was doing in the way of celebrations.

There was a furzy field near Puck's Cross, about half a mile from the last houses in Brainborough; a patch of bad land that was always available for sports and meetings of any kind. Here they had the hobby horses and the bonfire that Liam and Priscilla saw in the distance. It was blazing well by the time Tim reached it and coming into its own as the daylight faded. Shankey, the clerk of the fair, had lighted it by taking a sod of turf soaked in paraffin and setting a match to it and throwing it in among the twigs. Standing on the mount where the bonfire was, at the highest point in the field, you got a wide view over the hummocky up and down country, and on other little hills you could see other fires starting here and there. But these were private fires kindled by farmers for the children and the stay-at-homes who were too lazy or too blasé to walk to Brainborough to the real fair.

Hobbyhorse music and painted caravans, the rise and fall of the swing boats, people laughing and jostling, the noise and brightness round the fire, and all beyond, the soft pink dusk over the soft blue landscape, and summer holding her honey breath. There was some magic there, whether the same or different from that which was invoked by ancient rites. Tim had attended the fair year after year, beginning years before his mother knew or permitted it. When he was a little boy he had found it the door to adventure, and as an old man he might try to go back through the door to childhood. For enchantment lies on the future when you are young; on the past when you are old.

But Tim that night was twenty and lived in the now. He looked at the two tinkers' carts, needing a coat of paint; he watched a young farm laborer lose ten shillings or a day's wages on the three-card trick, that hoary old take-in; he saw the hobby horses break down as usual; and he was glad he had not brought his friend Marshall. Marshall was the English public school boy who had swapped the snails for *Aeneid* Book VIII. Tim could just hear him saying that all this was pretty primitive and rather a poor show.

He was sorry he had arrived too late for the auction of the goat. There was generally some fun over that. Cuddy, whom he met in the crowd, told him it had been most successful this year; the animal had fetched a record price. It had been knocked down to one James Gorman, a butcher, the man who bought Brainborough Castle with its demesne and deer park when the old lord sold up. Gorman had a license to export venison to England, so the future of the goat might be regarded as settled.

Cuddy was in a state of depression, not without reason, for he was due to appear next day at the District Court and answer for his sins in the matter of the onions. He would have preferred to spend the evening of Beltane in Devine's, comforting himself quietly in a corner, while his friends spoke tactfully among themselves of the nosiness of the Guards. But Mrs. Cuddy had reminded him of a promise to take Micky, their eldest, to the bonfire, and Cuddy with all his faults was a good family man. Micky had just been sick out of a swing boat, and while Cuddy and Tim were talking he fell into the fire and was pulled out with his jacket singed. A few minutes later anguished yells were heard above the noise of the crowd. People took their feet away and out rolled two small boys, punching and clawing and doing their best to ruin each other's appearance. When set up on end these turned out to be Caddy's Micky and Billy McGuirk. The fight arose out of Billy, the bigger boy, calling Micky's father a thief. However, McGuirk, who disapproved of fairs, could be relied on to take it out of Billy when he went home. Cuddy gave him a clip over the ear to be going on with, gave Micky another in the interests of fairness, and ordered his own son home. Feeling at liberty then to pursue his alternative program, he set off for Devine's after all.

Tim hung about a bit longer, but there was nothing much to stay for. He had a chat with the proprietor of the hobby horses about the difficulty of getting fuel to run his engine. He saw the machine started up again, and he bought a ride for Cuddy's Micky, who had sneaked back by himself. Then Tim felt he had seen it all. The crowd round the bonfire were singing, and there was a chap playing the piano accordion, but he did not play it as well as Marshall, and he did not seem to know any tunes under five years old. Tim felt out of it all. He thought he would go home.

He cycled slowly back through the dusk along a byroad that was one of his shortcuts. The crowd had made him feel lonely and the summer evening made him feel sad. He wished there was some other youth of his own age in Brainborough. He wished he had a dog. He wished he was not growing up so quickly. He knew he ought to make up his mind about his future, but how could he choose a career when he had the greatest difficulty in choosing even a Christmas present for himself without feeling afterwards that he had wasted the money? One thing that did seem to be off was detection. He was glad to leave that to the police in future, and he did wish they would hurry up and settle who was responsible for Cousin Rebecca's death. At present one did not know whom one could trust. It was a pity about those cakes at tea time, and life would not be worth living if one had to go on taking those kind of precautions.

Ahead of his front wheel was a patch of dark shadow on the road bank. No, it was a heap of old sacks. No, it was a person, or a person's body, lying at the side of the road. Tim dropped his bicycle on the grass and approached nervously. He did not have to touch; he knew by the clothes it was Mrs. Shegog.

She was breathing. In fact she was making a noise like a grampus. Relieved to find her alive, Tim gingerly lifted her head, but she gave no sign of consciousness, so he put it down again. It was pillowed on a slight rise in the bank and looked fairly comfortable. Tim thought the best thing he could do was to leave her there for the moment and go for Dr. Claffey.

As he rode back to Brainborough he was reminded of the last time he had gone scorching on his bicycle for help in a case of life or death. It seemed to happen every week now.

Dr. Claffey was used to sudden calls. He came at once without getting fussed. It was not more than twenty minutes before they stopped his car in the lane with the headlights turned on Mrs. Shegog. The doctor looked down at her reclining form and smiled slightly.

"That's an easy one," he said. "She's stotius."

"Oh," said Tim. "I did think she smelled of drink, you know, but then she always does a bit. I'm glad there's nothing worse the matter with her."

"Well, I'll just have a look," said the doctor, feeling professionally for the old woman's heart and pulse, "but I think you can put it down to the celebrations. I saw her earlier today and she was pluthered then. She must have had some more since. I don't know who she gets to stand treat for her. They shouldn't."

"She probably paid for it herself," said Tim. "She got a good price selling her goat."

The doctor finished his examination. "Well," he said, "she'll sleep it off. She has a remarkable constitution if she wouldn't take liberties with it."

"She's wonderful for her age, isn't she?" said Tim. "I suppose she's nearly as old as Cousin Rebecca."

"Ah, not at all. What makes you think that? She had her last child since I came here, and I'm not above fifteen years in this place. None of these old women are as old as they look. It's what a hard life does to you. Well, we may as well run her home."

Tim had the privilege of propping up Mrs. Shegog in the back of the doctor's car, and in a strong atmosphere of whiskey, with her head lolling on his shoulder, he traveled the few miles to the cottage at the back entrance to Hampton Court.

Dr. Claffey had found the key, a thing weighing several ounces, on a string round Mrs. Shegog's neck. They carried in the old woman, still sleeping, and dumped her on her bed. It was dark in the house, but Tim had his bicycle lamp and they found a candle end on the table.

While the doctor was loosening the patient's clothes and taking her boots off, Tim glanced curiously round the cottage interior. He shone round the ray of his bicycle lamp and picked out several articles salvaged from the Hampton Court rubbish dump. The corset which the police had unearthed in the kitchen now hung over the end of Mrs. Shegog's bed. The lamp beam traveled on to *Mrs. Lavender's Herbal Book.* Tim picked it up, as Priscilla Hoyle had done, to investigate the taste in reading of the poorer classes.

"She'll do now, I think," said Dr. Claffey. "It's well for her she hasn't to be at the inquest tomorrow."

"I could do without it myself," said Tim.

"I thought you were keen on police work."

"I was, but I've had enough. This has been such a rotten sort of case. It'd be different dealing with criminals, but there's nobody in this that you'd think could possibly ever have put poison in an old lady's dinner."

"There it was, all the same."

"Yes, I know. It couldn't have come without hands."

Tim only said that because people kept on saying it to him. It was a boring remark, he thought. So true.

He was still poring over *Mrs. Lavender's Herbal Book,* which he found a mine of information. Mrs. Shegog's thoughts had evidently been running on the same lines as everyone else's, for the book opened at a description of how snails were given to a young man without his knowledge and worked a remarkable cure. It described the preparation of the snails, including the French method of feeding them beforehand on apples and culinary herbs to improve the flavor. Tim slipped the book in his pocket. He thought he might borrow it for bedside reading.

Dr. Claffey blew out the candle and they went out. Tim was glad to be given a lift home; he had had a tiring day.

It might have been the result of overtiredness, but Tim could not sleep that night. He read snatches of Mrs. Lavender, then lay in the dark thinking about herbs and *héliciculture* and what would happen at the inquest. He churned over all the facts and deductions in his notebook again, without expecting to make anything of them. Then, just as his mother's Wyandotte cock started its first announcement of morning, and the prelude to the dawn song began in the lilacs under his window, Tim had an idea that stirred him out of bed and sent him off to Hampton Court to knock up the inspector.

CHAPTER TWENTY-FIVE
The Verdict

THE adjourned inquest was in Devines' Rooms, in reality one big room which had been built over the back yard as an annex. It was the inevitable place in Brainborough for inquests, meetings, whist drives and dances. Devines were used to everything of that kind and knew what to provide: chairs and tiles for the officials and reporters; chairs on one side for the jury, chairs on the other side for the witnesses and their friends; a high desk and stool out of the shop for a witness box; some benches for the general public. The chairs for the witnesses being placed sideways gave the general public the chance to study their faces and decide who looked most guilty.

Priscilla sat beside her mother, cut off from Liam by a rampart of humanity (Mrs. Hoyle, Mary, Mrs. De Vigne) and by a desert of empty chairs waiting for the Linacres and Dr. Claffey. As at the opening of the inquest, Liam had brought the Hampton Court household in with him in Shankey's taxi, but the three women had shared the back, and Liam had sat in front with Shankey, so all Priscilla had seen of him since yesterday was the back of his neck. She could not be sure he still loved her. After her mother's warnings she dared not look his way.

There were far more people than she had expected. There would have been many more if it had been any morning but the morning after Beltane. Brainborough had had a week to talk over the mystery and interest was so intense that though the inquest began at ten o'clock, several people got up early in order to come. Their faces glistened with the anticipation of seeing somebody arrested, either the young woman from Dublin, who looked to be a deep one, or the captain himself, who had always annoyed his neighbors by "cleverality."

Three reporters sent down by Dublin newspapers came and sat at the big table in the middle. They had to share it with Mr. Counsel, who had gone back home for his reading glasses. The coroner's clerk had a table of his own. He was very busy shuffling official forms.

The young Guard who had been helpful about the goat was on duty at the door. The county superintendent and the station sergeant were standing about, overawing everybody with their presence. George, in plain clothes, was leaning inconspicuously against the wall. There was no sign as yet of Inspector Devlin.

Mrs. Linacre came in, not quite her calmest self. She said, "Isn't Tim here? I don't know what's come over him. He was out till all hours last night, and this morning he dashed off early without his breakfast. I waited and he never came back, and I didn't want to be late so I came on without him."

"I do hope nothing's happened to him," said Mrs. De Vigne. "One feels so unsafe nowadays."

The room was stifling. As more people came in and the crowd breathed harder and harder, Priscilla began to be afraid she would faint, and this took her mind off the coming ordeal. Mrs. Hoyle produced smelling salts.

The reporters were looking at their watches and thinking how slack people were in the country, for it was after ten o'clock.

"Tim is late," said Mrs. Linacre. "Where can he be? I don't know what I ought to do about him."

George overheard her and came across to them. "Don't you worry, Ma'am, he's with the chief. Him and Dr. Claffey. They came in together half an hour ago. I understood they had some information."

"Some information!" repeated Mrs. Linacre blankly. "How very strange! My son never said anything to me."

At that very moment in came Tim, the inspector, Dr. Claffey and Mr. Counsel, all in a huddle. They were followed immediately by the coroner: The Court stood up and sat down again, and the proceedings opened.

Inquests are free of the theatrical trappings of other courts. There are no wigs and gowns; the atmosphere is that of an extra formal committee meeting. Most of the evidence is in the form of written statements, read aloud by the coroner's clerk. The witnesses listen to the reading, swear to their depositions, and sign them in the presence of the Court. Some of them may have questions put to them by the coroner or the jury or by solicitors representing interested parties.

The coroner on this occasion was a sound man with all the qualities of a good chairman and the knack of getting on with his job. He began with a short address to the jury, reminding them of everything they were supposed to know already. On the first day of the inquest they had had evidence of identification of the body by Captain Hampton, the diagnosis of atropine poisoning by the doctor who attended the deceased, the report of the Brainborough Guards on how they took charge, and, the report of the state pathologist who performed the post mortem. Two points had been brought out in the medical evidence: one, that a very small dose of atropine had been known to prove fatal, for instance, a teaspoonful of liniment, or a drachm of the tincture; two, that the form in which the poison was taken might affect the probability of a fatal result. Poison taken neat might be vomited quickly by the patient without leaving ill effects; poison mixed with food would be more thoroughly digested and harder to eliminate from the patient's system.

When the coroner had finished his summary, the county superintendent stepped into the witness box and read the analyst's report on the organs sent up for examination after the post mortem, and on the remains of the deceased's last meal. There was a sensation when he referred to the dish of snails. Everybody in Brainborough knew about this already, but still it produced a buzz of talk and the coroner had to call for order. The reporters scribbled industriously.

So now everybody knew the poison was in the dish of snails, and the next thing, Priscilla thought, would be for her to go into the witness box and say she had cooked it.

They were not quite ready for her yet, however. The analyst's report also mentioned the bottle of ABC Liniment, which apparently could not have been the source of the poison. Then Inspector Devlin came forward to describe the police search of the house and explain that nothing containing atropine had been found on the premises with the exception of this one bottle of liniment, which the analyst ruled out, and which, in any case, had not even been opened till after lunch.

All the same old story, the same set of facts that they had all gone over, over and over again. And one had to listen. It would never do to be caught not attending. "Will it be me next?" thought Priscilla. The palms of her hands felt sticky, and what was more serious, she could feel her face getting shiny. Her morale was at a low ebb.

But it was not her next. The inspector left the witness box and had a

confidential word with the coroner's clerk. Then the clerk called Timothy
Linacre.

Tim, who had been jigging in his seat with impatience, jumped up,
knocked over a chair, and landed in the witness box looking every bit as
nervous as Priscilla felt. His face was white and his ears were red. He
dropped the Bible they gave him to swear on and bumped his head on the
desk when he stooped to pick it up. He shifted from foot to foot several
times while the clerk hunted through papers for his statement, which had
been one of the last in the sheaf.

Tim's original statement was bald and brief. The superintendent, ob-
jecting to laughter in Court, had blue-pencilled all the part about how he
had pretended to eat the snails and had hidden them in his handkerchief.
He simply said that he had been there at lunch on the day of Miss
Hampton's death, and had eaten everything except the snails, and had
suffered no ill effects; that Miss Hampton had seemed in normal health
before lunch; and that he had not known there was anything wrong till his
mother brought her in from the garden. He also said that he remembered
seeing the bottle of liniment still unopened after lunch.

"Yes; that's all right as far as it goes," said Tim, breaking in as the clerk
concluded his reading, "but I've something much more important to add."

"One moment, Mr. Linacre," said the coroner. The clerk prepared to
take notes. The reporters' pens were poised. The general public gazed at
Tim like goldfish looking for crumbs.

"Would you prefer to put it in writing, Mr. Linacre?" said the coroner. "You know that anything you say will be taken down and may be
used in evidence if there should be a trial?"

But the patience of the Court was not to be tried in this inhuman
manner. Tim was as anxious to tell as they were to hear.

"I don't think anybody will have to be tried," he said, "unless it's me for
manslaughter. Because if anybody poisoned Cousin Rebecca it was me."

All the goldfish gasped. Mr. Counsel jumped up, looking horrified,
but the coroner let Tim go on in his own words.

"I'd have owned up at once if only I'd realized, but it only came to
me last night, in the middle of the night. I'd been reading a book called
Mrs. Lavender's Herbal Book that told how they flavor snails for table in
France by feeding them on herbs. Well, I suddenly thought, what happens
if instead of feeding them on culinary herbs the snails eat something poisonous? Because when I sold those snails to my cousin at the flower show,
I filled their box up with greenstuff for them to eat. I remember taking the
nearest thing handy, and that was my mother's exhibit of deadly night-

shade. Those snails lived on that stuff for three days. By Wednesday there was nothing left of it but stalks. By that time the snails must have been transformed into crawling lumps of atropine."

Tim stopped for breath, and there was dead silence, then a general sigh of relief. "Sensation!" wrote the reporters. Mrs. De Vigne said in a loud whisper to Mrs. Hoyle: "I know one can't be too careful with oysters." Priscilla leaned forward to smile at Liam, who was leaning forward to smile at her.

The coroner said he thought the jury would be glad to hear Dr. Claffey's opinion. Dr. Claffey stood up. He said, "I should say that what Mr. Linacre suggests is perfectly possible. I never heard of it before, but then I never heard of anyone in this country eating snails before either. It's a different matter from oysters," he shot a reproving glance at Mrs. De Vigne. "The danger there would be from bacteria. But there certainly have been cases of people being affected by eating the flesh of poisoned animals."

"I know of one, sir," said Tim, interrupting. "Do you know a book called A *Textbook of Forensic Medicine and Toxicology* by R.J.M. Buchanan? It tells in that how some people were poisoned by eating Canadian partridges that had eaten poisonous berries in a hard winter."

"Is that so?" said Dr. Claffey. "Case I was thinking of, there was a whole family died of eating atropine in rabbit pie. The rabbit had eaten deadly nightshade. A man called Sprague was tried over that for murder, and he was acquitted."

The jury were having a consultation. Something was bothering them. The foreman wanted to know, "Why didn't the snails die?"

"I can't tell you why," said Tim loftily, "but if you'd spent yesterday afternoon the way I did, picking deadly nightshade by the sackful, you'd know that slugs and snails live and thrive on it. Incidentally, I don't suppose you know much, about fungi, but you can take it from me that slugs and snails eat the deadliest, most poisonous varieties."

"Thank you, Mr. Linacre," said the coroner, and Tim's evidence concluded.

That was not quite the end of the argy bargy. Legal procedure involves the dragging in of all possible minor details, regardless of anticlimax. All the other witnesses had to swear to their own statements as previously arranged, and the lovely morning wore tediously away as first one aspect of the case and then another was presented to the jury. When at last they had the whole facts the coroner summed up, and if they had not already made up their minds he did it for them. They only retired for a moment. They trooped out, trooped in again, the foreman passed a slip of paper to the coroner, and the coroner said he accepted that verdict and read it aloud to the Court:

"Accidental death."

II

Priscilla found Liam, who still loved her, standing at her elbow. "Come on," he said. "What you need now is a drink."

They repaired to the section of Devine's establishment where you can have "Superior Drinks" in a "Select Lounge," but select as the lounge was, they could hardly hope to have it all to themselves on such an occasion. Shankey was there already; Dr. Claffey wandered in just after them with Mr. Gahan; Mr. Booley Browne put in an appearance; Mr. Counsel was discovered in a quiet corner. So Liam made the best of it and stood drinks all round. Then Tim came to find Priscilla for Mrs. Hoyle, and they made him have a Club Orange; then Mrs. Linacre came looking for Tim, and Mrs. Hoyle peeped round the door and said over her shoulder: "Do come in, Mrs. De Vigne, it's all right, we're not the only women." Once inside, the ladies were induced to take sherry, and everybody drank Tim's health.

Liam shook hands with him. "You did a good day's work today, Tim," he said. "I suppose, now, you'll be joining the detective branch?"

Tim shook his head. "No, thank you very much. I think I'll stay home and keep ducks."

"Maybe you're right," said Liam. "Nothing like staying down on the farm. If you still feel like that when you're through college, come and talk to me. One of these days I'll be needing an agent, and I could train you for the job."

"Oh, Liam!" said Mrs. Linacre, glowing. It was what she had longed and schemed for, to have Tim settled near her for good. Tim said cautiously: "I believe I'd like that. Thanks awfully, Liam. It's very decent of you." They shook hands again on it.

Inspector Devlin wandered in and Liam bought him a drink too.

"*Slainte*, Inspector!"

"Same to you," said the inspector, raising his glass, "and congratulations to you and Miss Hoyle."

Priscilla looked confused. Liam laughed.

"Thank you, Inspector. So you guessed."

"Guessed what?" said the inspector. "I was congratulating you on the satisfactory way the case was cleared up. I don't mind telling you it had me puzzled. Do you know, there were moments now and then when I almost suspected it was one or other of you?"

"No, Inspector, you don't say!"

But Dr. Claffey was quicker in the uptake. He had noted Priscilla's blush. He slapped Liam on the back.

"What's this about congratulations? Come clean, you two! Hey, Biddy! Same again all round, and this time it's on me."

Protests. Exclamations. "You really must excuse me," said Mr. Counsel. "Oh, not another at this time of day," said Mrs. Linacre. "Oh, please no, I mustn't," gasped Mrs. De Vigne.

"Indeed you must," said Dr. Claffey. "Hurry up there, Biddy, we're drinking another toast. Here's to you, Liam, and here's to Miss Hoyle! Another good nurse gone wrong!"

"Speech!" cried somebody. Priscilla looked at Liam. He acted promptly, opening the door behind them. He had forgotten that it led into the public bar. His appearance was greeted with a cheer, and when he took Priscilla by the arm the cheers redoubled. Behind them, Dr. Claffey called out, "Here's to the happy pair!"

"Dear me," said Mrs. De Vigne, tentatively sipping her second sherry, "do I understand that those two are engaged?"

"I hadn't been informed of it," said Mr. Counsel, "but I really think they must be."

THE END

Rue Morgue Press titles as of October 2001

Common or Garden Crime by Sheila Pim. Lucy Bex prefers Jane Austen or Anthony Trollope to the detective stories her brother Linnaeus gulps down, but when a neighbor is murdered with monkshood harvested from Lucy's own garden, she's the one who turns detective and spots the crucial clue that prevents the wrong person from going to the gallows. Set in 1943 in the small town of Clonmeen on the outskirts of Dublin, this delightful tale was written by an author who was called "the Irish Angela Thirkell." Published in Britain in 1945, the book makes its first appearance in the United States here. *Booklist* (published by the American Library Association) described it thus in its May 1, 2001, edition: "Amateur sleuths are led down the primrose path in this American debut of Pim's first detective novel, published in England in 1945. Set in the outskirts of Dublin during World War II, this horticultural whodunit cultivates a bumper crop of quirky characters, nearly all of whom become suspects when Lady Madeleine suddenly dies. It's a case of murder by monkshood when the lethal Aconitum Ferox inexplicably seasons her Sunday meal. In the best tradition of Agatha Christie, this tale will prompt readers to dig deep for clues as conjectures bounce from the dashing Lord Barma to the daffy Miss FitzEustace; not even the victim herself is beyond suspicion. Although Irish Guard detectives are called in to get to the root of the matter, it's the village's own charming yet sensible Lucy Bex who, in the course of attending to the daily rituals of Irish country life, unearths the murder's true identity. Pim's mystery becomes as much a novel of manners as murder, yielding a rich harvest of uncommon intrigue." "Crisp first novel."—*Publishers Weekly.* "This wonderfully leisurely tale set in 1943 Clonmeen, a village on the outskirts of Dublin, is a delight."—*Booknews*, The Poisoned Pen.   **0-915230-36-4 $14.00**

A Hive of Suspects by Sheila Pim. *Booklist*: The mining village of Drumclash, Ireland, circa 1950, is all abuzz when irascible curmudgeon Jason Prendergast dies after dinning on honey taken from his own hives. In a town filled with eccentric characters, suspects abound, including the bees themselves. There's Penrose, the morose chauffeur, and Vera, the vamping maid; throw in a couple of traveling thespians, some curious cousins, and a peculiar partner, and you have a typical Pim crew of lively candidates. Not on to fly off course, the head of the investigating Civic Guards gets a particular bee in his bonnet and suspects Phoebe, Prendergast's niece and caregiver. Doubting that sweet Phoebe was involved in murder, professional lawyer and amateur apiarist Edward GIldea makes a beeline to come to her defense, a task that keeps him busy as a bee. Whether she's holding forth on beekeeping lore or explaining the traits of mineral ore, Pim enthusiastically educates as much as she entertains." First published in 1952. "This is a good puzzle mystery from the 50's. The author allows us to become involved with all her characters; there is gossip, romance, intelligent detective work by the police; everything necessary in a vintage mystery. Interestingly enough, the environmental concerns strike a very modern note. . .fun to read."—Mary Ann Steele, *I Love a Mystery.*   **0-915230-38-0 $14.00**

Murder a Mile High by Elizabeth Dean. When Emma Marsh is asked by her old pal Mary, a visiting diva at the Central City, Colorado, Opera House, to desert the summer heat of 1942 Boston to help her with a little romantic problem, Emma smells trouble. After all, Mary of all people ought to know better than to get involved with a tenor. But Emma dutifully kisses her boyfriend Hank Fairbanks good-bye, reluctantly turns over the running of J. Graham Antiques to its owner, and boards a train for the Rockies. Besides, it just might help her get over the pending loss of Hank—who enlisted shortly after Pearl Harbor—to Army Intelligence. Soon after she arrives in Central City, Emma stumbles across the body of the tenor, encounters a very strange old man who seems to run the town, and spots what she thinks could be a nest of German spies. The old man offers to help catch the murderer, but Emma can't help but think he just might be covering his own guilty tracks. There are also plenty of candidates for murderer among the members of the opera company, including Mary, who appears to be keeping company with yet one more tenor—one with a decidedly Germanic bearing. If only Emma could account for the movements of all the suspects—but that, unfortunately, would require that she stay awake through one entire performance of the opera, a feat that seems beyond her abilities. *Murder a Mile High* was first published in 1944 and is one of the earliest detective novels to fully utilize Colorado as a setting. "Good fun."— *Murder Most Cozy.*   **0-915230-39-9 $14.00**

Murder is a Collector's Item by Elizabeth Dean. "(It) froths over with the same effervescent humor as the best Hepburn-Grant films."—Sujata Massey. "Completely enjoyable."—*New York Times.* "Fast and funny."—*The New Yorker.* Twenty-six-year-old Emma Marsh isn't much at spelling or geography and perhaps she butchers the odd literary quotation or two, but she's a keen judge of character and more than able to hold her own when it comes to selling antiques or solving murders. Originally published in 1939, *Murder is a Collector's Item* is the first of three books featuring Emma. Smoothly written and sparkling with dry, sophisticated humor, this milestone combines an intriguing puzzle with an entertaining portrait of a self-possessed young woman on her own at the end of the Great Depression.   **0-915230-19-4 $14.00**

Murder is a Serious Business by Elizabeth Dean. It's 1940 and the Thirsty Thirties are over but you couldn't tell it by the gang at J. Graham Antiques, where clerk Emma Marsh, her would-be criminologist boyfriend Hank, and boss Jeff Graham trade barbs in between shots of scotch when they aren't bothered by the rare customer. Trouble starts when Emma and crew head for a weekend at Amos Currier's country estate to inventory the man's antiques collection. It isn't long before the bodies start falling, and once again Emma is forced to turn sleuth in order to prove that her boss isn't a killer. "Judging from (this book) it's too bad she didn't write a few more."—Mary Ann Steel, *I Love a Mystery.*   **0-915230-28-3 $14.95**

The Black Paw by Constance & Gwenyth Little. Thanks to some overly indulgent parents, Callie Drake was "brought up soft" and doesn't know the first thing about doing housework, which makes it a bit of a stretch for her to pose as a maid in the Barton household. She's there dressed in the skimpiest maid's outfit this side of Paris to snatch some compromising love letters written by her friend Selma, who's afraid that her brute of an estranged husband just might use these adulterous missives to reduce her alimony. Altruism isn't a big part of Callie's makeup, and she agrees to the scheme only after Selma offers to hand over the keys to her hot little roadster in exchange for this bit of petty larceny. But when murder erupts in the Barton mansion, the police think it's a little odd that the bodies started falling only hours after Callie's arrival. Even worse, Selma's soon-to-be-ex is on to Callie and seems to take perverse enjoyment in forcing this spoiled debutante to continue her domestic chores. In between long hot baths and countless cigarette breaks, Callie stumbles across mysterious pawprints in a house without animals and comes upon rocking chairs that move even when there's no one in the room. It's enough to make this golddigger start digging for clues in this 1941 charmer. "Thank heavens for The Rue Morgue Press."—Peggy Itzen, *Cozies, Capers & Crimes.* **0-915230-37-2, $14.00.** Other Little books available from The Rue Morgue Press: *The Black Gloves* **(0-915230-20-8)**, *The Black Honeymoon* **(0-915230-21-6)**, *Black Corridors* **(0-915230-33-X)**, *The Black Stocking* **(0-915230-30-5)**, *Black-Headed Pins* "For a strong example of their work, try this very funny and inventive 1938 novel of a dysfunctional family Christmas."—Jon L. Breen, *Ellery Queen's Mystery Magazine.* **(0-915230-25-9)**, *Great Black Kanba* **(0-915230-22-4)**, and *The Grey Mist Murders* "Sophisticated humor."—*Publishers Weekly.* **(0-915230-26-7) ($14.00 each).**

Brief Candles by Manning Coles. From Topper to Aunt Dimity, mystery readers have embraced the cozy ghost story. Four of the best were written by Manning Coles, the creator of the witty Tommy Hambledon spy novels. First published in 1954, *Brief Candles* is likely to produce more laughs than chills as a young couple vacationing in

France run into two gentlemen with decidedly old-world manners. What they don't know is that James and Charles Latimer are ancestors of theirs who shuffled off this mortal coil some 80 years earlier when, emboldened by strong drink and with only a pet monkey and an aged waiter as allies, the two made a valiant, foolish and quite fatal attempt to halt a German advance during the Franco-Prussian War of 1870. Now these two ectoplasmic gentlemen and their spectral pet monkey Ulysses have been summoned from their unmarked graves because their visiting relatives are in serious trouble. But before they can solve the younger Latimers' problems, the three benevolent spirits light brief candles of insanity for a tipsy policeman, a recalcitrant banker, a convocation of English ghostbusters, and a card-playing rogue who's wanted for murder. "As felicitously foolish as a collaboration of (P.G.) Wodehouse and Thorne Smith."—Anthony Boucher. "For those who like something out of the ordinary. Lighthearted, very funny."—*The Sunday Times*. "A gay, most readable story."—*The Daily Telegraph*.**0-915230-24-0 ($14.00)**. It was followed by **Happy Returns.** The ghostly Latimers and their pet spectral monkey Ulysses return from the grave when Uncle Quentin finds himself in need of their help—it seems the old boy is being pursued by an old flame who won't take no for an answer in her quest to get him to the altar. Along the way, our courteous and honest spooks thwart a couple of bank robbers, unleash a bevy of circus animals on an unsuspecting French town, help out the odd person or two and even "solve" a murder—with the help of the victim. The laughs start practically from the first page and don't stop until Ulysses slides down the bannister, glass of wine in hand, to drink a toast to returning old friends. **0-915230-31-3 ($14.00)**. Next comes **Come and Go.** The third and final book featuring the ghostly Latimers finds our heroes saving an ancestor from marriage and murder in a plot straight out of P.G. Wodehouse. **0-915230-34-8 ($14.00)**. Coles alwo wrote one stand-alone ghost story, **The Far Traveller.** The Herr Graf was a familiar sight to the residents of the Rhineland village of Grauhugel. After all, he'd been walking the halls of the local castle at night and occasionally nodding to the servants ever since he drowned some 86 years ago. No one was the least bit alarmed by the Graf's spectral walks. Indeed, the castle's major domo found it all quite comforting, as the young Graf had been quite popular while he was alive. When the actor hired to play the dead Graf in a movie is felled by an accident, the film's director is overjoyed to come across a talented replacement who seems to have been born to play the part, little realizing that the Graf and his faithful servant—who perished in the same accident—had only recently decided to materialize in public. The Graf isn't stagestruck. He's back among the living to correct an old wrong. Along the way, he adds a bit of realism to a cinematic duel, befuddles a black marketeer, breaks out of jail, and exposes a charlatan spiritualist. In the meantime, his servant wonders if he's pursuing the granddaughters of the village maidens he dallied with eight decades ago. "If. . . you enjoyed books like the Topper series by Thorne Smith, you'll love this book. I laughed until I hurt. I liked it so much, I went back to page 1 and read it a second time after I finished it. Such a good book. Such fun. What a giggle. Again I have to say, 'Thank God for Rue Morgue Press for bringing back these books so more of us can laugh and laugh and laugh"—Peggy Itzen, *Cozies, Capers & Crimes*. **0-915230-35-6 ($14.00)**

The Chinese Chop by Juanita Sheridan. The postwar housing crunch finds Janice Cameron, newly arrived in New York City from Hawaii, without a place to live until she answers an ad for a roommate. It turns out the advertiser is an acquaintance from Hawaii, Lily Wu, whom critic Anthony Boucher (for whom Bouchercon, the World Mystery Convention, is named) described as "the exquisitely blended product of Eastern and Western cultures" and the only female sleuth that he "was devotedly in love with," citing "that odd mixture of respect for her professional skills and delight in her personal charms." First published in 1949, this ground-breaking book was the first of four to feature Lily and be told by her Watson, Janice, a first-time novelist. No sooner do Lily and Janice move into a rooming house in Washington Square than a corpse is found in the basement. In Lily Wu, Sheridan created one of the most believable—and memorable—female sleuths of her day. Highly recommended."—*I Love a Mystery*.

"This well-written. . .enjoyable variant of the boarding house whodunit and a vivid portrait of the post WWII New York City housing shortage, puts to lie the common misconception that strong, self-reliant, non-spinster-or-comic sleuths didn't appear on the scene until the 1970s. Chinese-American Lily Wu and her novelist Watson, Janice Cameron, are young and feminine but not dependent on men."—*Ellery Queen's Mystery Magazine.*   **0-915230-32-1 $14.00**

Death on Milestone Buttress by Glyn Carr. Abercrombie ("Filthy") Lewker was looking forward to a fortnight of climbing in Wales after a grueling season touring England with his Shakespearean company. Young Hilary Bourne thought the holiday would be a pleasant change from her dreary job at the bank as well as a chance to renew her acquaintance with a certain young scientist. Neither one expected this bucolic outing to turn deadly, but when one of their party is killed during what should have been an easy climb on the Milestone Buttress, Filthy and Hilary turn detective. Nearly every member of the climbing party had reason to hate the victim, but each one also had an alibi for the time of the murder. Filthy and Hilary retrace the route of the fatal climb before returning to their lodgings where, in the grand tradition of Nero Wolfe, Filthy confronts the suspects and points his finger at the only person who could have committed the crime. Filled with climbing details sure to appeal to expert climbers and armchair mountaineers alike, *Death on Milestone Buttress* was published in England in 1951. "You'll get a taste of the Welsh countryside, will encounter names replete with consonants, will be exposed to numerous snippets from Shakespeare and will find Carr's novel a worthy representative of the cozies of two generations ago."—*I Love a Mystery.*   **0-915230-29-1 $14.00**

Murder, Chop Chop by James Norman. "The book has the butter-wouldn't-melt-in-his-mouth cool of Rick in *Casablanca*."—*The Rocky Mountain News*. "Amuses the reader no end."—*Mystery News*. "This long out-of-print masterpiece is intricately plotted, full of eccentric characters and very humorous indeed. Highly recommended."—*Mysteries by Mail*. Meet Gimiendo Hernandez Quinto, a gigantic Mexican who once rode with Pancho Villa and who now trains *guerrilleros* for the Nationalist Chinese government when he isn't solving murders. At his side is a beautiful Eurasian known as Mountain of Virtue, a woman as dangerous to men as she is irresistible. Together they look into the murder of Abe Harrow, an ambulance driver who appears to have died at three different times.   **915230-16-X $13.00**

Death at The Dog by Joanna Cannan. "Worthy of being discussed in the same breath with an Agatha Christie or Josephine Tey...anyone who enjoys Golden Age mysteries will surely enjoy this one."—Sally Fellows, *Mystery News*. "Skilled writing and brilliant characterization."—*Times of London*. "An excellent English rural tale."—Jacques Barzun & Wendell Hertig Taylor in *A Catalogue of Crime*. Set in late 1939 during the first anxious months of World War II, *Death at The Dog*, first published in 1941, is a wonderful example of the classic English detective novel that flourished between the two World Wars. Set in a picturesque village filled with thatched-roof cottages, eccentric villagers and genial pubs, it's as well-plotted as a Christie, with clues abundantly and fairly planted, and as deftly written as the best of Sayers or Marsh, filled with quotable lines and perceptive observations on the human condition. **0-915230-23-2, $14.00.** The first book in this series is **They Rang Up the Police** by Joanna Cannan. "Just delightful."—Sleuth of Baker Street Pick-of-the-Month. "A brilliantly plotted mystery...splendid character study...don't miss this one, folks. It's a keeper."—Sally Fellows, *Mystery News*. When Delia Cathcart and Major Willoughby disappear from their quiet English village one morning in July 1937, it looks like a simple case of a frustrated spinster running off for a bit of fun with a straying husband. But as the hours turn into days, Inspector Guy Northeast begins to suspect that she may have been the victim of foul play. Never published in the United States, *They Rang Up the Police* appeared in England in 1939.   **0-1915230-27-5 $14.00**

The Man from Tibet by Clyde B. Clason. Locked inside the Tibetan Room of his Chicago apartment, the rich antiquarian was overheard repeating a forbidden occult chant under the watchful eyes of Buddhist gods. When the doors were opened it appeared that he had succumbed to a heart attack. But the elderly Roman historian and sometime amateur sleuth Theocritus Lucius Westborough is convinced that Adam Merriweather's death was anything but natural and that the weapon was an eighth century Tibetan manuscript. **0-915230-17-8 $14.00**

The Mirror by Marlys Millhiser. "Completely enjoyable."—*Library Journal.* "A great deal of fun."—*Publishers Weekly.* How could you not be intrigued by a novel in which "you find the main character marrying her own grandfather and giving birth to her own mother?" Such is the situation in this classic novel, originally published in 1978, of two women who end up living each other's lives. Twenty-year-old Shay Garrett is not aware that she's pregnant and is having second thoughts about marrying Marek Weir when she's suddenly transported back 78 years in time into the body of Brandy McCabe, her own grandmother, who is unwillingly about to be married off to miner Corbin Strock. Shay's in shock but she still recognizes that the picture of her grandfather that hangs in the family home doesn't resemble her husband-to-be. But marry Corbin she does and off she goes to the high mining town of Nederland, where this thoroughly modern young woman has to learn to cope with such things as wood cooking stoves and—to her—old-fashioned attitudes about sex. In the meantime, Brandy McCabe is finding it even harder to cope with life in the Boulder, Colorado, of 1978. **0-915230-15-1 $14.95**

The Mouse in the Mountain by Norbert Davis. There have been a lot of dogs in mystery fiction, from Baynard Kendrick's guide dog to Virginia Lanier's bloodhounds, but there's never been one quite like Carstairs. Doan, a short, chubby Los Angeles private eye, won Carstairs in a crap game, but there never was any question as to who the boss was in this relationship. Carstairs isn't just any Great Dane. He is so big that Doan figures he really ought to be considered another species. He scorns baby talk and belly rubs—unless administered by a pretty girl—and growls whenever Doan has a drink. His full name is Dougal's Laird Carstairs and as a sleuth he rarely barks up the wrong tree. He's down in Mexico with Doan, ostensibly to convince a missing fugitive that he would do well to stay put. The case is complicated by three murders, assorted villains, and a horrific earthquake that cuts the mountainous little village of Los Altos off from the rest of Mexico. Doan and Carstairs aren't the only unusual visitors to Los Altos. There's Patricia Van Osdel, a ravishing blonde whose father made millions from flypaper, and Captain Emile Perona, a Mexican policeman whose long-ago Spanish ancestor helped establish Los Altos. It's that ancestor who brings teacher Janet Martin to Mexico along with a stolen book that may contain the key to a secret hidden for hundreds of years in the village church. Written in the snappy hardboiled style of the day, *The Mouse in the Mountain* was first published in 1943 and followed by two other Doan and Carstairs novels. "Each of these is fast-paced, occasionally lyrical in a hard-edged way, and often quite funny. Davis, in fact, was one of the few writers to successfully blend the so-called hardboiled story with farcical humor."—Bill Pronzini, *1001 Midnights.* **0-915230-41-0 $14.00**

About The Rue Morgue Press

The Rue Morgue Press vintage mystery line is designed to bring back into print those books that were favorites of readers between the turn of the century and the 1960s. The editors welcome suggestions for reprints. To receive our catalog or make suggestions, write The Rue Morgue Press, P.O. Box 4119, Boulder, Colorado 80306 (1-800-699-6214).